THE ESCAPE

By the time Thalia realized what was happening, it was too late to react. Ashtyn had drawn even with her and leaped forward, catching her in his arms and taking them both to the ground.

"What did you think you were doing?" he demanded.

She tried to throw him off, but it was impossible. "L...let me up."

Ashtyn took both her arms and manacled them over her head. "Not until you stop struggling." He was angry, and she stilled as she stared into silver eyes that reflected the moonlight. She felt the raw strength in him and knew she had no chance of escaping. His face was very near Thalia's, and she felt his breath on her mouth. Fear was forgotten and other, more troubling feelings, swamped her—unfamiliar feelings that took her completely by surprise.

Thalia had never been this close to a man, and her body reacted to his in a most shocking way. She raised her hips in an age-old movement dictated by instinct. She felt his hands gentle on her wrists, and she felt him swell against her.

Why did she have the urge to take his face between her hands and grind her mouth against his?

"I shall never yield to you."

His eyes glittered. "I think you shall."

Other *Leisure* books by Constance O'Banyon:

SWORD OF ROME
LORD OF THE NILE
HAWK'S PURSUIT
HAWK'S PLEDGE
THE MOON AND THE STARS
HEART OF TEXAS
MOON RACER
THE AGREEMENT
RIDE THE WIND
SOMETHING BORROWED, SOMETHING
BLUE (Anthology)
TYKOTA'S WOMAN
FIVE GOLD RINGS (Anthology)
SAN ANTONIO ROSE
TEXAS PROUD
CELEBRATIONS (Anthology)

Constance O'Banyon

Daughter of Egypt

LEISURE BOOKS   NEW YORK CITY

A LEISURE BOOK®

July 2008

Published by

Dorchester Publishing Co., Inc.
200 Madison Avenue
New York, NY 10016

ISBN 10: 0-8439-6006-X
ISBN 13: 978-0-8439-6006-8

Dedication

Did you ever guess how wonderful you are in my eyes, my son, Jason Bryant Gee, or why I always smile when you walk into a room, or how much I have been touched by your kindness, strength and wisdom?

Did you ever guess that the day you were born I not only had a daughter, but a best friend as well, Pamela Adele Monck?

Did you ever guess, Rick Gee, how I watched in awe as you become exactly the kind of person every man should strive to be?

Did you ever guess, Linda Kaye Henderson, how special you are to me? How many hours you sat with me at the computer editing a book? Little did I know when I married your brother I would be getting a family to treasure—you being one of the dearest treasures.

Did you ever guess, Jo Ann McCormick, how much I have always admired you, and when I grow up, I want to be just like you? You are very dear to me.

Did you ever guess, Mary Dot Pinto, how your e-mails brighten my days, even on those days when the sun does not shine? How long ago was it you volunteered to be my sis, since I had no sister of my own?

Did you ever guess, Evan Marshall, how much I admire you as a person and treasure you as my agent? You stepped beyond what is expected of you and became a friend who is always just a phone call away.

Did you ever guess, Alicia Condon, that you are the most amazing editor I have ever had? I feel fortunate that when my books leave me they fall under your sharp, creative care.

DAUGHTER
OF
EGYPT

❧ PROLOGUE

Rome
44 B.C.

The night was dark, the shadows deep in the recesses of the catacomb. A ragged urchin stumbled in that direction, head hung low with weariness, footsteps faltering in the driving rain. Darker than the night was the gaping entrance on the lower course of the Tiber River. To the child, the mouth of the cave yawned like the looming jaws of a monster ready to devour anyone who stepped inside. Were not the streets of Rome an even greater threat than those that waited in the darkness?

Each night the frail urchin waited until Brace and his gang of thieves were asleep before sneaking inside. One of the child's worst fears was of oversleeping and being discovered hiding behind the huge boulder at the mouth of the cave.

Rain pelted the small child, who cautiously crept forward, eventually gathering the courage to enter the black void. Once inside, the child paused, hoping to remain undetected in the shadows.

"You there, brat," a harsh voice cut through the

darkness. "Didn't I tell you to find another place to sleep? If you won't work for me like the rest of the lads here, you can't enjoy my protection. Get out now unless you want another beating!"

Brace was no more than fourteen, but he was a person to be feared. As leader, he'd trained his pack of thieves to prey on the marketplace crowd and even sneak into the houses of unsuspecting citizens. Brace often boasted of killing three men in a fight, and also an old woman who caught him slipping into her home one night.

"I'm not a thief! I take only what I need," the urchin said, taking a quick step backward, "while you take all you can get."

"Shut your mouth!" Brace bellowed, looming out of the shadows, stalking toward the child. "You scrawny little brat, you'll feel the weight of my rod if you don't get out of here now."

"I just want a dry place to sleep. It's raining." The child's eyes were bright with hope. "Let me stay, and I won't tell anyone who you are, or where to find you."

"You dare threaten me?" Brace raised his rod, and the child cringed, waiting for him to strike. But the blow did not fall. Instead, Brace aimed a hard kick, and the child fell to the ground, moaning in pain.

"That'll be your last warning, boy," Brace snarled. "If I ever see you again, I'll beat you senseless and throw your carcass to the dogs."

The urchin rose, trembling with fear and pain, then, after taking a deep breath, managed to hobble out into the night. At least Brace had not yet discovered the secret she guarded so carefully. Thalia had learned early on that young girls didn't live long on the streets of Rome—they were taken either for slaves or for some darker purpose.

The rain stung her face as she stumbled down the hill. Shivering with cold, Thalia huddled behind a thornbush, and tried not to think about how painfully her ribs ached. She rested her head on her folded arms, her tears mingling with the rain. She was weary of the daily threats that shadowed her every step. There was always Brace and his gang to contend with, as well as the guards at the marketplace. Then there was her most relentless pursuer, the man with a patch over one eye. Thalia did not know who he was or what he wanted with her. She trembled with fear and weariness. How would she ever manage to avoid him with sore ribs?

It was as if they were playing a game of wits that she had to win. On the days he lay in wait for her, it was only her small frame and speed that helped her escape. Even her disguise as a lad had not fooled him for long. Some days she did not see him at all, and those were her good days. But when he did appear, it took all her skills to lose him in the twists and turns of the brick streets.

Although it had stopped raining, Thalia shivered on the damp ground. Turning onto her back, she stared at the opening in the clouds where she could see the stars.

Who was she—where did she come from?

Latin was not her original language, because she'd had to learn to speak it after she came to Rome. She was beginning to forget the language she'd once spoken, and when she tried to remember her past, it was like looking through a veil. She had distant memories of living in a house outside Rome where an old woman had taken care of her. Then one morning she'd found the old woman dead.

Thalia rubbed her teary eyes with grimy fists and tried to think beyond the dark shroud covering her past. There was an elusive memory of a fire, and a beautiful woman who had made her feel safe, but nothing that could answer her questions.

She lay awake until the first ray of sunlight struck the Tiber River, turning it to a silver ribbon that meandered to the sea. With weary steps she made her way down the embankment and cupped her hands, taking a deep drink. Reaching into her belt, she retrieved a crumbling honey cake and took small bites so it would last. When she licked the crumbs from her hands, her stomach still rumbled with hunger.

Today would be just like the one before and the one before that. Each step she took was rife with danger. There was no one in the world she could depend on but herself.

Placing her tattered cap on her head, she pushed her hair beneath it to disguise the fact that she was a girl. Thalia reached down to tie her worn sandals, thinking her first task after eating would be to steal some new clothes—hers were so ragged they were falling down her waist and off her shoulders. She stood, gazing downstream, knowing the exact street where she would find clothing hanging to dry.

Pain shot through her side each time she took a step, and slowly, Thalia made her way toward Rome.

At Trajan Marketplace, she slipped through the crowd virtually unseen. As always, Thalia was on the lookout for the man with the eye patch, but thankfully he was not here today—at least not yet.

Meandering toward a cart where date cakes and fruit were displayed, Thalia clasped her hands behind her and pretended to study the sky when the merchant looked at her suspiciously. Shortly thereafter, the merchant turned her attention to a woman who was inquiring about the fruit. It was Thalia's chance— she quickly snatched one of the cakes and tucked it into her sash. She saw her mistake immediately: she'd been watching the merchant and had overlooked the guard.

Fear gave wings to her feet as her pursuer was joined by two companions.

"Stop, thief!" the merchant called, which only made Thalia run faster. Darting around a corner, she attempted to outrun the men, but the pain in her side forced her to slow her pace.

Running past the fountain, she saw a beautiful young noblewoman watching her. As she slid behind the woman, Thalia begged for help.

To Thalia's relief, the stranger hid her until the men had disappeared around a corner. Thalia was not accustomed to kindness, and she was suspicious when the woman invited her to accompany her. She reluctantly agreed.

From that day forward Thalia's life changed forever. She never had to worry about finding enough food to survive or a safe place to sleep at night. At last she had a home.

Her savior was Lady Adhaniá, who was from a high-ranking Egyptian family with close ties to Queen Cleopatra. During the dark day of Julius Caesar's assassination, it was Thalia's courage and daring that saved her benefactress, and when Lady Adhaniá left Rome, she took Thalia with her.

When they reached Egypt, Adhaniá's family welcomed Thalia. It was the happiest day of Thalia's life when Adhaniá's mother, Lady Larania, adopted Thalia, making her a sister to Adhaniá. She even had a brother, Lord Ramtat, Queen Cleopatra's most trusted general, who doted upon her.

But there were still nights when Thalia woke up in fear.

Would the one-eyed man still come for her?

Thalia chided herself for allowing her thoughts to return to her childhood fear. Her old nemesis would never find her in Egypt. . . .

❦CHAPTER ONE

The Island Kingdom of Bal Forea
36 B.C.

The afternoon sun fell across the island, sending shards of light reflecting off aqua-colored water. Although the practice field was crowded with men honing their skills with sword and bow, not one of them noticed the huge man who slipped through a side door of the fortress and entered a seldom-used passage.

Turk's shoulders were so wide they scraped against the narrow tunnel on both sides, and he was glad when he emerged at the other end into a small windowless chamber that was the designated meeting place for the leaders of the rebel forces. The room was large and sparsely furnished. Maps of the island dominated one wall, pinpointing the areas held by the rebels.

The big man made his way across the cracked mosaic floors toward the lone occupant. Lord Sevilin, the leader of the rebellion, watched with narrowed eyes as Turk came toward him.

"I was surprised when I was informed you had arrived . . . alone. Where is the girl?"

Turk looked uncertainly at his lord. "Did no one

inform you that I have located her?" He thought Lord Sevilin would be pleased with the information, but the frown that marred the young man's handsome face suggested otherwise.

The rebels had rallied to Lord Sevilin's call to re-unite the country and move away from the bitter civil war that had divided Bal Forea for over a decade. Lord Sevilin was popular with the young people, who were easily swayed by his golden hair and deep blue eyes. Handsome of face, the young lord ignited loyalty in those with a rebellious spirit. All he lacked to gain the rule of the island was a royal bloodline, which he did not have. It was his stepfather, not his father, who had been the king's son.

"Are you certain the woman you saw is my cousin?"

Turk knew that even though Lord Sevilin claimed the young lady as his own kin, there was no blood tie between them. "There is no mistake. She is the very one I've been tracking for years. Although I haven't seen her since she was a child, I know it is Princess Thalia. She is as still as slippery as ever. One moment she was standing alone in the marketplace, but before I could approach her, she disappeared."

"So you came back to me empty-handed."

"Nay, lord. I watched the marketplace for seven days—she did not return. I need more men to help me in my search."

"Fool!" Lord Sevilin said, shaking his head in disgust. "Why did you leave Egypt if you knew she was there? She is the throne princess, and he who holds her rules Bal Forea. For now, I control all the young men who rebel against the old king, but the day will come when not even I can control them. I need her at my side to legitimize my claim. Those that follow me already know my grandfather is an inept king who has let bitterness and guilt rule his life and wreck his kingdom. I am the only one who can save the people and stop this war. But to do so, I must have the princess."

"If I could have taken her, I would have."

"So you keep telling me," Lord Sevilin said in disgust.

Turk bowed, but his eyes showed anger at being criticized. "You should be advised that there was another man searching for the princess—I managed to dispose of him, but I fear he'd already sent word to the king before I ended his miserable life."

"You should have remained in Egypt."

With an irritable frown, Turk said, "I left my best man behind to keep watch. I thought it was more important to inform you that she is in Egypt."

Lord Sevilin steepled his long, shapely fingers. "It is fortunate that my mother had great foresight and sent you after Princess Thalia years before the war began. However, the princess managed to elude you then, as she still does. Perhaps I should find someone else to bring her home."

Turk gritted his teeth and replied with a grimace, "I know Princess Thalia better than anyone, and I know her habits. Who but me understands how important she is to your cause? If she reappears at the marketplace while I am here, my men will follow her to her destination. It is but a matter of time before I have her."

"You would not be so sure of yourself if you knew the identity of the man that the king summoned to the palace this very day." Lord Sevilin's eyelids flickered the merest bit. "You are aware of the general they call the Destroyer?"

Turk's jaw tightened. "You speak of Count Ashtyn. Although we have never met, I know of him. His father was ruthless, and I'm told the son is much the same."

"My mother has placed one of our own in the king's household, and the spy overheard a conversation between two guards. The king means to send Count Ashtyn to Egypt to find my cousin. It is said the Destroyer uses his charm as well as his sword to gain his will." Lord Sevilin stared at Turk, thinking he had no charm at all, but he could be merciless, and he was still useful. "Be wary of him at all times. If you can, eliminate him."

"That is a deed I would relish," Turk replied, thinking about the pleasure he'd derive from slaying the king's most trusted general. "His death would devastate the Royal Army and deal them a blow from which they might not recover."

"Take care," Lord Sevilin warned. "Count Ashtyn is not so easy to kill, or the deed would already be done." Lord Sevilin's eyes narrowed. "He stands at the right hand of my grandfather. Thus he stands between me and the throne."

"I will sweep him out of your way."

"Don't boast of what you will do—just do it!" Lord Sevilin waved Turk away. "Board a ship for Egypt at first light."

As Turk left, the curtain behind Sevilin stirred and his mother, Lady Vistah, emerged. She had once been a handsome woman, but gluttony had thickened her waist and plumped her features. "I do not think you should have sent that man after the princess. He has tried and failed for years."

"He is the only one who knows her on sight. We are running out of time, Mother."

Her clawlike hand curled around his shoulder, and when Sevilin brushed it away, she shrugged and moved to a chair beside him. "You already know the need to marry the girl and get her with child as soon as she is brought to you."

"Aye. Not a pleasant thought. Living on the streets of Rome will have hardened her. Now, if she lives on the streets of Egypt, who knows what she has become?"

"What can that matter? She has the royal blood—you do not. But if you have a child by her, the child will be royal and will need its father to act as regent, which will be the same as sitting on the throne."

Lord Sevilin's eyes narrowed. "You are saying the princess will only be necessary to me until she gives birth?" He eased back in his chair, his gaze fixed on his mother's face. "Are you prepared to become grandmother to the next king or queen of Bal Forea?"

A ripple of excitement coursed through Lady Vistah's body, and her eyes flared with expectation. Uncurling her fingers from the arm of the chair, anticipation threaded her words. "We shall have her, and all will be ours!" She reached for a platter of date cakes and took a bite. Although her cheeks bulged with the cake, she reached for another and popped it into her mouth. "You do not need the princess after the child is born," she mumbled. Lady Vistah sunk back against her chair. She was a jealous mother and had no intention of sharing her son with any other woman.

He looked at her sardonically. "Aye, Mother. I do. With Princess Thalia, I will start a dynasty."

Dark shadows flickered across chipped marble walls. A sudden gust of wind burst through an open window, causing an oil lamp to flicker and almost go out before it flamed to life with renewed brightness. The old man sat hunched on a chair, staring at a scroll spread before him, his gnarled fingers stained with ink. He was king of a war-torn country, and he'd spent the last ten years trying to reunite his divided land.

King Melik nodded at the man who had suddenly appeared out of the shadows. "My good Count Ashtyn, you have come at last." The old man's eyes narrowed as he stared at his most trusted warrior. "Did I not summon you days ago? Did my messenger not inform you my need was urgent?"

Count Ashtyn was a mere shadow as he bowed to his sovereign. "I was three days away with our patrols on the eastern border when your messenger found me. My men had just located a rebel camp and although we were outnumbered, surprise was on our side. We wiped them out to a man. I stand before you with the dust of the road still clinging to my armor and blood on my sword."

The king waved the explanation aside. "What I need of you is far more important than a few dead rebels. I have a grave situation that requires your attention. My agent in Egypt sent a message that he has located my granddaughter." He sighed wearily, as if the years rested heavily upon his frail shoulders. "It seems the man disappeared after sending the message."

"Then we can assume he died in your service," Count Ashtyn said matter-of-factly.

"Aye, else he would have brought my granddaughter to me by now." A deep cough racked the old man's thin frame, and it took a moment for him to catch his breath. "I feel mortality shadowing my steps—my burdens are heavy, and I cannot keep death at bay for much longer. I would see my country free of civil war before I die."

Count Ashtyn was sympathetic, but he feared the king would be devastated if the young woman in Egypt was not his granddaughter. "Majesty, years have passed since the princess was last seen. She has grown into a woman, and we have to question how she could be in Egypt, when she was living on the streets of Rome eight years ago."

"It *is* my granddaughter, I feel it in my heart." The king seemed to shrink as he leaned forward and hung his head. "It must be her."

Count Ashtyn had other concerns. "Sire, you must consider that even if this person is the princess, she may not be . . . capable of ruling."

The old man stared at the lamp, the harsh light reflecting in his faded blue eyes. "That is of little matter; she is my heir and must take her place."

"Many will die if you bring her home. Sevilin will see to that."

King Melik's voice had a hard bite to it when he said, "No price is too heavy to pay when so many have already died in this war. The one fear that robs my sleep is what will become of my people if Sevilin finds her first. She will become his pawn. Bring Thalia to me so I may see her for myself. Never doubt I shall know flesh of my flesh when I see her."

Tension mounted between the two men. "Surely you are not sending me to Egypt. I have a war to fight. I cannot just leave!"

The king raised his head, urgency driving his words. "You must! If we can show the people that I have a living heir, she will be the steadying force that reunites Bal Forea. The people will rally behind her because she is of the true blood—not a usurper like Lord Sevilin, who sets my people against each other and proclaims himself their deliverer."

"The people have been without hope for so long. How can this young girl bring peace to our land?"

"Maybe she cannot. But I don't need to remind you what will happen if she is captured by my dead son's stepson. Sevilin would proclaim her queen, and himself king!"

Count Ashtyn nodded in resignation.

The king's blue-veined hand trembled as he clutched the arm of his chair. "Find her for me—keep her safe, no matter what the cost. Bring her to me with all haste." The king raised his wavering gaze to the only man he trusted to complete this mission. "Should something happen to me, you must make certain she is crowned queen. Thalia has been your responsibility since the pledge you made to me and your father before his death. She is yours to keep from harm."

Count Ashtyn gazed steadily into the king's watery eyes. "Majesty, I was but a lad when you and my father had me betrothed to the princess."

"Nevertheless, you gave your word, and I hold you

to it. When you bring Thalia home, she will need a strong man beside her—that man will be you."

Count Ashtyn swept into a bow. "I have not forgotten my pledge. If she is in Egypt, I shall find her and do what is expected of me."

The aged king shifted his weight and groaned in pain as he reached out and grabbed Count Ashtyn's arm. "Over the years your father was my loyal mainstay. I depended heavily on his wisdom and strength. Now that he's gone, I place my hopes in your hands. To this day you have not disappointed me in any task I have set you." His gaze hardened. "Do not fail me now."

"In all things, I serve you."

"Fly with the wings of haste. Use your cunning—do whatever you must to capture her." The king eased his grip on Ashtyn's arm, and his hand dropped away. "One thing more—if I die before you return, you must kill Sevilin." He met the young man's eyes. "That is another pledge I expect from you. Then you will do all that is necessary to help the true queen."

"I will guide her in any way I am able."

"Aye. You will guide her as her husband. You will sit at her side."

Count Ashtyn jerked his head toward the king, wanting to declare his aversion to being wed to a woman who had grown up on the streets. He shunned the thought of what she'd been forced to do to stay alive. He said instead, "I have never chosen to stand near the throne—I was given no choice at all."

"If you love me as your king, as soon as we know the young woman is of my blood, you will take her as your wife and consummate the marriage." The king suddenly dropped his head, as if it was too heavy to hold upright. "I know you are not as reluctant as you seem. It is said that you sometimes go into the fountain room and stare at the statue of Thalia's mother. Do you envision Thalia to look like her?"

"Aye. Sometimes I do," the count confessed.

The king sighed heavily and handed Ashtyn a scroll. "This describes the young woman in Egypt, and if the description is true, she is very like her mother."

Ashtyn read the scroll several times. "Then she is of great beauty," he admitted.

"Go. Bring her to me."

With hardly a sound, Count Ashtyn faded into the shadows and was gone.

The old king bowed his head, his heart heavy. He lamented the harshness with which he'd dealt with his daughter when she had proclaimed her love for the captain of his guard and refused to marry the nobleman of his choosing. His anger had caused his beautiful Jiesa to go into hiding. He could hardly bear to think of her tragic death, and not a day passed that he did not mourn her. But the gods had been merciful: his daughter had borne a child. If she was not found, his house would die with him, and his kingdom would fall to a lesser man.

❧ CHAPTER TWO

Tausrat Villa
Outside Alexandria, Egypt

Lady Larania of the house of Tausrat glanced across the room at her adopted daughter and smiled. Even from a distance, Thalia's golden hair and blue eyes stood out among all the dark-haired beauties. As usual, she was surrounded by young lords who vied eagerly for a place beside her.

There was something about Thalia that Lady Larania could not put into words, an aura that drew people to her. Lady Larania frowned as she watched one of the young gentlemen hold a sugared date out to Thalia, who took the fruit in her mouth, leaving the man blushing and stammering. She turned to speak to her son Ramtat, who stood at her side, smiling at his sister's antics. Her son was her pride: he was tall, as his father had been, with the same dark eyes, and just as handsome of face. Her attention briefly turned back to her daughter, who was laughing at something one of the men had said.

"I must speak to Thalia about her behavior: what I permitted her to do when she was a child is no longer acceptable. She will be known as a flirt if she continues to tease those young gentlemen."

Ramtat glanced at his mother and smiled with amused tolerance. Her black hair was peppered with white, and her high cheekbones gave evidence of her Bedouin heritage. Soft lines fanned out from her eyes and mouth, but she looked ten years younger than her true age and was still a handsome woman.

"I see no harm in my sister's actions. I have taken notice that she is careful not to be alone with any of the men. Thalia is young and a favorite with everyone—she does not seek them out, they find her." He glanced at the young woman who was lurking near his sister—Marsada was considered a renowned beauty, and Ramtat noticed the hatred and envy reflected in the young woman's dark eyes. "Perhaps not everyone loves her," he amended, nodding at the woman whose intended husband was lavishing attention on Thalia. "Soon we must find a suitable husband for Thalia, lest all the men in Egypt attach themselves to her. Until then, allow her to have fun before she settles into the duties of a wife."

Lady Larania's expression softened. "Thalia has been a joy to me from the moment she entered this house. She made me laugh at her antics as a child, and she warms my heart with her kindness. It will be difficult when the time comes for her to wed and leave me."

"When I look at her now, I don't know how she survived the cutthroat streets of Rome at such an early age."

"She seems carefree enough now, even though it grieves her that she has no past. There is strength in her and a tenacious will."

Ramtat noticed how pale his mother was, and he

feared her health was failing. "Do not fret, Mother. We cannot give Thalia back her past, but we have given her a future. Has she shown marked attention to any young man in particular?"

"Not in the least. She is content to entertain them all but does not favor one above another."

"It will take a man of strength and patience to conquer our Thalia's resistance." Ramtat surveyed the room. "All I see here are those she would dominate without even trying."

Lady Larania sighed. "Will you be leaving us in the morning?"

"Nay, I leave tonight. Our Badari will begin their migration within weeks, and I must be there to greet each chief as they arrive." His heart ached because this would probably be the last time his mother would join the desert tribes. She was much too thin, and he could tell it was an effort for her to remain standing, so he led her to a stool and made her comfortable.

Lady Larania's trembling hand rested on her son's strong arm. "Thalia and I shall be joining you in ten days' time."

"The Badari are always happy to welcome home their princess."

Thalia hardly had room to breathe. To her way of thinking, the men who surrounded her only talked nonsense when they were with a female, most probably because they thought a woman did not possess enough knowledge to have an intelligent conversation. Did they think she really cared that they compared her hair to spun gold or argued over which were more perfect, her lips or her eyes?

Untangling her fingers from one of the men who had dared touch her, she shook her head at him, moving away when he tried to recapture her hand. Rising amidst the protests of her would-be suitors, she hurried out of the banquet room and into the corridor.

Jamal, the guard, nodded to her—he would stop any gentleman who tried to follow her.

The gatherings were always the same—the women her age snubbed her, and the men persistently annoyed her by following her wherever she went. She never invited them to join her—they just seemed to attach themselves to her.

Thalia moved quickly through the marble corridor until she came to her bedchamber. Badaza, the housekeeper who ruled the villa and the other servants, was placing fresh linens in a trunk at the foot of Thalia's bed.

Heaving her heavy bulk around the bed and plumping a pillow, Badaza stared at the young mistress. "Was the party not to your liking?"

"It wearied me," Thalia said with a sigh, and then slipped out the arched doorway into the garden. She gazed up at the stars, wondering why she was so restless.

And why none of the men of her acquaintance touched her heart.

❧ CHAPTER THREE

Night had fallen, but the garden was illuminated by hanging lanterns that cast a soft glow along the pathway. Kicking off her shoes and carrying them with her, Thalia felt tranquility flow around her as her bare feet sunk into the cool grass. She paused beneath an acacia tree, reveling in its sweet scent. In her heart, she could feel the stirring of the night as the pulsebeat of the land flowed through her very being.

Egypt was her home, and she never wanted to leave it.

Her footsteps didn't slow until she reached the far end of the garden where she had often played as a child. The pond was filled with lotus blossoms, and several kinds of fish darted through the thick foliage. Thalia paused to pick up a fallen palm frond and fanned herself with the broad leaf. It was a lovely evening, with a full moon casting its glow upon the stone walls. Nuit, the ancient goddess of the sky, had sprinkled stars across the silken night. The sweet scent of lemon blossoms filled the air, and Thalia dropped her shoes and lowered herself onto a marble bench to bask in the beauty of the sounds and smells that surrounded her.

Closing her eyes, she fanned herself while pondering

her actions tonight. Thalia knew she would face a lecture from her mother for leaving the banquet early, but she could not have stood another moment of boredom. Lately, her mother had been pressing her to marry, and had paraded in front of her what seemed to Thalia like all of the eligible nobles in Egypt. Since the thought of spending an evening with any of them was so objectionable, how could she be expected to spend her *life* with one of them?

With a sigh, she emptied her mind and let the night close in around her.

"You seek solitude," a heavily-accented voice said in perfect Egyptian.

Thalia jumped to her feet, startled by the man who seemed to have appeared from the shadows. He was unknown to her, and his accent unfamiliar.

When the stranger turned his head toward the house, moonlight crowned the obsidian hair that fell to his shoulders. His white tunic was of good quality, though not what a man of wealth would wear to one of her mother's gatherings. She could not imagine this man living the superficial life of a courtier; strength clung to him like armor—perhaps he was a soldier.

"Are you one of my brother's friends?"

"Lord Ramtat," he said, as if testing the name.

Thalia paused, trying to gather her thoughts. The stranger was staring at her so intently it made her uneasy. At last she said, "Ramtat is my brother, do you know him?"

"I have heard much of him. Queen Cleopatra favors him."

Thalia was disappointed. He *was* a courtier, perhaps a visitor to Queen Cleopatra's court.

"I cannot quite place your accent, and yet it is somehow familiar to me," she remarked, merely to have something to say to cover the long silence.

"I am from an island far away. I think you may not have heard of it."

He stepped further into the light, and Thalia saw his shoulders were broad and muscular. She could not tell what color his eyes were, but they were sharp, and she doubted he missed anything that went on around him. At first glance he did not appear handsome, but on closer examination she reconsidered—his features were honed with stark planes and severe angles. His jaw was like granite. He must have realized she was studying him, because he was watching her just as closely.

There was a hint of danger about the man.

Never taking her gaze off his, she reached for her shoes with the intention of leaving. She saw coldness pour into his watchful eyes.

"You need not fear me," he told her.

Thalia dropped her shoes and slid her feet into them, thinking she should return to the house. She took a step before he stalled her with a question.

"Why did you leave the banquet?"

She answered before she could think. "I was not enjoying it."

He nodded, his brow creased into a frown. "I have been observing you for some time and came to that same conclusion. There were many men who wished to catch your notice, yet you eluded them."

A touch of fear stirred in Thalia's mind. Had her past come in search of her?

Of course this man wasn't from her past—he was too young, she reasoned. Besides, he had made no threatening move in her direction, though he admitted he'd been watching her.

She was reluctant to leave him until she discovered who he was and what he was doing in her garden. "The party was too noisy," she told him, "and I love it here in the garden this time of night."

"And why is that?" The stranger's voice was soothing and somehow seductive.

"It was on the very place you're standing that my brother-in-law, Marcellus, asked my sister, Adhaniá, to become his wife."

"Ah, your sister who married a Roman officer."

Thalia pressed her lips together, wondering why she had talked about her sister to this stranger—what was there about him that encouraged trust when she didn't know him? Even when the man said nothing at all, charm flowed from him and caused a breathless stirring within her.

"Marcellus is a Roman general."

"I wager I can guess your name," he said in a deep whispered tone, his gaze centered on the dimple in her chin.

"That would be no great feat, since everyone at my mother's party knows my name." Suspicion crept up her spine, and she frowned. "Are you an invited guest?"

"Nay, I am not. Yet I wager I know more about you than you can imagine. I could probably tell you things you don't even know yourself, Thalia."

She should have trusted her first instinct! She had a hard time finding her voice past the tightness in her throat, so her words came out in a whisper. "Do not speak my name again until you tell me yours."

His eyes half closed as he continued to study her,

beginning at her sandaled feet, lingering longer on the swell of her breasts before moving to her face and again centering his attention on her dimpled chin. "I seek one who is called Lady Thalia."

Stark terror poured into Thalia like water over a waterfall, and she shook with dread. "You should leave," she said, inching toward the path.

He took a step toward her, and she took one back.

"I would not have you fear me," he said with concern.

"You are a stranger, yet you speak too familiarly to me."

He paused in mid-stride. "Forgive me. I feel as if I know you. I have thought of you so often, and now to actually . . ." He watched the way the light from the torches fell on her golden hair. "You are the one I seek."

Fear crawled down Thalia's spine. Three days ago she'd accompanied her mother to the goldsmith's shop, and she'd felt nagging unrest, as if she was being watched. Although she had scanned the crowd, she had seen no one. At the time she had not wanted to upset her mother, and had quickly pushed the incident to the back of her mind. She should have trusted those instincts that had kept her alive as a child. Taking a quick step toward the path, Thalia gauged her escape route. "Why are you here in my garden?"

"I was sent by someone who fears for your safety."

Thalia's hand went to her throat as she stared into silver eyes that reflected the moonlight. A chill stole over her, and she inched farther away with the intention of running. "Please go away."

"Thalia, the last thing I wanted to do was frighten you. Can you not think of me as a friend?"

"You are not my friend, or you would not have come under cover of night."

He reached out to her, then let his hand fall. "If I had meant to harm you, the deed would already be done."

Ashtyn stared at the woman whose life had been tied to his. She was not what he'd expected—she was more. There was no sign that she'd ever been an urchin on the streets of Rome. She had grown up cherished and protected, and was so beautiful it took his breath away.

The words kept echoing in his mind.

Mine.

She is mine.

❦ Chapter Four

Thalia attempted to look away from the stranger's scrutinizing gaze, but she was held fast like a mouse cornered by a cat. Just when she thought she could not stand the tension another moment, she heard a footfall on the graveled path. Her courage returned and she faced her terror, asking the question that had haunted her all the years she had been pursued as a child. "Who sent you, and what do you want with me?"

"My allegiance is to a man who cares greatly for your safety. If you do not heed my warning, you will find yourself in grave danger, Lady Thalia. Come with me—trust in me to keep you safe."

Like a dark foreshadowing of dread, a sudden gust of wind struck, tearing at the trees, stripping leaves and sending them careening to the ground to gather at Thalia's feet. Her gaze met silver-blue eyes, and she seemed to have no will of her own.

She had been watching him so closely, she noticed the moment he became alert to the footsteps on the pathway. Relief washed over Thalia when her maidservant, Safra, called to her.

"Mistress, your honored mother has asked that you join her to pay your respects to the departing guests."

With profound relief Thalia answered, "I am here—wait for me." She had looked away from the intruder for a mere instant, but when she turned back, he was gone. There had been no sound to announce his departure; not a leaf stirred, not a twig snapped. The only sound she heard was her own ragged breathing.

The stranger had faded into the shadows and disappeared as if he'd never been there.

With fear driving her steps, Thalia fled toward Safra. "Let us go inside at once."

Safra had been her personal maid since she'd first come to Egypt, and the woman's concerned gaze swept Thalia's face. "Is something wrong, mistress? You seem distraught."

Thalia considered asking Jamal to search the garden, but instinct told her he would find no sign of the intruder. "Let us hurry," she urged, glancing over her shoulder. Instinct also warned her she'd not seen the last of the stranger.

When they passed the archway, Jamal, the stern-faced captain of the guards, lowered his gaze to Thalia, and she feared he'd sense something was wrong. "Post an extra man in the garden tonight. But say nothing about it to my mother. I do not want to worry her unnecessarily."

The Badari guard frowned. "Has something occurred I should know about?" he asked, his gaze already sweeping across the darkened corners of the garden.

Jamal was too shrewd to miss anything, so Thalia decided to tell him a half-truth. "I thought I saw a stranger lingering at the back of the garden. To be safe, have a look around."

Jamal frowned. "If there was an intruder, Lady Larania must be told at once."

Thalia shook her head. "Nay. Do not mention it to my mother. It was probably nothing more than my imagination."

Jamal's brow creased with worry. "As you will, Mistress." He bowed and stepped away to allow her to pass into the house. He then hurried down the pathway to search the garden.

When Thalia joined her mother, most of the guests had already departed. Determined to conceal her fear, Thalia pasted a smile on her face.

"You look pale," her mother commented.

"With so many people in the chamber it was sweltering, so I sought the cool of the garden. I just got overheated, that's all."

Lady Larania turned to Thalia so she could look into her eyes. "Heat never bothered you before. You love the desert."

"That is true."

Lady Larania sighed. "I had so wanted you to enjoy the evening."

Thalia's face brightened as she sought to distract her mother. "Soon we shall be leaving for the Badari encampment, and I will be happy to join the rest of the family." She dared not tell her mother that someone had breeched the garden walls, because her mother would worry.

"I am always contented when I am with my Badari," Lady Larania replied, watching the servants cleaning the room. "Aye, it will be wonderful for all of us to be together." Her gaze settled on Thalia. "I will be happy when you are settled with a man you can love and respect."

"There is no such man in my future. I could never be as fortunate as my brother and sister in their choice of life-mates." She smiled, linking her arm through her mother's. "But like you, I am content. I will be happy to remain with you forever."

"Nonsense. Your future will take you in another direction. One day you will meet a man who will make you happy."

"Where is Ramtat?" Thalia said, looking around desperately. "I wanted to hear how the children are faring."

"Ramtat was eager to rejoin Danaë at the encampment, so he left early. He asked that you go to the marketplace next week for the ring the goldsmith is crafting for Danaë. He does so love to surprise her."

"If I could find a man with the honor and intelligence of my brother, or my brother-in-law, I might consider marriage. But I have seen no one who can make me want to leave my home."

"Dearest daughter, have patience. The man you speak of is looking as hard for you as you are for him."

"Do you really believe that?"

Lady Larania gripped Thalia's hand and led her down the corridor.

"Indeed I do."

Thalia's mind wandered back to the man she'd encountered in the garden. Eight years had passed since she'd arrived in Egypt. The stranger was not one of the men who had pursued her as a child in Rome, but she knew the old fear was back. Danger had found her even in Egypt.

"Thalia?"

Her attention returned to her mother.

"Did you hear what I said?"

"I'm sorry, my mind was wandering."

"I merely mentioned that you should seek your bed. You look tired."

Thalia touched her mother's hand and moved to the door. "We are both weary, Mother."

Lady Larania nodded tiredly. "Sleep well, Daughter."

Thalia smiled. "Just think of it—Adhaniá and Marcellus will be arriving from Rome very soon. Their two sons must have changed greatly in the last year. And you shall see your new granddaughter for the first time."

Her mother smiled. "It will be a joyous reunion."

As Thalia made her way down the corridor, fear still lingered in the back of her mind. The man in the garden was a threat. There was no doubt in her mind he'd come for her. When she stepped into her bedchamber, she was glad to find Safra waiting for her. Thalia leaned her head against the door and watched the maid pull down the covers and plump the pillows.

Why was this happening to her? she wondered, trying not to give in to the terror that lurked at the back of her mind.

What was it that kept people searching for her after so many years?

Thalia didn't know who to fight or who to run from. How could she battle what she could not see?

Lying on her bed, Thalia fought against the sleep that tried to claim her. She was still frightened. Her thoughts traveled back to her childhood and the one-eyed man who had been determined to capture her.

Since she'd left Rome, he had only appeared in her nightmares. And what about the man who had invaded her garden? Was he somehow connected to the one-eyed man?

Thalia realized she had been too complacent in thinking she'd left that frightening part of her life behind in Rome.

Her eyelids were so heavy, and still she fought against the drowsiness that threatened to take her. She clutched her hands, digging her fingernails into her palms, hoping pain would hold back the dream.

Shadows swallowed the sunlight, casting her into total darkness—her head was spinning, and terror tightened inside her because she knew what came next—it was always the same, never deviating in any way. The same beautiful woman grabbed her up in her arms and ran down a long hallway. Thalia did not know who the woman was, but she could feel her fear, and she knew the woman was trying to save them. Flames licked at the walls, all but devouring the house. The woman stumbled and fell. Thalia felt pain rip through her body as she hit the stone floor. The woman scrambled to her feet, gathering Thalia in her arms once more, then handed her to the serving woman. Shoving Thalia into the servant's arms, the beautiful woman spoke in a language Thalia understood, although it was not Latin. "Take her to safety. A ship is waiting to take you both away—they will be expecting you."

At this point the nightmare always worsened.

A horrible man with long stringy hair and a twisted expression blocked their escape. The servant ran with Thalia

*clutched in her arms, but the man drew steadily closer. The
wind tore at her hair, tangling it about her face, and Thalia
could not see what was happening. A dark void yawned before her, and she was sliding toward it, clawing and trying
to save herself.*

She was falling, falling.

It always ended the same way, and try as she might,
Thalia could not push aside the dark curtain that
shrouded the past, because there was nothing behind
the black void.

She took a deep gulp of air, not realizing until that
moment that she'd stopped breathing. Even as darkness swallowed the dream, her heart was thundering
inside her. Terror kept her pinned to the bed, then
slowly Thalia was able to raise up on her elbows. She
searched her chambers, not because she thought anyone was lurking in the shadows, but because she was
still cautious after all these years.

This was her home—a place that was dear and familiar to her—a place where she had found love and
kindness, and until tonight she'd thought she had escaped her past.

Easing off the bed, she padded across the cool floor
and stepped out into the garden. Obviously her encounter with the man earlier in the evening had caused
her nightmares to return. Even if he was not the scarred-
faced man she feared, he was a threat nonetheless.

Thalia remained in the garden until soft light chased
away the shadows and dark clouds moved away from
the moon. Fear had invaded her home, and the past
had caught up with her.

A sudden movement across the pathway made her

cringe until she recognized one of the guards. Good Jamal had taken her fear seriously and posted more men around the villa.

What could be so important about her that whoever pursued her would not stop?

The man in the garden had said she was in danger.

From whom?

From him.

Thalia was still pondering what she should do as sunrise struck the garden walls. If only Ramtat or Adhaniá's husband Marcellus was in Alexandria, they could advise her.

Danger was stalking her, waiting for her to become careless.

❦ CHAPTER FIVE

In the light of day the bad dream had faded, leaving Thalia feeling somewhat foolish. Walking toward the stables, she'd convinced herself that she had overreacted to the stranger the night before. She even smiled when she remembered how frightened she'd been. The poor man must have thought her reaction to him was odd.

But how was she supposed to react when he warned her of danger?

Moving beneath a grape arbor, she reached over her head, snatched a cluster of grapes and bit into one, savoring the taste. The sun was just dropping below the horizon, and the workers were coming in from the fields. She knew many by name and waved to them as they passed her.

The family had many holdings, but here at Tausrat Villa, near Alexandria, was where she had spent most of her time. The estate was substantial, with fields, outbuildings and stables. As she ambled along, enjoying the quiet of the evening, one of her sandals came unlaced and she almost tripped. Thalia bent to retie it, and a shadow fell across her face. Thinking it was one of the workers, she glanced up and smiled.

But this man was not one of the slaves that toiled in the family fields. He was the same person who haunted her nightmares. He was older now, and his long hair had thinned on top, but his one good eye was just as piercing, and the scar on his face just as frightening.

She stepped back, glancing over her shoulder, wondering whether anyone would hear her if she called out for help before the man overtook her.

"It's been a long time, lady," he said, stepping closer. "Many times you eluded me in Rome though you were but a child. But no matter; I have found you. You will come with me now."

His accent was different from that of the man she'd encountered in the garden the night before—this man's voice was guttural and less cultured. Anger, more than fear, prompted her to take a step toward him. "You must be crazed. I have no intention of going anywhere with you."

"I would prefer if you came willingly, but it matters little. I shall take you by force if need be."

Thalia's only thought was to escape—there were no catacombs where she could hide, but she was no longer alone. Far to her right were the workers' dwellings, but most of them had already gone inside. Between her and the safety of the garden walls was a long stretch of open ground.

Without pausing to think, Thalia turned and ran, her heart pounding, her pulse racing. She heard the man's lumbering footsteps behind her—he was gaining on her. When Thalia reached the grape arbor, she saw Jamal hurrying toward her, his sword drawn—but would he reach her in time? Suddenly the workers were coming out of their houses, and they too were racing to help her. Knowing rescue was near at hand, Thalia turned back to face her pursuer—something she had never had the courage to do when she was a child. "Who are you, and what do you want with me?"

The man held up his hands as if in surrender. "We shall meet again, lady."

"If you come near me again, my guards will slay you."

When he smiled, his scar tugged at his lip, and it looked more like a frown. "Until we next meet," he said, moving back down the tilled row. For such a big man he moved with surprising agility as he ran to his horse and rode away.

By the time Jamal reached her, Thalia was still trembling. "Are you harmed, Mistress? Who was that man?"

"I am not harmed, but he frightened me," she said, pressing her hands together to stop their quaking.

"What did he want of you?" Jamal asked, knowing he could not catch the man since he was on foot and the intruder had a horse.

Thalia could do no more than whisper. "He wanted me to go away with him."

"Come," the guard said, motioning for the workers to go on their way. "I will escort you to your mother. Describe the man for me, and I will send out a search for him."

She paused. "I would not have you cross swords with that man even if you could locate him—he is dangerous. And something more, Jamal—say nothing to my mother of this incident. I do not want to worry her."

He frowned. "She must be told that you are being threatened."

"I will explain it to my mother in my own time."

"What can you tell me about that man, Mistress?"

"When I was a child he ruled me through fear—I will not allow him that much power over me now that I am a woman." Her words were brave, but she was frightened.

"But, Mistress, we must tell—"

She held up her hand to silence him. "We will tell my brother when next we see him. But I forbid you to upset my mother."

By now they had reached the gate to the inner garden, and Thalia turned her gaze on Jamal. "I will be safe when we reach the desert. Until then, I shall be careful."

"I will double the guard."

Thalia nodded in agreement. "Do it in such a way that will not draw my mother's attention."

His breath hissed through his teeth, but the habit of obedience was strong within him. "As you will." Jamal bowed stiffly and stalked away.

When Thalia reached her bedchamber, she dropped down onto a stool and removed her sandals. Could there be *two* men after her? she wondered. Were they collaborators or enemies? Perhaps the man in the garden *had* been trying to warn her about the one-eyed man.

Her dimpled chin went up a notch. Until she could talk to Ramtat, she must either conquer her fear or give in to it, and she was not of a temperament to admit defeat.

The noonday sun beat down on the streets of Alexandria in white-hot waves as crowds of people moved through the marketplace. Unnoticed, a man mingled with the crowd, his gaze sweeping the marketplace for any trouble that might come his way.

Count Ashtyn quickly stepped beneath the shade of an overhanging palm frond that projected out from the front of the Green Jackal Inn. He waited and watched, making sure he was not being followed, before entering the taproom. His gaze swept the faces of the people seated at tables until he saw the man he sought. It was difficult to miss Captain Darius, a huge man with broad shoulders and hands that were larger than most men's heads. Ashtyn motioned for the captain to join him upstairs.

Opening the door to the small chamber, Ashtyn ignored the strong odor of unwashed flesh that permeated the room. He avoided the filthy straw bed that was probably lice-infested and moved to the window, throwing wide the shutters and taking a deep breath of fresh air.

Ashtyn didn't have long to wait before he heard Captain Darius's unmistakable lumbering gait coming down the corridor. The door was thrust open and the big man stepped into the room, glancing back over his shoulder to make certain he'd not been followed. Before he spoke, he glanced about the filthy room, curling his lip in distaste.

Ashtyn knew that his captain's past experience as a prisoner locked in a dank dungeon had made him uncomfortable in enclosed places, and this inn was no exception. "Has the scribe told you anything that can help us?"

Captain Darius moved to the window to stand beside his lord. "Commander, I had to ply the man with two jugs of wine in hopes of loosening his tongue. He told me nothing. But I believe he's ready for you to question him."

Ashtyn braced his hands on either side of the window, staring at the rubbish-littered alleyway. When he spoke, it was obvious he'd chosen his words with care. "I believe I made a grave mistake last night." He turned back to Captain Darius. "I went to the Tausrat Villa and climbed the wall into the garden. The family was having a celebration, and I thought I might blend in long enough to find a servant who would talk to me about their young mistress."

Captain Darius was shocked. His commander didn't usually make such a mistake. "Did you find out what you wanted to know?"

"Unfortunately, it wasn't a servant I encountered," Ashtyn admitted. "The lady herself came upon me, taking me by surprise. Her tread was so soft, she was standing beside me before I could react."

Captain Darius looked worried. "It is not easy for anyone to sneak up on you, Commander. You have the ears of a fox."

"And the young woman has the tread of a cat."

"What happened?"

"I frightened her." Ashtyn looked at the big man. "I tried to warn her that she was in danger, but I did more harm than good. She didn't believe me. I feel sure the guards have been doubled around the perimeter. I am forced to find another method to trap her."

"You are sure she's the one you seek?"

"She is King Melik's granddaughter. Of this I have no doubt."

"Then we can take the princess home at last."

Ashtyn continued to speak as if he had not heard Captain Darius. "Although it was dark, I could see her hair was golden in color, and her eyes are definitely blue. Although she passes for a daughter of the Taus-rat family, she is not of Egyptian blood."

Skepticism crept into the captain's voice. "Com-mander, many wealthy Egyptians have slaves from other countries—here you cannot judge them by hair or eye color."

"Princess Thalia is no slave, but is considered a daughter of the house. She is the image of the statue of her mother, just as I knew she would be."

"Do you still wish to question the scribe before he sobers?"

"Where is he?"

The big man leaned his shoulder against the wall and folded his arms over his broad chest. "I left him with his head on a table, attempting to make the room stop spinning. I gave the innkeeper a gold piece to keep him there until you are ready to interrogate him."

"Take him to our camp and wait for me there. I want him out of the city so we will not be interrupted."

"Will you not come with us?"

"Nay, we must separate. Leave my horse at the back door—I'll join you later. I have a feeling we are being watched."

Captain Darius nodded. If the commander thought they were being watched, they were. "Have a care—there might be more than one."

"There are more, but there is only one who watches this place."

Acting on instinct, when Ashtyn left the Green Jackal Inn, he doubled back, hiding in the courtyard in the shadows of a mud-brick storage house that gave him a view of both the back and front doors of the tavern.

His instincts had kept him alive in many dangerous situations. As was his habit, he made decisions without pausing to consider. Now he waited and watched as the evening shadows lengthened and night approached.

Ashtyn's patience was rewarded when a man exited the inn, his gaze cautiously sweeping the courtyard, and Ashtyn recognized him as a rebel spy. Waiting until the man drew near, Ashtyn grabbed him around the neck and dragged him behind the shrubs. With a quick twist, Ashtyn heard a snap and dropped the limp man to the ground.

Gathering the reins of his horse, he mounted and rode toward the desert. If Turk and his followers were in Egypt, Ashtyn had to act quickly.

❧ Chapter Six

Night had fallen by the time Ashtyn reached camp. He'd chosen a site on raised ground so he could see in every direction and spot the enemy before they approached. When he dismounted, Captain Darius was waiting for him.

"He's beginning to coming around, Commander, and starting to ask questions. He wants to know why I brought him here."

Ashtyn glanced at the man huddled close to the fire, shivering. Dressed in a simple linen tunic, the man was lean and short with thin lips. His black wig was askew on his head, and his dark eyes looked to Ashtyn for answers.

"You'll not need to use force on this one, Commander," Captain Darius observed. "I believe charm will work on him."

The scribe tried to scramble to his feet as Ashtyn approached, but dizziness overcame him. Holding his head in his hands, he asked, "Lord, can you tell me where I am? The last thing I recall was drinking wine at the Green Jackal Inn with that man." He pointed to Captain Darius. "And now here I am, and my head feels like it's cracking."

Ashtyn flashed a friendly smile, picked up a blanket, draped it around the scribe's shoulders and sat down next to him. "So, good sir, wine makes your head ache, does it?"

"Not usually, Lord. But for whatever reason, I drank more than usual. Even now my head swims." He looked up with blurry eyes, holding his hand over his mouth. "Why am I here?"

"Since you had consumed so much wine, you were vulnerable to every robber and cutthroat who frequented the inn. My man, Darius, brought you to our camp where you would be safe."

Captain Darius nodded to himself. The commander had a method that always bore fruit: He would gain the person's confidence by making them feel he was their friend and plying them with compliments until they were willing to spill their deepest secrets. He had seen hardened warriors tell Count Ashtyn everything he wanted to hear, and afterwards, thank him for the pleasure of doing so. Of course, when that didn't work, there was always force, and he was good at that as well. But force would not be needed with this man.

"Darius would have taken you home," Ashtyn continued, "but you were in no condition to tell him where you reside."

Lady Larania's scribe held his head, grimacing in pain while trying to settle more comfortably beneath the blanket. "I am not accustomed to the richness of the date wine. My pecuniary resources most oft run to grog or barley beer." He looked shamefaced for a moment. "You may find this hard to fathom, but it is not my usual habit to drink so much." A sudden thought must have occurred to him, because he reached for his money belt as if he feared he'd already been robbed.

The scribe smiled and jabbed his elbow into Ashtyn's ribs. "I beg pardon. I wrongly had the notion you and your man there might have brought me here to rob me." He juggled his money pouch and shook his head. "Forgive me, eh?" he asked, his expression contrite.

"There is nothing to forgive," Ashtyn assured the man. "We are all friends here."

"I should go home," the scribe said, trying to stand and falling back, his head bobbing to the side. "My mistress and her daughter will soon be leaving for the desert, and they will need my assistance to get the household in order."

"My friend," Ashtyn said, clapping the scribe on the back. "It is not safe to be about at this time of night. The roads are hazardous with footpads and scoundrels. Rest the night with us, and we will see you safely on your way at daybreak."

Ashtyn's advice must have seemed sound to the little man, because he relaxed a bit and settled lower into the blanket. "Why would you show such kindness to a stranger? You have an accent unfamiliar to me, so you cannot be from Egypt."

"I am but a traveler in your country," Ashtyn admitted. "I welcome this chance to speak with someone of intelligence who can explain your wondrous land to me."

"I am an educated man," the scribe said, warming to Ashtyn's praise. "I am scribe for one of the most prominent families in all Egypt."

Captain Darius was tethering the horses. "What did

I tell you, Commander—Did I not say this was a man of some import?"

"Commander?" the man asked, now alert.

" 'Tis but a title of respect," Captain Darius quickly amended his statement. "I sometimes speak before I think."

The scribe's head was clearing, and he looked from one man to the other with distrust. "From where do you hail, and why are you in Egypt?" he wanted to know.

Ashtyn spoke in a calming voice. "We dwell on a small island beyond the great sea. I doubt you have heard of it."

The scribe compressed his lips. "I have never been out of Egypt. But I would like to travel one day."

Captain Darius saw that Ashtyn had completely won the scribe's trust. He was glad, because he'd taken a liking to the little man and didn't want to see him hurt.

"By what name shall I call you?" Ashtyn asked, his gaze sweeping across the man's face.

"I am called 'Klama, the scribe'."

"And I am Ashtyn."

"It's fortunate that the two of you befriended me, else I would surely have been robbed."

"Do you live in the city?" Ashtyn asked, knowing full well where Klama lived.

"Nay, nay. I dwell just a bit south of the city on a large estate belonging to the Tausrat family. I have but newly been hired to see to the mistress's household finances. I count myself fortunate to work for such a fine family. I can tell you it is not always so with men in my profession."

"Tell me about the family you work for, my new friend Klama. What are they like?"

Captain Darius smiled to himself as he sliced cheese and placed grapes in wooden bowls, handing one to each man. The commander continued to weave his magic. The poor foolish scribe would tell Count Ashtyn everything he wanted to know, and never be the wiser for it.

"The head of the Tausrat family is Lord Ramtat. He is adviser to Queen Cleopatra herself—you may not believe this, but Lord Ramtat's wife is half-sister to the queen. On his mother's side of the family, Lord Ramtat inherited the title of sheik to the Badari Bedouin." Klama took a bite of cheese and mulled over his next words. "As you see, I have ties to a most important family. The eldest daughter is married to a Roman lord and spends half her time in Rome and the other half in Alexandria. I have not yet met her—but the whole family will be gathering at the desert encampment for some kind of celebration."

Captain Darius handed Count Ashtyn a wooden cup of wine and offered one to the scribe as well, but the little man refused with a shake of his head. The scribe continued to speak with pride of the Tausrat family, and Captain Darius smiled to himself, thinking the commander wouldn't be able to keep this man from talking if he tried.

Ashtyn took a sip of wine and leaned back on his blanket. "I thought the queen's sisters and brothers were all dead. Had I heard wrongly?"

"I don't know the particulars, but the queen is very fond of this sister." He prattled on without the slightest urging. "I have actually seen the queen on two occasions when she visited Tausrat Villa. Queen Cleopatra is magnificent in all her finery, but she acts like one of the family when she visits. Of course, the queen took no notice of me, and why should she?"

Ashtyn met Darius's gaze as they both realized that the Egyptian queen having such close ties with the family was not welcome news. There was danger in rousing Cleopatra's anger, for her husband was Mark Antony, the most powerful man in the world.

Antony and his Roman legions could swarm over Bal Forea like a destructive wind. And in truth, the Roman Proconsul would not hesitate to draw the island's population under Roman domination. The only reason Rome had paid no heed to Bal Forea thus far was because it was too insignificant for them to bother with. And those who had tried to conquer the island in the past had given up when they discovered how difficult it was to fight their way through the inhospitable mountainous regions.

"So there is but the one brother and sister in the Tausrat family?" Ashtyn continued to prod.

"Nay, there is one other. Lady Thalia is quite the beauty—sweet and kind as well. One does not always find those qualities in such a grand young lady. She always speaks my name in greeting."

Ashtyn glanced at the campfire, watching it die to smoldering embers. "This daughter, Lady Thalia, is she wed?"

"Nay. But it is not because she has had no suitors. Young gentlemen hang around her like bees drawing nectar from a flower, but so far she will have none of them. I am not saying she discourages them, but she does not encourage them either."

"Then she is a flirt."

The little man's face reddened in defense of the lady.

"No one would dare called her that, except perhaps some of the young ladies who are jealous of her comeliness. She is just too kind to send anyone from her side."

"So your mistress has two daughters and one son."

"That is not exactly the way of it," Klama said, finally reaching for the cup of wine and taking a sip. "This is an interesting story, and you may not believe me, but I swear it is the truth. My mistress's younger daughter, Lady Thalia, was actually rescued from the streets of Rome when she was but a child. Lady Adhaniá brought my little mistress to Egypt. Lady Larania adopted her, and I have seen for myself how Lady Thalia is loved, just as if she'd been born of their blood."

Ashtyn's eyes gleamed. This was his final proof. His search was over.

He had found the lost princess!

His princess.

Captain Darius tried not to smile as he gathered the bowls and scraps of food. "I suppose we'll be leaving before sunup," he said loudly.

"Aye. That we shall."

"You know," the little scribe said, with brow furrowed, "speaking of Lady Thalia, I heard her talking to Jamal, the head guard, and she believes someone is trying to kidnap her."

Ashtyn looked at him sharply. "Why should she think that?"

"As I heard it, a one-eyed stranger came upon her in the fields and was intent on capturing her. I can tell you Lady Thalia is not one to spook easily. After all, she survived on the streets of Rome." He popped a grape in his mouth and waited until the sweet juice ran down his throat, not seeing his host stiffen. "My mistress has been ill lately, and Lady Thalia refuses to upset her. She has ordered the servants not to speak of the one-eyed man to her mother."

Ashtyn drew in a deep breath. "Surely your young mistress understands the danger to herself."

"She still goes about like nothing happened. I can tell you the head guard, Jamal, is plenty worried."

"Tell me about this man with only one eye."

"I know nothing but what I overheard."

Ashtyn clenched his fists, and his gaze met Captain Darius's. Turk had found the princess! They must act quickly before he had a chance to capture her.

Ashtyn rose to his feet and gazed back toward Alexandria. He must strike fast and hard!

❧ CHAPTER SEVEN

Dressed in a short white tunic with gold ribbon crisscrossing beneath her breasts and golden amulets clasped about her upper arms, Thalia laced her sandals to her knees. For the past few days, she had allowed fear to keep her confined to the safety of the house. But today she had awakened determined that nothing was going to keep her from going into Alexandria on an errand for Ramtat.

A short time later, a hot breeze kissed her face and tangled her hair. She maneuvered her chariot down the rutted road, delighting in the high-stepping gait of the matching whites. The horses were born and bred by Ramtat's fierce Bedouin tribe and were the most sought-after breed in all Egypt, perhaps in the world. They were so graceful that everyone stopped what they were doing to stare after the horses when her chariot passed.

Safra, however, did not admire them. When her young mistress swerved around a corner, Safra swayed, gripping the top side of the chariot, her face the color of paste. Jamal and six mounted guards rode behind Thalia, scanning the countryside for any sign of danger.

The guards had been added at Jamal's insistence, and Thalia was glad for the extra protection.

Poor Safra trembled with concern when Thalia urged her whites to a swifter pace. Nervously, she tugged at Thalia's sleeve. "Mistress, are we not going too fast?"

"You worry too much," Thalia assured her, smiling and sweeping around yet another corner with controlled ease. "Did you not hear my brother Ramtat say I was almost as good a charioteer as those who race in the great Circus of Rome?"

"Aye, he did say that," Safra admitted, tightening her hold even more. "If you do not have a care, we will surely tip over!" she cried, clinging tighter to the golden rung.

"Fear not. I shall get us to the goldsmith's and back home without mishap." Thalia's expert young hands held firmly on the reins. "Trust in me to keep you safe."

"*Aiee*, I trust *you*, but not those great brutes," Safra cried, her eyes widening. "Suppose they take it in their heads to race through the streets, crushing people as they go!"

"My whites are as gentle as newborn lambs and respond to the slightest tug on the reins."

"Those beast are not lambs, they're thistle thorns!"

Thalia's laughter danced on the wind as she reflected on the poor woman's fear and slowed the stallions to placate her. The chariot was black with gold trim, and had been a gift from Queen Cleopatra. The four Badarian whites that pranced at the end of the red leather reins were a gift from Ramtat and had been specially trained to draw a chariot.

Thalia loved the freedom she experienced when

she could allow her whites to run full out—she loved the wind in her hair and sun on her face. But poor Safra was frightened out of her wits, so Thalia slowed their pace even more for the maid's sake.

Thalia artfully swerved to miss a row of tethered donkeys laden with wares for the marketplace. She laughed aloud when Safra groaned. The jingle of harnesses turned many gazes in her direction, and those who knew Thalia respectfully bowed as she passed.

As they neared Alexandria, the roadway became more congested, and Thalia slowed the horses to a canter. She never tired of the sight of the numerous marble obelisks that vied for space against the background of the great lighthouse. In the distance, sunlight reflected off the Mediterranean Sea, giving the appearance of melted turquoise. The very air she breathed was charged with excitement.

Thalia had always loved the sounds and smells of the marketplace of Alexandria and thought of it as the heartbeat of Egypt. The fishmonger called out that his fish was a fresh catch. A basketmaker's artful fingers wove spindly reeds into shape. The potter's wheel turned as masterful hands shaped a fat blue jug. Thalia loved Egypt as much as any daughter who had been born to this ancient land.

When they reached the center of the marketplace, the press of humanity was so great that Thalia was forced to slow the whites to a walk. The goldsmith's shop was just ahead, and she halted the team in front of it. Tying the reins off, she stepped from the chariot, instructing Safra to wait for her. The guards halted their horses to await her return.

When Thalia entered the shop, she paused to watch

the goldsmith lift a crucible of melted gold and pour it into a mold the shape of a coiled asp. She knew the piece was being crafted for Queen Cleopatra. When the goldsmith saw her, he immediately stopped what he was doing and bowed low. "Have you come for the ring Lord Ramtat ordered, Lady Thalia?"

"Aye, Master Craftsman. My brother is anxious to make a gift of this to his wife."

The goldsmith bowed once more and handed her an ebony box that contained the ring. When Thalia stepped out of the shop, the sights and sounds reminded her of her childhood on the streets of Rome. But Alexandria was the queen of cities, with marble buildings reflected against blue skies, while Rome copied the architectural styles of those she conquered. Of course, Thalia's Roman brother-in-law, Marcellus, was the newest Master Architect of Rome, and he copied no man's work. She was proud of his accomplishments, which were admired by many around the world.

Noticing her whites were growing restless and stomping their hooves, Thalia mounted the chariot and took up the reins.

On the homeward journey, the streets were more congested, and it soon became necessary for Thalia to rein her horses to a full stop. Without movement, the heat was like the inside of an oven and sweat ran down her face, stinging her eyes.

A sudden unease touched Thalia's mind—at first it was just a prickle of disquiet, and then a trickle of edginess. Her gaze quickly moved over the faces of the people that surrounded her, but she saw nothing threatening. There was a sea of faces, all unknown to her, but no one who seemed to wish her harm. Then she swung her head to her left, and he was there.

The one-eyed man.

Thalia tensed, fear tingling all over her like ants crawling her skin. She glanced over her shoulder to see how close Jamal and his guards were, and her heart plummeted—they were some way back, attempting to manoeuver though the crowd.

Swinging her head back in the direction of her old nemesis, she watched him pushing his way through the throngs of people in an attempt to reach her.

Since Thalia was hemmed in by the crowd, she could go no farther lest her horses trample the people in front of her. Her grip tightened on the whip, and she spoke quickly to Safra. "Step out and go quickly to Jamal. Tell him I need him at once!"

"Mistress?"

All the fear Thalia had experienced as a child now resounded in her mind, and panic took over her reasoning. "Go now. Hasten!"

Safra looked confused. "Mistress, the guards can do nothing to clear the people from your path. Would it not be better to wait until the crowd thins?"

Losing patience because the servant questioned her at such a time, she shoved Safra out of the chariot. "Bring the guards to me at once. Tell them I am in danger!"

Thalia, still at a standstill, was vaguely aware that Safra was attempting to elbow her way to the guards. Frantically, she searched the crowd and was somewhat relieved that she could not see the one-eyed man. Perhaps she'd only imagined him? No, there had been no mistake—she'd clearly seen his deeply scarred face.

Where was he?

Just as the crowd began to thin and Thalia could take a deep breath, she felt a presence behind her. He was there—she could feel his chill gaze upon her.

And then he emerged from the crowd. With heavy tread, he closed in on Thalia.

Raising her whip, she tried to strike him, but he grabbed her wrist and jumped into the chariot beside her.

From their mounted horses, other eyes watched the incident in the marketplace. Ashtyn's voice vibrated with anger as he spoke to Captain Darius. "Turk got to her before us. Follow him and find out where he takes her, then return to me at once."

"Aye, Commander."

Captain Darius nudged his horse around the edge of the crowd, taking a little-traveled alleyway and coming out the other end, in sight of the disappearing chariot. He stayed far enough behind Turk so the man wouldn't realize he was being followed. From the looks of it, Turk was having a difficult time subduing the young woman while trying to keep the spirited whites under control.

Ashtyn watched Thalia's confused guards scatter in every direction. They would never reach the princess in time to rescue her.

Fools, he thought, as he helplessly spun his horse around. *Why hadn't they stayed close enough to protect her?*

Dark clouds were gathering in the north, and the smell of rain was in the air as Thalia struggled against the hateful man, fighting for her freedom. But he was too strong for her and managed to press her between him and the chariot. He wrenched the whip from her hand and applied it to the horses. The whites, not accustomed to the whip, leaped forward, and the crowd scattered to avoid the flying hooves.

Thalia would not admit she was beaten. She shoved against the man, but with his heavy bulk, he merely smiled at her futile attempt.

"Cease struggling," he told her, grabbing her wrists in a tight grip. "I mean you no harm. Your safety is my one concern."

Fat raindrops pelted Thalia as she continued to struggle. "Why do you do this?" she cried, trying to loosen her hands so she could strike him. "Answer me!"

He stared straight ahead. "Your questions will all be answered when the time is right."

Thalia thought of her mother and how grieved she would be when she heard what had happened. "If you mean me no harm, allow me to give a message to my servant to take to my mother. She is unwell."

The stranger merely looked down at her with that cold, colorless eye, and she felt fear clog her throat. He seemed to know all the twists and turns of the side streets and alleyways that took them away from the crowds. He refused to slow the horses when some unsuspecting person was in his path, and Thalia thanked the gods that thus far no one had been trampled beneath the hooves of her whites.

He was pressing against her so tightly she could hardly draw a breath, and she could not move at all.

"Where are you taking me?" she asked in a trembling voice. "I demand to know."

"A place where no one will look for you until I can safely get you onboard a ship."

Now she was really frightened. "You are taking me out of Egypt?"

He fixed her with his rheumy eye. "I am taking you home to the island of Bal Forea."

"What do you mean?" she asked, trying to squirm loose. "Are you mad?"

"Nay, Lady—I will be greatly rewarded for capturing you."

She stilled and fell silent while a tremor shook her. The person she had run from for most of her childhood had finally caught her.

"Who will pay you for my capture?"

"You will learn in time."

She was in real trouble. No one would know where to look for her.

"It will mean your life if you don't set me free," she told him.

"I'm in no danger—your family will not miss you for hours, and by that time, we will be out of the city."

All the rooms at the villa were lit and the estate was a beehive of activity. Lady Larania's guards swarmed throughout Alexandria, questioning people and searching every building in the marketplace, but they could find no trace of Thalia.

Fierce Bedouin warriors surrounded the house and gardens, their swords unsheathed, ever alert for trouble. With trembling hands, Lady Larania finished the message she was writing to Ramtat, urging him to return at once. Rolling the scroll, she tapped it against the palm of her hand, wondering helplessly if there was more she could do.

Jamal entered Lady Larania's chamber with a heavy tread, his head bowed low in shame. "Mistress, you have every right to blame me for Lady Thalia's abduction. But the man who took the young mistress timed his plan well. With the crowds swarming around us, there was no way we could reach Lady Thalia in time."

"I do blame you," she said, standing and pacing. "I'm told you knew she had been approached by strangers on two different occasions and did not inform me. Why is that?"

"Mistress," he said, his gaze hitting the floor. "Not wanting to worry you, Lady Thalia ordered me not to say anything. She can be very persuasive when she puts her mind to it."

"Tell me everything that happened. My son will want to know when he arrives. Who was the man? Why did he take my daughter?"

"I can think of no one who would wish her harm. But whoever did this was brazen—he took her in open daylight among a multitude of people, with her guards just behind her. He jumped into the chariot with your daughter and spirited her away. Before we could reach her, they had disappeared."

Lady Larania stared at the man. "No one just disappears."

Once more Jamal bowed his head, unable to meet his mistress's accusing gaze. It was his responsibility to protect the Tausrat family. He had failed, and now bore the shame.

"Mistress, what is it you wish me to do?"

"I wish I knew." Lady Larania turned her tear-bright eyes away so he would not see her cry. "If anyone is to blame, it is I." Her shoulders hunched with weariness. "I should have remembered her telling me she had been followed as a child. But I thought her safe here. It never entered my mind that anyone would take her away from us."

"Mistress, be not concerned for your own safety. My warriors will not allow anyone to cross these lands."

She spun around to face him, anger choking her. "Do not think I worry about my own safety—I want my daughter back! Don't waste valuable time and men guarding me." She handed him the scroll. "Give this to your fastest rider and instruct him to travel night and day to reach my son. Have him inform Lord Ramtat of what has happened and ask in my name that he come here in all haste."

Jamal took the scroll, bowing low. "If Lady Thalia is still in the city, we will find her."

Lady Larania's spine stiffened. "And if she is not?"

Jamal gave a hopeless gesture and said glumly, "Then we will widen the search."

❦CHAPTER EIGHT

When Thalia's captor lifted her into his arms, she struggled and twisted, trying to get away from him. She could see that he intended to abandon her horses and chariot in a dank, narrow alley. "Let go of me," she commanded.

Turk laughed down at Thalia. "Someone will sell the chariot and steal the horses," he said, carrying her away. "That will make it more difficult for anyone to trace us."

"My guards are Bedouin; they are not so easily fooled, as you shall soon discover."

His mouth thinned. "If the men who guarded you today were Bedouin, they deserve neither your praise nor my admiration. They did not protect you very well, did they?"

Thalia fell silent.

The big man carried her through twisting and turning alleyways that were unfamiliar to her. Near the outskirts of Alexandria, they were suddenly joined by three mounted men, one of whom led an extra horse.

When the one-eyed man attempted to lift Thalia on one of the horses, she reached up and tore at his

face with her fingernails. He smashed his huge hand
against her jaw, and she knew no more.

Thalia wasn't sure how long she had been unconscious. She groaned and blinked her eyes, tenderly
touching her throbbing jaw. She heard a buzzing in
her ears and closed her eyes against a wave of nausea.
Her captor held her in front of him on a horse. She
was jolted against the man and cried out in pain.

"I did not want to hurt you," he said.

"You're a swine," she spat, the sheltered noble-
women reverting in an instant to the child of the
streets who had to fight to survive. She pulled herself
up stiffly, not wanting him to know how frightened
she was or that she was silently crying.

Once, the stranger's horse stumbled, and he caught
Thalia by the arm to keep her from falling. She felt
the strength in his callused hands, and knew he was
capable of killing her if he decided to.

As the city disappeared behind them, so did
Thalia's hope. They were racing across the desert, and
she watched as sunlight broke through the clouds and
struck against the sand, turning it the color of bur-
nished gold.

It was long after sunset when they finally halted at
an abandoned limestone quarry. Thalia had ridden
past the site many times on her way to the Badari encampment. It was a crude campsite, with only one
tent. When her captor lifted her off the horse, she noticed his companions avoided looking at her and wondered why.

The big man motioned the others away, then led

Thalia to the tent. When she balked at the opening, he gave her a shove, and she almost lost her footing. She expected him to follow, but he did not. Thalia wondered if, after all these years of trying to elude this man, she would finally find out why he had hunted her so relentlessly.

A lantern that had been placed on a small stool did little to brighten the darkened corners inside the tent. After pacing until she was weary, Thalia finally dropped down onto a cot, taking notice of her surroundings. To her surprise, the tent was well furnished; there was an ebony cushioned stool and the cot was covered with a valuable tiger-skin robe. A pitcher of water sat on a low table, and she reached out to examine a jade drinking cup with precious stones inlaid in its curved handle.

Thalia frowned, wondering why the man had taken the trouble and expense to add such comforts for a captive. By the gods, what could this man want with her? He said he was taking her home—what did that mean?

Thalia paused at the tent opening and listened to the murmur of voices. Although she did not speak their language, she understood enough words to recognize that they were speaking Greek. If they were not Romans, who were they?

Thalia cringed and stepped quickly away from the opening when she heard heavy footsteps crunch against loose limestone. Her breath caught when her captor's deeply-accented voice called out to her.

"May I enter, Lady?"

His question made no sense—he had captured her,

struck her hard enough to render her unconscious, and now he was asking her permission to enter the tent?

"Go away."

"I will only take a moment of your time."

Thalia tugged at her short tunic, trying to cover as much of her legs as possible. "It is not for me to invite you in since I am your prisoner. Were I your hostess, you would certainly not be welcome."

"Nay. You are not my prisoner, but an honored guest. I want to ease your mind by explaining some things to you. Would you not welcome answers to the questions that have surely plagued you for years?"

Though she cringed at the thought of being alone with him, Thalia did want answers, so she capitulated. "You may enter."

He eased the opening aside, and since he was so tall, had to stoop to enter. The flickering lantern cast half his face in shadow, and he looked even more menacing than usual. Thalia scrambled backwards until she reached the far side of the tent, watching every move he made, lest he come too near her.

He seemed to sense her unease and kept his distance. "Again I ask forgiveness for striking you. But I had to silence you. It is my hope that you will learn to trust me," he said gruffly. "I will never do you harm; I want only to serve you, most high lady. Will you not sit so we can talk?"

"If you wish me no harm, you will allow me to go home."

"I *am* taking you home." He motioned to the stool near the opening. "Do you mind if I sit in your presence? I am not as young as I once was, and today has been hard on these old bones."

Thalia crossed her arms over her breasts. "Do not expect pity from me. If you are asking for my forgiveness, I cannot give it."

He remained standing and drew in a weary breath. "We have a long journey ahead of us, and I do not want you to spend it in fear. I was told by he who sent me to explain some things to you."

"You are the one who filled my childhood with terror," she lashed out at him. "What do you want with me?"

He rubbed his thumb across his chin in thoughtfulness before he nodded. "I have spent the better part of seventeen years searching for you. At last I have accomplished my task. You have been a worthy adversary."

"I ask you again—why?"

"Please, Lady, sit. It is not proper for me to sit until you do, and I don't know how much longer I can stand."

Raising her chin to an obstinate angle, Thalia examined the face that had haunted her nightmares. Then she met his onyx gaze. "And why is that? I am not Queen Cleopatra that you must stand in my presence."

"Your blood is as royal as the queen of Egypt's, perhaps even more so. I am but a soldier on a mission, which is to take you back to those who await your homecoming."

Her mouth fell open. "Either you toy with me, or you have made a grievous mistake. I'm certainly *not* who you think I am. I *am* a daughter of the house of Tausrat. If that does not strike fear in your heart, then you have not heard of my brother, Lord Ramtat, or the power he wields."

"I must disagree with you, most esteemed lady. You are not who you think you are."

She folded her arms across her chest and glared at him. "And who do *you* think I am?"

"You are the throne princess of the island kingdom of Bal Forea, as was your mother before you."

"Are you crazed? I am not that person!"

"But you are." He bowed deeply. "And I honor you as such."

Dismayed, Thalia shook her head. "I have never heard of such a place."

"Nonetheless, it exists."

She gave him a disbelieving glare. "You are either crazed, or you have been so long in the sun it has addled your brain."

"Nay, Royal One. I am as sane as you. If you doubt me, ask yourself what I would have to gain by speaking falsely."

"Your brain *is* addled if you think I will believe such a falsehood. You kidnap me, hold me prisoner, and then ask me to trust you. I do not even know your name or anything about you."

"Many refer to me as Turk."

She met his dark gaze and saw distress—either he was a good actor, or he was trying to trick her. "How can I call you by such a name? Surely you have a true name."

"If I had any other name, it has long been forgotten."

She was intrigued. "And why is that?"

"As a young man, I was captured from my homeland and taken to Rome, where I was trained to be a gladiator. When I was too old to fight, I became the personal guard of a woman of royal blood. I served her loyally until her death. I serve another now, just as loyally."

Thalia eased down on the cot and felt the soft fur against her skin. She watched him nod and sink gratefully onto the stool.

"Whatever you were paid to capture me, my family will pay more to get me back. Take me home."

"My mission is a noble one, so do not think to tempt me with wealth. Shall I tell you about your family, and why they want you back?"

Thalia nodded reluctantly.

He folded his huge hands in his lap and looked directly at her. "I served your mother, Princess Jiesa. Her father, the king of Bal Forea, was forcing her to marry a man she despised. Your mother loved the commander of the royal guard and fled with him to Greece, where they were married. A wide search was made for the princess, but she could not be found—her lover hid her well."

"I don't believe you," Thalia said, but with less conviction than before. "You weave a story, and not even a good one."

"Nay, I speak only the truth."

"I would hear more of this fable."

Turk dropped his huge head for a moment and then glanced back at her. "Not long after your mother fled Bal Forea, the island slipped into civil war. Many people rose up against your grandfather and labeled him a tyrant. Even today the island is torn in half by two warring factions—two men claim the throne, and neither will yield to the other. As the true throne princess, it is hoped that your presence on the island will end this war and reunite the people." Turk met her gaze, and Thalia lowered her eyes. "Every man, woman and child is sick of bloodshed," he continued. "Brothers fight against brothers, and no one has the heart for war, but it continues to feed on itself. Only you can bring it to an end, Princess."

Thalia stood, her fists clenched. "Do not call me that! You fabricated this tale. I do not believe one word of it. This island does not exist, or I would have heard of it."

He rose like someone had pulled a string and jerked him upward. "But it does exist, Highness."

"I told you to stop calling me that!" She walked over to him and poked her finger in his chest. "Enough lies. Tell me the truth!"

He looked thoughtful for a moment. "I knew where to begin my search for you because I had helped your mother escape. She despised your grandfather so much that when the war began she sent me back to help the rebels."

"And where did my mother hide?"

"At a small villa outside Athens. Your father died before you were born."

She held up her hand. "Stop! If you are truthful, you tell me my father died with no more emotion than if you were discussing the weather."

Turk looked startled, as if he could not guess why she was upset. "Forgive me. I know of no other way to say the truth. I have lived with this so long, I forget what it means to you."

"I am not saying I believe you—but if I did, how did the man you say is my father die?"

"From wounds he'd received in the escape from Bal

Forea. He left your mother enough money to survive on if she lived meagerly. She had me sell her jewels, which were worth a great price."

"Does this woman you say is my mother still live?"

He shook his head sorrowfully, or so it seemed to Thalia. "I am sorry to tell you Princess Jiesa died in a fire."

Thalia placed her hands over her ears. "Say nothing more of this travesty. I want to go home to the only mother I have ever known."

"That will not be possible."

A prickle of guilt assailed Thalia. How could she be expected to grieve for a father and mother who may or may not have existed? Still, she could not help but be curious. "Tell me more of this fabrication," she said, as she took her seat once again.

Turk eased his bulk back onto the stool. "When your mother sent me back to Bal Forea, she sent a message to her brother, who she trusted. Unfortunately, her brother had died. His wife, Lady Vistah, sent me back to Athens. Little did I know that your grandfather's spies followed me. A struggle ensued with the king's agents. A lantern was overturned and started a fire. Your mother fought to save you, but the ceiling caved in, trapping her beneath it. The house went up in flames, and your mother perished, but not before she ordered your nurse to flee to safety with you."

"And why did you not follow the nurse?"

"Unfortunately, I was injured, and it was many months before I could search for you. By then the nurse had hidden you well, leaving no trace." He reached up and absentmindedly rubbed his finger across the scar on his face.

"That is how you lost your eye?"

He nodded.

Thalia buried her fists into the tiger-skin as a vague memory of flickering flames tugged at her mind. This could explain her nightmares about a burning house. For the first time, she had to admit there might be some semblance of truth in Turk's words.

"Tell me more."

"Your uncle's wife, Lady Vistah, took up the search for you and enlisted my help. When next I happened upon your trail, I was led to a small house outside of Rome. I was told by a neighbor that the old woman who lived there had died, and they did not know what had happened to the small child. You would have been very young at the time."

The face of a woman flashed through Thalia's mind but soon faded. "I remember the nurse. I awoke one morning to find her ill." Suddenly, memories flowed through Thalia's mind like a dam bursting. "She told me I had to make my way to Rome and petition someone—I do not recall who. I was too young to re-member the details."

Turk watched her closely as he spoke, "Since you are of royal blood, she most likely sent you to Pompey or Julius Caesar."

"I only remember it took me days of walking to reach Rome. I was frightened and lost with no one to befriend me. I was hungry and ill when I finally reached the city." Bits and pieces of her memory kept falling into place. She could actually remember the old nurse's careworn face. Her name was Rainia! How could she have forgotten such a kind and gentle woman?

Thalia looked into Turk's eye—he was telling the truth, at least about her time in Rome. She still did not believe she was of royal blood. "How old am I now? I never knew."

His hard gaze softened. "At the time you walked to Rome you were only in your sixth summer. You are now in your eighteenth season. On the Ides of Junius, you will turn eighteen."

She looked doubtful. "I had thought I was two years older."

He actually chuckled. "Many a female would like to take two years off her age."

Thalia suddenly froze, and her fear returned. "There may be some truth to what you say, but I am no princess."

"If I had any doubts about who you are, I have only to remember your beautiful mother. You have the same look and coloring, and the deep dimple in your chin that is so common in the royal family of Bel Forea."

"What if I told you I am not interested in going with you? I don't care about your island or your war. I only want to go home to my family."

"You have no choice, and neither do I."

"What will happen to me?"

"I will be taking you onboard a ship when it is safe to return to Alexandria."

"To the man my mother detested?"

"Nay, nay. I would never take you to King Melik, nor would your mother want me to. You have a cousin, Lord Sevilin. He is a handsome young man who cares what happens to you. He is but five years your senior."

"How do you claim we are related?"

"His mother, Lady Vistah, married Prince Kalavera, your mother's brother."

She studied Turk's face, trying to understand. "If that is so, you do not need me. This Sevilin must be the true ruler of your island."

"Indeed he should be. But it is complicated. Your uncle, Prince Kalavera, was Lord Sevilin's stepfather. Unfortunately, your uncle died without issue. Lord Sevilin holds out hope that he can one day ascend the throne and unite the people."

Thalia was trying to untangle the web of information that whirled through her mind. "It seems to me that if your Lord Sevilin is who you say he is, he has no legitimate claim to the throne."

"It grieves me to tell you that your grandfather is not loved by the people. You must understand that if you fell under King Melik's influence, he would use you for his own gain."

Thalia was clever enough to see what Turk had left unsaid. "And the lord you represent would use me for *his* gain."

"You misunderstand. Lord Sevilin's only hope is to reunite the country—with your help, that could be accomplished."

"You are asking me to choose between two men I have never known, both of whom want to rule an island I have never heard of."

"In truth, Princess, you have no choice. Others will make that decision for you. When you meet Lord Sevilin, you will know that his cause is just."

"I have a family I love here in Egypt. By now they will be frantic with worry. They must be told that I'm safe."

Turk stood and towered over her. "That is not possible."

"I order you to take me home."

"I cannot do that."

"If what you say is true, and if I am this throne princess, should you not obey me?"

His sudden smile curled his lips. "I will obey you in most everything, but not when it goes against your obligation to Bal Forea."

"Then the title is meaningless."

He looked perturbed, but his one good eye slowly widened. "I almost forgot—I have a gift I was told to present to you." He reached inside his robe, withdrew an ivory box and handed it to her. "Lord Sevilin wanted you to have this as a token of his goodwill."

Thalia merely stared at the ivory box, making no attempt to take it from him. "I do not want his trinkets."

Turk opened the box himself and withdrew a shimmering gold chain with an amethyst shaped like a huge teardrop. It was stunning, but she had no desire to own it.

"Return it to your lord and tell him I refuse his gift as well as the offer of his . . . hospitality. I have jewels of my own at home. Some of them were a gift from Queen Cleopatra, and quite valuable."

Turk dropped the necklace back into the box and slammed the lid shut. "You have no desire to come with me even after I have told you that your presence could end a civil war?"

"Why should I believe you? I am not an innocent to be lured by treasures. I have only your word that I am of royal blood."

His jaw hardened, and the jagged scar became more pronounced. "You should want to accompany me, if for no other reason than to exact revenge upon the man who is responsible for your mother's death."

"Again, I have only your word for that. If you speak truth, accompany me to my home and tell this to my family. Then we shall put your case before Queen Cleopatra and allow her to decide what I should do."

"My orders are to bring you directly to the island."

"As a child I was frightened of you, and I still am. If you want to gain my trust, do not take me away from my home. Let us seek my queen's advice."

"As much as I would like to gain your trust, I will certainly not be seeking an audience with the Egyptian queen. It saddens me that you rail against your duty. When we reach Bal Forea you will know I speak the truth." He moved to the tent opening and shoved it aside. "I suggest you get some sleep."

"By now all Egypt will be looking for me," Thalia warned.

"That is true, but they will not find you. You might like to know that an agent of the king has arrived in Egypt and is also searching for you."

Thalia looked bemused. "It would seem I am more important than I could ever have imagined."

"You are fortunate it was I who found you. The Destroyer would not have been as patient with you as I have been."

Thalia stared at him. "I know of whom you speak. He approached me in my garden. He said I was in danger—" Her eyes widened with understanding. "The danger he was warning me of was you!"

Turk's face actually whitened. "The Destroyer has a

reputation of always getting what he goes after. "How did you escape him?"

"I learned to survive, thanks to you. If I had taken that man's advice, you would not have caught me."

"Know this. The Destroyer will not care about anything but taking you to your grandfather. Be warned, you do not want to fall into his hands."

❦Chapter Nine

The hour was late, and Jamal hesitated in front of Lady Larania's chamber, wishing he had better news to give her. Gathering his courage, he rapped softly on her door and called, "Mistress, may I speak with you?"

Badaza opened the door and gazed worriedly at the guard. "The mistress will see you," she said, nodding toward the small sitting room. "Wait for her in there, and she will come directly." The servant saw the grim expression on the guard's face. "You must not upset our lady."

"I would not if I could do otherwise—there is no help for it." Jamal had hardly entered the small chamber when his mistress came rushing in, clutching her green dressing gown, her hair uncombed, her eyes red from weeping. Her worried gaze settled on his face. "Tell me quickly—have you found my daughter?"

Jamal avoided her eyes. Lady Larania was held in great esteem by the Badari Bedouin: As a princess of the blood, her father had been the sheik, and now her son held that honored position. She was beloved by all, and her pain was their pain. "One of my men found the horses and chariot. A family living just outside the city recognized who they belonged to. The father approached one of my men and led him to the chariot." Jamal handed her the ebony box, his eyes sad.

"What is this?"

"It is the ring Lady Thalia picked up from the gold-smith today."

Lady Larania felt heavy despair. "Then the motive could not have been robbery, or the man would have taken the ring. If that is so, we will not be receiving a ransom demand either."

Jamal was loath to dash Lady Larania's hopes, but he had no choice. "I believe we can rule out both of those reasons," he said cautiously.

Her face paled, and she clutched the back of a chair. "Then what can be the motive? My daughter—what can that horrid man want with her?" She could think of many reasons a man would want Thalia, and her fear escalated.

"Mistress," Jamal said with concern, "will you not be seated? Allow me to call your maid to fetch you a cup of wine."

She waved him away. "Think not of me. It is my daughter that must be foremost in all our minds."

"We questioned the family who found the chariot, but none of them were at home when it was abandoned."

Lady Larania bowed her head, her loose hair falling across her face. "Was there . . . did you see any blood on the chariot?"

The fierce warrior's voice was gentle. "No, Mistress. Nothing like that."

She paced the room, dragging her hair out of her face and sweeping it behind her ears, then drawing her shawl across her shoulders. "Thalia will be frightened."

Her voice shook with emotion and took on a pleading tone when she cried, "Bring her home to me!"

Jamal avoided her eyes, which swam with tears. "Be assured I will not rest until she is found, Mistress."

Queen Cleopatra stood on her balcony, her unadorned ebony hair rippling in the wind blowing off the Mediterranean. She lowered her head in sadness, clutching the leather-skin message she had just received from Lady Larania.

The Tausrat family had stood at her side in those dark days when she had returned to Egypt after Caesar's death. At that time, she had fallen into deep mourning because she'd lost the man she loved, and with his passing, their plans for the future of a world ruled by Egypt and Rome. But always in her grief, Lady Larania had been at her side, as had the rest of the family. Thalia had been but a young girl at the time and had been a loving companion to Cleopatra's son, Caesarion.

As time passed, Cleopatra had emerged from her grief with the help of her half-sister, Danaë. Under Ramtat's skillful guidance, Cleopatra had signed new trade agreements with old allies, and Egypt's economy now thrived. Because of the bounty from the Nile, Egypt had two growing seasons; therefore, Egyptian grain filled the bellies of half the world, and Cleopatra's coffers were full.

She owed the Tausrat family more than her life.

Cleopatra heard footsteps and turned to face Mark Antony. She held her hand out to him and he gently pulled her into his strong arms. Nestling against his shoulder, she felt sheltered from the world, and for the moment, from her troubles.

Antony was of medium height, not tall as Caesar had been, but to Cleopatra, he cast a long shadow. He was not the unimpeachable architect of war that Caesar had been, but she loved Antony more deeply than she had ever loved any man. She ran her hand through his curly black hair, thinking he had a face and body that attracted the attention of women. He had scars and battle wounds, but those only intrigued her more. He was a relentless warrior, and since Caesar's death, Antony had become one of most powerful men in the world—a power he shared with Caesar's sickly nephew, Octavian. Antony was a battle-hardened soldier respected by the armies, and therein lay his real power.

At the moment Cleopatra had an uneasy alliance with Rome. But she was confident Antony would one day take the whole of Rome under his control, and together the two of them would rule the world.

Antony smiled tenderly down at her and traced her cheek with his thumb. "Why is it you grow more beautiful each time I see you?"

"Perhaps it is because you love me more with the passing of time—I know that is how it is with me."

He lay his rough cheek to her smooth one. "To think I almost lost you when I returned to Rome. How bleak that time was without you at my side. I feared you would never forgive me for my mistake."

"If you speak of your marriage to Octavia, I was hurt and angry at the time, never wanting to look upon your face again."

"And you made me suffer for it. Poor Octavia, she had no husband in me—my thoughts were always of you."

"My real anger came from the fact that you allowed Octavian to trick you into marrying his sister. He thought he could control you through her and make you forget me."

"Yet it had the opposite effect." Antony raised her face to his. "I want to live every day beside you, and when death claims me, let you be at my side."

"My dearest love," Cleopatra said, her gaze moving over his beloved face. "I never knew love could hurt so much. It tears at my heart like thorns."

"I set Octavia aside, and you are now my wife. Does that not prove my love for you?"

She searched his dark eyes and saw love shining there. "I have no doubt that you love me, but our marriage is not recognized in Rome. In the eyes of the Senate, you are still married to Octavia."

He placed his arm about her waist and turned them both toward the sea. "You do not know what suffering is. I was tormented while you were with Caesar. I was never jealous of anything he had, with the exception of you."

"I loved Caesar," she admitted, "but not with the all-consuming love that I feel for you." She knew in her heart that Antony would never have Caesar's driving ambition, but she had enough ambition for them both. It took so little to guide Antony gently in the right direction. "I have never told you this, but when you sent for me to come to you at Tarsus, I had my barge prepared with every luxury and went in hopes of seducing you. In truth, you seduced me, and I felt love such as the world has never known."

"You seem troubled tonight," Antony observed. "What is the matter?"

She focused on the great lighthouse and the beacons that swept far out to sea, guiding ships to Alexandria's shores. "You know of the Tausrat family."

"Aye. My general, Marcellus, married a daughter of the family."

"News reached me tonight that the youngest daughter has been kidnapped right here on the streets of Alexandria."

Antony stiffened. "How could such a thing happen? Surely she had guards with her."

Cleopatra told him all she knew. "I have sent men to sweep the city and try to determine what happened."

"What have they discovered?"

"Many people in the marketplace saw Lady Thalia captured, but no one recognized the man, or knew where he took her."

"Would you like me to send Roman troops to help find her?"

Cleopatra turned to him, clutching his tunic. "Please. Lady Thalia is a favorite with me and is sister-in-law to my beloved Danaë, the only family I have left. Though she was but a child when Caesar was assassinated, Thalia almost lost her life in an attempt to help save him from death."

"Then most certainly I shall order my men to scour the city and ask questions from house to house. Surely someone will have seen something."

"I fear for her. Who has done this, and why?"

Antony's arms tightened about her. "No one can disappear completely. Have you posted guards at every road leading out of the city?"

"A mouse could not slip through without detection." Cleopatra frowned. "When I find who has done this, I shall crush him!"

"And I shall help you."

❦ CHAPTER TEN

The full moon was riding high as Ashtyn flattened his body against the sand, motioning Captain Darius forward. The stone pit just ahead looked deserted but for the dying campfire. Ashtyn spied the two guards posted outside a small tent and smiled to himself.

"That's their camp," he told his companion. "Make your way around to their horses and untie their hobbles so we can drive them away. I don't want them chasing us after they discover the princess is missing."

"Aye, Commander," Captain Darius said, looking troubled. "'Tis a pity we had to leave our supplies back in Alexandria."

"There was no time to go for them. We had to rescue the princess from Turk." Ashtyn glanced up at the moon and watched a cloud pass under it, casting the night in deep shadows. "Go now!" he commanded, jumping to his feet and hurrying silently toward the limestone quarry.

Thalia laid awake for hours, acquainting herself with the sounds around her. She heard a man cough just outside the tent, and later she heard the changing of the guards. It was futile to think she could escape—they were watching her too closely. When weariness swamped her, she could no longer keep her eyes open and fell asleep.

At first her sleep was dreamless, but suddenly she groaned, reliving her childhood nightmare. She was jarred awake when a hand clamped over her mouth and strong arms dragged her to her feet.

"Do not make a sound," an accented voice hissed near her ear. "Not one sound—nod if you understand."

Through her terror, Thalia managed to give a small nod.

Gripping her arm, he forced her to the back of the tent where moonlight poured through a wide slit. Although she had not seen the man's face, she knew he was the intruder who'd come into her garden. Turk had called him the Destroyer. And now she was his prisoner.

When they cleared the tent, he lifted Thalia in his arms, cautioning, "Do not utter a word."

Thalia's throat was closed off with fear, and she couldn't have made a sound if her life depended on it. She lay frozen in his arms as he carried her up the hill to where another man was waiting with three horses. The clouds that covered the moon drifted away, and Thalia saw that her captors wore Bedouin head-coverings and robes, though they were not desert dwellers.

Thalia tried to wriggle out of the man's arms. "Why are you doing this?"

"You have been warned to remain silent," he whispered fiercely, his grip tightening on her arm. "Say nothing more—is that understood?"

Thalia nodded. Now was not the time to rebel

against this man. But she was not beaten, as he would discover.

She was compliant when he lifted her onto one of the horses, then she watched him toss her reins to his companion while he mounted his own horse.

"I suppose you can ride," he whispered. "I saw you drive the chariot and aptly control those great beasts without trouble."

"I can ride," she answered haughtily.

Instead of heading in the direction of Alexandria as Thalia expected them to, they rode directly toward Turk's encampment. The man who rode beside Thalia gave a loud yell when they neared Turk's horses, scattering the animals in every direction.

As they rode past the camp, Thalia heard loud shouts as Turk's men tried to pursue them on foot. The camp came to life, and men chased after them as they galloped into the night.

Thalia was holding tightly to the reins and kept her legs clamped around the belly of her horse so she wouldn't be unseated. "Where are you taking me?" she asked, but her words were carried away by the brisk wind.

They rode silently until the first streaks of daylight illuminated the landscape. When they stopped, her captor dismounted, then reached up to her and placed her on the ground.

"We will walk and rest the animals," he told her.

Thalia was taken by surprise when he halted, reached for her and studied her face. "Who hit you?" he demanded.

So much had happened, Thalia had forgotten how much her jaw hurt. "What concern is it of yours?"

His thumb ran smoothly over her injured jaw. "It matters," he said, as his eyes burned into her. "Turk will pay for this."

Thalia wondered why this man should care. At the moment her pain was her least worry. She was so weary she stumbled, and the man reached for her, keeping a steadying grip on her arm.

"We will walk but a little farther." He shook his head. "This desert seems limitless. Is there no end to it?"

"I hope you lose your way and have to wander aimlessly for years," Thalia told him.

"Aye, I know what you think of me. I would be grateful, however, if you would keep such thoughts to yourself."

Thalia stopped to shake the sand out of her shoes.

The man frowned as he saw her dainty sandals, meant more for fashion than function. "You are certainly ill-prepared for the desert."

She stared at him in amazement. "You will forgive me," she said, "but when I dressed this morning, I had no notion I would be kidnapped twice and taken into the desert against my will."

Thalia turned and stalked away as best she could in her flimsy sandals, sand pouring through the straps with each step she took.

Her throat felt parched and she shivered from the cold.

The Destroyer, which was the only name Thalia had for him, caught up with her and gave her a hard look. "Why did you not tell me you were cold?" Without waiting for an answer, he removed his outer robe and draped it about her.

Thalia's first thought was to throw off the robe, but

the warmth of it seeped into her body, and she reconsidered. "I scorn your concern. Why would you care how I feel?"

His tone was deep and heavily accented when he spoke, "I care."

"Then may I please have a drink?"

The Destroyer snapped his fingers at the other man. "Bring the waterskin."

After Thalia satisfied her thirst, she thought about her situation. Turk had refused to listen to her pleas, and she felt this man would as well. But she had to try to reason with him. "Will you take me home to my family?"

He paused for a moment before he said, "That is not our destination."

"Then take me to Queen Cleopatra. Allow her to hear your story, if indeed your story is the same as Turk's."

"You talk too much. Voices carry in the desert."

Thalia unfastened the amulet from her upper arm and held it out to him. "Take this and let me go, and I'll find my own way back to Alexandria. Look closely at the workmanship," she said, shoving the amulet toward him. "It's very valuable; the gold and gems are real."

The sun was rising higher, but she couldn't see much of the man's face, which was still covered by the Bedouin headpiece.

"Do not think you can tempt me with jewels. All that you have belongs to you, and no one will take it from you. Come, we must resume our journey."

Thalia dropped to her knees. "I refuse to go one step farther until you tell me where you are taking me."

Without ceremony, the man lifted her onto her horse and climbed onto his. "You have no choice in the matter."

Thalia had the feeling the Destroyer was much more dangerous than Turk.

CHAPTER ELEVEN

As the morning sun rose higher in the sky, the heat became unbearable. The horses were lathered and had slowed to a walk. After a silent gaze into the distance to make certain they were not being followed, Ashtyn gave a quick nod, indicating they should dismount. "Let us rest the animals."

He stood on the sand and reached up for Thalia, but she pushed his hand away and slid off the horse on her own. Stretching her stiff muscles, she glanced at the distant sand dune. If anyone was tracking them, they were staying out of sight.

Thalia was thirsty, and when she reached for a water-skin, she saw there were only two, and the one she lifted was only half-full. She frowned with concern. Surely these men must know this was not enough water to keep them and the animals alive until they reached the first village.

Hot sand sifted into her sandals, making it uncomfortable for her to walk. Thalia leaned against the horse and lifted the long robe so she wouldn't stumble as she trudged along. Once she had to pause to empty the sand and retie her shoes, while the two man waited patiently for her to continue.

Gazing sideways at the Destroyer, Thalia studied him, but she looked away quickly when his silver eyes stared back at her. "Where are you taking me?"

He gave her a perfunctory gaze, his mouth set in a firm line. "I will tell you all when the time is right."

"I am not asking if you are taking me to my so-called 'grandfather' or my 'cousin.' What I'm asking is where are you taking me *today*? You do have a plan, do you not?"

Ashtyn sighed in exasperation, unaccustomed to having to explain his decisions to anyone. "We are headed for the village of Osage, where the Nile meets the sea. A ship will be waiting offshore to take us aboard."

"Since we are crossing the desert, you should have been better prepared. I know the village well. Be warned, you do not have enough water to reach Osage."

When the Destroyer spoke, he sounded irritated. "I did not have time to make plans," he admitted. "When we discovered Turk had taken you captive, I had to act fast, or he would have whisked you out of Egypt before I could stop him."

"It matters little to me whether I am your prisoner or his, except that he was better prepared." Thalia nodded at the sky where a hawk circled. "If I had the wings of that bird, I would fly home and leave the two of you to die of thirst. It would be no more than you deserve."

The man frowned. "It does matter that you are under my protection, and no longer in Turk's power."

Her eyes focused on the signet ring the Destroyer wore on his right hand. It was a thick band of gold, with a noble's crest that had a red shield with a golden arrow through it. Unlike Turk, who was a servant, this was no ordinary man. "Please help me. I know nothing about the island Turk told me about, and I don't care about any of the people who fight against each other. I want to go home."

He said nothing.

Ashtyn was aware of every breath Thalia took. In truth, he was so aware of her, he could think of nothing else. For years she had been real to him, while she had never known of his existence. He closed his eyes and thought of what her presence on the island would mean to the people, though she had just admitted she cared nothing about them.

And why should she? She was merely a pawn between two rival factions in an island kingdom far from her home. Ashtyn's life was tied to hers by a pledge she didn't even know existed, and she saw him only as the enemy.

She stumbled, but her eyes dared him to touch her. Ashtyn ached inside, knowing she was bone-weary, yet he was forced to push her beyond endurance. His gaze fell on her shapely lips, and he wanted to press his mouth against them. She belonged to him, and he to her. As he stared at her beautiful face, the ache inside him became deeper. He swallowed hard, knowing she despised him. While he . . . what did he feel for her?

He was a commander of men and knew how to fight a battle and bring down his enemy, but he was at the mercy of the desert, having no experience with arid land. He ground his teeth, fearing that he must seem like a total imbecile to her.

They walked for a time in silence, the big man trudging behind them. When Thalia looked at the man beside her, he seemed angry about something, but little she cared—she was angry herself.

Finally, Thalia could hold her tongue no longer. "You are apparently not accustomed to the desert, else you would know that if we don't soon reach shade and water, we shall all perish."

That got his attention.

"I already told you when I saw Turk had captured you, I was forced to rescue you and had no time to gather supplies," he said in exasperation.

Her laughter was bitter. "Rescue me! Do you call this a rescue? The horses will die first—probably before sundown. Both your waterskins are near empty, so we will probably die before sunrise."

He fell silent, and she found his attitude disquieting. But she was still sure she had his attention. "Have you ever seen a man die of thirst? Nay, you have not," she said before he could answer. "I have, so allow me to explain how it happens: First you become delirious, imagining ponds and puddles of water tormenting you everywhere you look. Your tongue will swell, and you won't be able to swallow. Your body will soon begin to roast like meat cooked over a campfire."

His silver gaze pinned her. "Since you are so knowledgeable about the desert, what would you suggest we do?"

Thalia glanced around until she found what she was looking for. She knelt and picked up several small pebbles. "Put these in your mouth and suck on them. Remember to keep your mouth closed. I don't know why this helps, but it is my brother's advice, so if I were you, I would take it as truth."

Ashtyn took the pebbles in his hand and stared

down at them as if they were some foreign object. Then he handed some to Darius and put the rest in his mouth. "Do what she says." Turning back to Thalia, he asked, "Now what?"

"I know of an oasis nearby, though I can't promise there will be water this time of year. Some years the watering hole is completely dry, but it is our only hope of survival." She bit her lower lip, knowing the oasis was too small to be on the caravan route. She could not expect help for herself from that direction.

"How do I know I can trust you not to lead us further into the desert?"

"You cannot. But I want to live as much as you do. You will have to trust me, although I care naught if you do."

She could not see his expression because his lower face was covered. She wished she could lead them to the Badari encampment, but it was many days away.

The Destroyer swept his hand forward. "It seems we are at your mercy. Lead the way."

Thalia lowered her head. "We should all take a drink now, but no more than a sip. And give the horses water. We cannot allow ourselves to become too thirsty. The horses will need a bit more water than we do. It is also important to keep your body covered as much as you can. I have your outer robe, and I can give it back to you since I am more accustomed to the heat."

She started to pull it over her head, but The Destroyer stopped her. "Keep it. You are wearing less clothing than either of us," he said in a voice that would brook no argument.

In irritation, she dropped the robe back around her body as they mounted their horses.

Her captor might not know the desert, but she would not want to challenge him in other matters.

"I always like to put a name to a face, and the only name I have for you is Destroyer," Thalia said when they started moving. "Surely you have another name."

"I am Ashtyn." He nodded toward his companion, who still hung back, watching for danger. "He is Captain Darius, my second-in-command. He does not speak much, but he will look after your welfare."

For the first time, Thalia allowed herself to study the big man. He was completely bald, and his nose was hooked. He had dark eyes, and whenever he caught Thalia looking at him, he lowered them. "The only people I need protection from are you and him," Thalia told Ashtyn pointedly.

His jaw tightened. "You say this because you do not know what awaits you on Bal Forea," he said, glancing back over his shoulder.

"The night you came to my garden, you spoke my name, but you are mistaken about my identity. I am not the person you seek."

"Have you known any other with your name?"

"Nay. But—"

"It is a name from the royal family of Bal Forea." He lowered his gaze to her dimpled chin. "There is no mistaking who you are." He gazed ahead of them. "How far is this oasis?"

Thalia calculated the distance they'd traveled from Alexandria. "I could be mistaken, but I believe it is no more than two or three hours ahead. Depending, of course, on how swiftly these untrained horses can move through the sand. I am usually mounted on one of my brother's Badarian horses. They can cover much ground in a short amount of time."

"Lord Ramtat," he said, nodding. "I know of his Badarian horses—their fame has reached as far as Bal Forea. The whites that pulled your chariot were of that breed, were they not?"

"Destroyer, Ashtyn, whatever you are called, if you do not fear my brother, you are a fool. He has men who can track an ant across the highest sand dune. If you believe he will not find your trail, you are mistaken. There is nowhere you can hide that he will not follow."

"I am sure you speak the truth. But put no hope in being rescued. The sea leaves no tracks."

She raised her chin defiantly. "Right now we are in the desert, and you had best look over your shoulder." Ashtyn appeared unconcerned, and she fell into silence, knowing Ramtat would come as soon as he heard what had happened to her. But would he be too late? Thalia's shoulders drooped in hopelessness. The Destroyer might not know how to trek through the desert, but he was no fool.

Thalia glanced at the man. He wore brushed trousers tucked into high-top boots. His linen shirt was open at the neck, and she caught a glimpse of smooth skin. Muscles rippled across his broad shoulders, and she knew he was indeed a warrior. If she had not been afraid of him, she would have thought he was the most handsome man she'd ever seen.

Tearing her gaze away from him, she stared straight ahead. It was nearing sundown and Thalia thought she sighted the top of a date palm just ahead. She slid off her horse and jerked the reins out of Ashtyn's hand, practically dragging the animal toward the oasis. After Thalia allowed the horse to drink, she dropped to her knees, cupped her hands and took small sips. Then she fell back on the ground, taking a deep breath, and watched as the two men satisfied their thirst.

Ashtyn gazed up at the lacy palm fronds that fluttered in the scorching breeze. "I am glad you were truthful about the oasis. I was unsure where you were leading us," he remarked as he knelt beside her, a look of concern on his face. "Are you ill?"

She sat up and braced her back against the rough bark of the date palm, noticing Ashtyn's second-in-command sprawled beneath the shade, wiping sweat from his brow. Neither of these men were accustomed to desert heat. "I am not ill—just weary. And as for being honest with you, know this—in my eyes you are naught but my captor and deserve no such courtesy from me."

He glanced at her as if weighing his reply. "That may be the way I look to you now, but when you know me better, I hope your opinion will change. Thank you for leading us to water."

He watched her swing her head in his direction, her golden hair sliding across her shoulders. He saw the anger brightening her blue eyes. "Do not make the mistake of thinking I wanted to save your lives. To me you are a villain," she nodded at his companion, "and so is he. I led you here because I did not want to die of thirst."

Instead of being angered by her words, Ashtyn laughed. "If I had any doubts as to your true identity, you just swept them aside. Your words are like sharp nettle, reminding me of your grandfather."

Thalia turned away from him, crossing her arms over her chest. "Go away."

Ashtyn reached into his leather satchel and withdrew dried meat and cheese, handing some to her. Then he settled beside her. "You must be confused by all that has happened to you."

"More angry than confused."

"What did Turk tell you?"

"That man is crazed. His claims are outrageous."

"Tell me about them."

She tore off a chunk of dried meat with strong white teeth, and watched him as she chewed. "I would like to hear who *you* think I am."

"I know who you are. Your mother, Princess Jiesa, was the throne princess. She was expected to wed a great prince of a neighboring country, but she defied her father and fled the island."

"Are you sure you and Turk aren't cohorts?"

Ashtyn laughed. "Never doubt that Turk and I are enemies. But we both know you are King Melik's only living descendant, and the only person who can legitimately succeed him on the throne of Bal Forea."

"If what you say is true—which I doubt—my mother did not want to be queen, and neither do I."

He gazed into her eyes. "Sometimes we have no choice in what is decided for us."

"I spit on your king—both him and the cousin. I want to go home and live the life I had before you and Turk interfered. I have a family I love and miss. I do not want this cousin, or a grandfather I don't know. You must let me go."

"I cannot do that."

"Neither you nor Turk have told me anything that would make me want to accompany you to this island. If the king you speak of is my grandfather, would he not arrange a marriage for me as he did for my mother?"

Ashtyn gazed into the distance. "I cannot speak for the king."

"Apparently this half-cousin is an usurper who is trying to steal the throne. I say let him have it. Leave both those men to their war."

Ashtyn took a deep breath. "What about the people who need leadership? Your grandfather is old and ill—he cannot hold on for much longer. As for Lord Sevilin, his one drive in life is power. He is consumed by the notion of ascending to the throne of Bal Forea. The rebels that follow him do not realize that Sevilin can never wear the crown. His slight hold on power will slip through his grasp as fleetingly as a great fire devouring a forest and leaving only ashes."

He spoke with great passion, and almost made Thalia believe in his cause. Then she remembered Turk had told her this man had a reputation for seducing with words, and she shook herself mentally. "I am sorry for the king, and I am sure he will eventually crush this Lord Sevilin, or he may decide to allow him to succeed him on the throne. It could be that he will make a good king."

"That will never happen!" Ashtyn sounded appalled. "You have no love for your own people if you believe that."

"I do not know those people, and they are not mine. I may not be Egyptian by birth, but in my heart, I am a true daughter of this land. Your people mean nothing to me."

Ashtyn tossed his dried meat angrily into the fire and sparks flew. "You may be able to stop the war merely by standing at your grandfather's side. How can you not care?"

She heard the disappointment in his tone, but what did he expect? She wanted more than anything to be in her mother's arms. "If I chose to stand at the side of my half-cousin, what would happen?"

"That, too, might end the war," Ashtyn admitted. "Sevilin would most certainly use you for his own ambitions."

"Turk said much the same to me about King Melik. And he certainly warned me to be wary of you." She met his steady gaze with her own. "I am suspicious of anyone called 'The Destroyer.'"

Ashtyn chose to ignore her reference to the name the rebels had attached to him because he was ruthless and unyielding in the service of his king. "I cannot convince you which one is right or wrong—this you will have to decide for yourself. But if you are as wise as I think you are, you will remember Lord Sevilin has no true claim to the throne." He gripped her hand and made her look at him. "No claim at all except through you."

"And that would be a bad thing?"

"Judge for yourself. Sevilin has gathered about him a force of thugs and malcontents who take the spoils of victory to increase their wealth at the expense of the common people. The Bal Foreans know the king is ill, and they fear what will happen to them if he dies without someone to succeed him. Many now clamber to Lord Sevilin's side because he has threatened to punish those who resist him."

This caught Thalia's interest. "This Sevilin is in no way related to me, if I am who you say I am."

"His only connection to you would be that his mother married your uncle. I doubt Turk told you Lord Sevilin plans to make you his wife, thus legitimizing his claim to the throne."

Thalia's mouth opened in horror. "No one can make me marry against my will. Not that man, and not your king." She shook her head. "But why should I tell you this? You are no more than a hireling for the king."

Ashtyn spoke softly and without anger. "In that you are not far from the truth. I am the king's man."

"Something perplexes me: Turk has been searching for me most of my life, yet he says this man, Sevilin, is no more than five years older than myself. How could such a young man have plotted to capture me in Rome?"

"The ambition to rule Bal Forea did not begin with Lord Sevilin. His mother, Lady Vistah, is ruthless and ambitious. When her husband died, her ambitions died with him, until she realized she could still get to the throne through you. She planted those ambitions in her son, and as he grew to manhood, they took seed."

Thalia watched the sun drop low in the west and hung her head, weary of plots and stratagems. "The way I see it, I have a choice between bad or worse. Why should I want a life such as you offer me when I am happy with my own life?"

"The road you must travel was chosen for you at

your birth. To be born royal is to make sacrifices for those who depend upon you. You will be called upon to take up the scepter of Bal Forea, and you must not deny what is best for your people."

Thalia leaned forward, her hands clasped tightly in her lap. "My people are Egyptian! How many times must I tell you I have no interest in the people you speak of?"

"You may deny it all you want, but the blood that runs in your veins is pure Bal Forean. 'Tis a pity you cannot know how your people need you."

While this man frightened her, the sound of his voice sent shivers across her skin, and she loved to hear him speak. But she must be on guard against his power to persuade. "Tell me about the island."

He gazed toward the sunset as if he were seeing Bal Forea in his mind. "One side of the island has thick woods and mountains, while the other side slopes to the sea. There is a rocky coastline that sweeps upward to a mountainous area with many waterfalls spilling down the steep sides." He rubbed the back of his neck as if he was weary. "Sevilin never actually leads his band of cutthroats and rebels into battle, but instead stays holed up in a fortress in the mountains, making it difficult to drive him out. But we never stop trying."

Thalia turned her back to him, not wanting to hear anything more of this island. There had to be a way to escape. Watching Captain Darius fill the water skins, Thalia's gaze went to the horses that grazed on the sweet grass along the watering hole. If she could wait until both men fell asleep, she might be able to make it to the horses and ride away.

She would wait, bide her time, hoping to find the right moment—then she would strike!

The moon shone brightly across the oasis. Thalia watched the campfire die into smoldering embers. In the distance she could hear the sound of jackals. The wind was blowing out of the north, and she smelled the strong scent of sulphur that told her they were very near the Nile. The river always had this particular scent during the flood season when it brought life-giving bounty for the farmers.

Huddling beneath Ashtyn's robe, she inhaled his clean spicy scent that still clung to the rough linen. He lay facing her, and she watched him, waiting for the moment his eyes closed in sleep.

Captain Darius, however, was another matter. He had gone twice to check on the horses, and he'd now settled down with his back against the date palm. She would have to wait a bit until he was asleep.

Moments passed, and Thalia's gaze fastened on the dagger Ashtyn kept close to his body. She stiffened as she watched him take a deep breath, and she wondered what drove a man such as he. He'd removed the *kaf-fiyeh*, so Thalia stared at the thick black hair that fell about his handsome face. His brows were dark and his lashes were long for a man. His mouth was beautiful. She felt herself blush as she considered touching him.

Was she crazed? He was the enemy.

He definitely had a way of seducing with words, and she had almost believed everything he'd told her. Almost.

Night shadows crept across the oasis, and the moon climbed higher. Thalia watched Captain Darius's head fall sideways, and then he jerked awake, sitting upright. Finally Thalia's patience was rewarded—his head fell sideways and he did not move. Still she waited, too frightened to act.

If she didn't make the attempt to escape soon, she might not get a better chance. . . .

❧ CHAPTER TWELVE

Thalia silently inched her hand toward Ashtyn's dagger, watching him closely for any sign that he was waking. As a child, the streets of Rome had tutored her in the skills she needed to survive. She was apt at picking locks, skilled as a pickpocket, and she'd learned to strike quickly and move without anyone detecting her. Of course, she had not used those skills in many years.

Quietly, Thalia reached forward and gripped the hilt of Ashtyn's dagger, then eased it toward her. She waited a moment to make sure neither man had detected her actions. To her relief, both were still asleep.

Rising to her knees, she waited a moment before gaining her feet. Holding her breath, she cautiously took a step in the direction of the horses, then dashed silently across the camp.

When she reached the horses, Thalia cut the tethers with the dagger, and then tucked it into her sash. Carefully she eased herself onto a horse, still watching the two men. Thus far neither of them had moved, and she congratulated herself that she had not lost her ability to survive. Nudging the horse forward, she whirled it around and urged the animal into a gallop.

She rode in the direction of Alexandria without looking back.

Thalia was grateful for the bright moonlight that lit her way. When she reached the first sand dune, the horse slowed its pace, laboring to make it to the top. How she wished she was mounted on one of her brother's Badarians, who could outdistance any horse in the desert. When the animal finally made it to the top of the dune, Thalia's heart lightened with a feeling of triumph.

She was free!

That was when she realized she'd made a mistake: She hadn't taken a waterskin with her. She would never make it home without water.

But Thalia had no time to worry about thirst because she heard another rider. Ashtyn!

With fear driving her, she jabbed her horse in the flanks, and the poor animal stumbled in the deep sand. Once she'd cleared the dune, she urged the horse to a faster pace, hoping to outdistance her pursuer. But he was gaining on her.

Her horse was at an all-out run, but still Ashtyn was drawing closer. When he drew even with Thalia, he ordered her to stop, but she had no intention of obeying.

"Halt!" Ashtyn called out once more.

"I will not!" she yelled back over her shoulder.

By the time Thalia realized what was happening, it was too late to react. Ashtyn had drawn even with her and leaped forward, catching her in his arms and taking them both to the ground.

Thalia landed hard, and pain ripped through her body. She couldn't move or breathe with his weight pressing against her.

"What did you think you were doing?" he demanded.

She tried to throw him off, but it was impossible. "L-let me up."

Ashtyn took both her arms and manacled them over her head. "Not until you stop struggling." He was angry, and she stilled as she stared into his silver eyes that reflected the moonlight. She felt the raw strength in him and knew she had no chance of escaping. His face was very near Thalia's, and she felt his breath on her mouth. Fear was forgotten and other, more troubling feelings swamped her—unfamiliar feelings that took her completely by surprise.

Thalia had never been this close to a man, and her body reacted to his in a most shocking way. She raised her hips in an age-old movement dictated by instinct. His hands loosened on her wrists, and she felt him swell against her.

Why did she have the urge to take his face between her hands and grind her mouth against his?

"I shall never yield to you."

His eyes glittered. "I think you shall."

Ashtyn had finally subdued the little tigress and knew the very moment she admitted defeat. He had never met a woman as stubborn and unwilling to listen to reason as this one. Thalia could strike out with the precision of an Egyptian asp, and be just as deadly. This was the woman the king required him to marry?

If he had been allowed to choose a wife, she would have been docile and compliant. This woman would never bend to any man.

"Let . . . me . . . up," Thalia said between clenched teeth.

"If I release you, I expect you to accompany me without argument." His voice was soft but menacing.

She twisted, trying to get loose. "I do not agree to anything."

"It seems to me you have little choice in the matter." His grip tightened on her wrists. "The sooner you comply, the sooner I release you."

Then Ashtyn felt her body arch toward his and desire slammed into him. Unthinking, he rubbed against her and watched her eyes widen. Her breasts were flattened against his chest, and he wanted to rip open the robe and expose them to his gaze. Yearning such as he'd never known burned within him, and he wanted her more than he'd ever wanted any woman.

Ashtyn tried to regain control over his passion when he saw the confusion in Thalia's eyes and reminded himself she was an innocent. Or was she? Perhaps she knew exactly what she was doing.

Burning need coursed hotly through him and he lowered his head, his mouth a mere breath from Thalia's. It took all of his willpower to resist the need to press his mouth against those soft parted lips. In exasperation, he released her hands and quickly stood, pulling Thalia to her feet. "Do not think you can use your womanly guile on me, little vixen. More experienced women than you have tried to turn me from my duty and failed."

Thalia shoved against Ashtyn. What was he talking about? She knew nothing of womanly wiles, and if she did, he'd be the last man she'd try to entice. She was so stunned by his accusation that she made no protest when he lifted her onto his horse and mounted behind her.

Taking the reins of Thalia's horse, Ashtyn headed back toward the oasis.

Thalia searched her mind, wondering what had just happened between them. There had been a moment her body had responded to his, and that disturbed her.

She glanced over her shoulder at Ashtyn. "You cannot watch me all the time. I will eventually make my escape," she told him tauntingly.

He halted his mount and gripped her chin, staring into her eyes. "I am not a patient man. Do not push me too far. You are in my care, and after your attempt to escape, I will never be farther from you than I am at this moment. Grow accustomed to it."

"Then what Turk said about you is true: you are a destroyer."

Ashtyn frowned and pulled her against his chest. "I can assure you no one in the king's service calls me that."

Although Thalia was not looking at him, she could feel those searching eyes on her.

"'Tis no more than a name the rebels call me to frighten young recruits." He paused. "Are you afraid of me?"

"I fear you no more than the desert scorpion." Thalia was quiet for a moment while she gathered her thoughts. "You are not what your humble clothing would suggest. Who are you really?"

"What do you mean?"

"There is evidence on your upper arms that you wear armbands. Did you purposely remove them before you arrived in Egypt? And I know that is a signet ring you wear on your finger."

Ashtyn urged his horse forward as he spoke in a tone swift and soft, "You see too much."

When they reached the oasis, Ashtyn ordered the camp struck although it was not yet daylight. Captain Darius glanced worriedly from one to the other but said nothing as he gathered their supplies.

"She'll be riding with me," Ashtyn told the big man.

Being forced to ride on the same horse with Ashtyn was a punishment. Thalia held herself stiff, and his laughter told her he knew what she was doing. But as the day wore on and the heat drained her strength, she fell back against him.

Ashtyn whispered close to Thalia's ear, "Tell me, little vixen, how far to the village where the Nile meets the sea?"

She looked over her shoulder at Ashtyn and watched him smile. "I will not tell you."

"Perhaps you do not know how far the distance is," he suggested.

Irked by his skillful prodding, she answered, "We will be there before sundown unless the horses go lame, or unless my brother and Queen Cleopatra's army sweep down on you."

He laughed softly. "You are a bloodthirsty little princess."

It was late afternoon when they rode through the ancient fishing village of Osage. Thalia glanced at the small mud-baked houses with palm-thatched roofs while listening to the rhythm of the life going on around her. Here, as in all Egypt, the people owed their existence to the bountiful Nile. The mud-colored flow hummed with life now that the seasonal floods were upon them.

The brush along the banks was so dense, Captain Darius had to hack his way through thick reeds as high as his head. They trudged through the marshes of papyrus rushes, making way for the villagers who were harvesting the valuable crop to sell at the marketplace in Alexandria.

When they reached the dock, they had to step around the heavy fishing nets drying in the sun. Thalia glanced about, looking for anyone who could help her. Captain Darius was speaking to a man about buying the horses, while Ashtyn stared out at the Mediterranean.

Thalia saw her chance when she noticed a young lad mending a tattered net. Bending down to him, she quickly pressed her ring into his hand and whispered, "Give this to Lord Ramtat, Sheik of the Badari, when he comes looking for me, and your family will be richly rewarded. Tell him you saw me, and that I am being forcibly taken onboard a ship to an island called Bal Forea."

The boy looked puzzled that such a grand lady would stop to talk to him. "We have heard news of a great one who was taken," he said, staring into her eyes. "Are you the one?"

"Shh," she cautioned, as Ashtyn turned to her with suspicion in his silver-blue eyes. "Say nothing that man can overhear."

Ashtyn stalked toward Thalia, grasping her hand and pulling her to her feet. "What did you tell the boy?" he asked, tightening his hand on her wrist.

Thalia's eyes met the child's, and she watched him quickly tuck her ring into his shabby linen belt. "I was noting what artful stitches he took." She nodded at the boy. "If you do not believe me, ask him." Her gaze met the lad's in understanding. "He will tell you what I said."

Thalia turned sharply away, lest the boy might confess all out of fear. She was relieved when Ashtyn followed her.

"It matters not what you told the lad. We shall be gone from here before sunset." He pointed to a ship that was little more than a small dot on the horizon. "Say farewell to Egypt. We shall soon put out to sea." When he saw her face whiten, he took her hand and said in a consoling tone, "I can assure you that you will have every comfort on this voyage."

Thalia glared at him as despair hit her. "I have sailed from Rome to Egypt on Queen Cleopatra's barge. And I have gone down the Nile on several occasions with my family and an entourage of servants." She tore her hand from his grasp. "Let us hope you are better equipped for a sea voyage than you were for a trek through the desert."

Ashtyn's eyes flashed, and Thalia was glad she'd made him angry. She glanced over her shoulder to watch the young boy she'd given her ring to scurry toward the village. Ramtat would look for her here, she had no doubt of that, but she could not be certain whether the young boy would give her brother the ring or just keep it for himself. She must face whatever fate awaited her at the end of the sea voyage.

Thalia turned back toward the sea with her hand shading her eyes from the glare of the setting sun. The ship now loomed larger, riding restless waves. How ominous it looked with its red sails and a prow shaped like a great bird of prey. She thought it might be a hawk, but the ship was too far away to tell for sure.

Ashtyn signaled the ship, and soon two silent crewmen rowed ashore. Knowing it would serve no purpose, Thalia did not resist when Ashtyn helped her into the small punt. She noticed the crewmen avoided looking at her and concentrated instead on plying their oars with vigor.

Thalia also noticed Captain Darius glancing back toward the shore, his face pale.

"I am not a sailor, Commander, I'm a soldier," the big man reminded him. "I do not like it on the sea."

Ashtyn nodded grimly. "You spent most of our voyage to Egypt below deck. Perhaps the sea will be calmer on our return."

The poor captain gripped the sides of the punt, his stomach already heaving.

Ashtyn fell into silence, staring straight ahead. When they reached the ship, he climbed up the rope ladder, then reached for Thalia. His strong hands clasped her arms, and he lifted her onboard. He kept a steadying hand on her shoulder until she became accustomed to the swaying of the ship.

"This is the royal galley, *War Bird*. Here you take your first step onto Bal Forea territory," Ashtyn told her.

With a heavy heart, it took Thalia a moment to realize the strange occurrence that had taken place. All the crew members had postured themselves in deep bows, and some had dropped to their knees.

She whirled around and stared at Ashtyn, anger boiling inside her. "You pass yourself off as a humble soldier, but I see the truth of your deceit. Those men would not bow to a common man."

"Nay, they would not," he agreed.

"They are almost groveling at your feet. And think you I do not see the reverence in their eyes?"

A smile curved his lips. "What you see is no tribute to me, but rather your countrymen paying homage to you." Ashtyn turned her around so she was facing the elevated prow of the ship. "Watch your subjects carefully when they see you watching them. They are so respectful of you, they cannot bring themselves to look upon your face. Those young men you see falling to their knees before you grew up with the hope that you would one day be found and brought home. The elder ones now have renewed hope for the future. Nay, Princess Thalia, they do not bow to me. 'Tis you they revere."

Thalia quickly lowered her own head, swallowing deep. Her body trembled, and she wanted to cry. There was so much to say, but words failed her. She stumbled forward, gripping the aft railing as tears dampened her eyes.

"Princess Thalia, may I present Captain Normah to you?" Ashtyn asked from behind her.

She turned to find a tall, thin man with a swarthy sea-weathered face and keen blue eyes. "Highness," he said, bending low. "I am blessed to have been chosen to take you to Bal Forea. If there is anything you wish, you have only to ask."

"I would ask that you take me ashore and sail away without me," she said ungraciously.

Captain Normah looked astonished as he bowed. "I shall see you safely home."

It was too much to bear. Thalia was aware that Ashtyn still stood beside her, and she glanced at him. "I am not the person they believe me to be. Please tell them to stop bowing."

His words were spoken in a kind tone, his gaze searching her face. "If you have never lost hope, you cannot know what these men have lived through. Now they look to you to change their lives."

"I am not responsible for anyone's life, save my own. 'Tis I who have no hope."

❧Chapter Thirteen

Ramtat dismounted at the oasis and stared down at the scattered ashes of what remained of a campfire. He glanced at his master of horse, General Heikki. "It appears to be two days old."

Heikki bent and sifted the ashes through his fingers. "Aye, at least that."

Ramtat traced the outline of his sister's small footprint. "I make out that there are two men with her."

Heikki observed a deep imprint. "One man is large."

"They will have gone to the village of Osage, and I suspect she will be taken out of Egypt by ship."

"Master, who are they, and what do they want with Lady Thalia?"

"If we knew the who, we might know the why," Ramtat said worriedly. "We ride to Osage with all haste. Perhaps someone there will have seen my sister."

The fierce Badarian warriors knew the urgency that drove their lord. They were the best trackers in all Egypt, and if they could not find Lady Thalia, no one could.

No man complained because he was tired. They had ridden for two days without stopping, leading fresh horses and changing mounts often. They ate as they rode, and some even fell asleep in the saddle, knowing their well-trained horses would follow the others.

When they reached the village, a young boy came rushing up to Ramtat, waving a ring at him. "Great Lord of the Badari, I know of whom you seek!"

Ramtat took the ring and dismounted. Bending to the boy, he said, "Tell me everything you know about the woman who gave you this ring."

The boy pointed toward the horizon where a ship was barely visible. "She was a great lady, Lord, and she gave me this to show to someone of importance, like you."

"Did she tell you their destination?" Ramtat urged.

The boy hung his head. "Aye, Lord, but I do not remember." Then his head snapped up and his eyes brightened. "It was an island!"

"Tell me about the men with her," Ramtat prodded, anger burning inside him because he had missed Thalia by mere hours.

"One was a giant of a man. The other appeared to be a lordly man, with cold eyes as silver as the underwing of a kilta bird." The boy's brow knitted. "They were different from us."

"In what way—taller, darker, lighter?"

"They wear their hair long. One man had no hair at all. But the strong one had hair to his shoulders. So did the man who came in the small boat to take the lady to the ship."

Ramtat could think of no country where the men wore long hair. "The ship, did you see any markings on the sails?"

"Aye. The sails were red and had the markings of a

huge black bird with wings spread. It was a hawk, clutching a gold crown."

Ramtat stood, glancing hard at Heikki. "I cannot think of any country that flies such a standard."

"Nay, Master," Heikki said. "Nor can I."

Ramtat glanced around at the flimsy fishing boats that were built to hug the shoreline. "We have no ship to follow, nor do I know in which direction they sail."

He glanced back at the boy and gave him several gold pieces, unmoved by the happiness that shone in the lad's eyes. His mind was on his sister and how frightened she must be.

Thalia stood on the deck staring out to sea, aware that Ashtyn was speaking privately with the captain, no doubt about her. Out of the corner of her eye she watched the crew members move away from her and go about their business of getting underway. She suspected Ashtyn had explained to the captain that she had been made uncomfortable by the crew's reaction to her.

With an ache in her heart, Thalia watched the coastline of Egypt grow smaller in the distance. After a time, she was unable to watch any longer and directed her attention to the bow. Her gaze swept upward to the tall red sails billowing in the wind, displaying a huge pattern of a great hawk. With the wind whipping at the sails, it almost seemed the bird was in flight.

"What do you think of the ship?"

Thalia had not heard Ashtyn come up beside her, and his voice startled her. " 'Tis a warship, is it not?"

"Aye. The *War Bird* is the pride of the fleet. She was built for ramming enemy ships. Many victories are attributed to the hawk figurehead."

Thalia stared upward at the billowing red sails. "It seems your country is obsessed with war."

"How can we be otherwise when war is thrust upon us?" Ashtyn said with a bite to his tone.

He noticed that Thalia's attention was drawn to the billowing sails. "The hawk is the symbol of Bal Forea. It is said by soothsayers that if the hawks leave the island, the royal house of Forea will fall."

Thalia cast him a skeptical glance.

"Of late the people have watched the birds more closely to see if they migrate from the island. There are those who say very few hawks are left on Bal Forea. They believe your coming will begin the return of the hawks."

"'Tis naught but a fabrication invented by those who foster gloom." She watched the sails ripple. "There is a soothsayer in Alexandria who swears Queen Cleopatra will be the last ruling pharaoh of Egypt. We all know that cannot be true because her majesty is young and healthy and has three children to succeed her. At least one of them will surely live to be pharaoh."

"But there are no such children on Bal Forea. Our king is of advanced age, and there is only you to stand in his stead."

Thalia confronted Ashtyn, her eyes blazing with anger. "Our every conversation ends in an argument, and I am weary of it. Can you speak on any subject but the plight of Bal Forea? Why don't you start by telling me who you really are."

He smiled, dazzled by her fiery spirit. "I am Count Ashtyn, of the house of Tyran, commanding general of his majesty's forces."

Her eyes widened. She had suspected he was more

than he seemed, but she had not thought him to have such high rank. "And I am Lady Thalia of the house of Tausrat," she said, bowing to him, the glint in her eyes daring him to challenge her identity.

Ashtyn decided not to contest the matter of her title at the moment. To her surprise, he touched her cheek. "The bruise where Turk struck you is still visible."

"And my shoulder aches where you knocked me off that horse and fell on top of me." She suddenly laughed. "It must have been a contest between the two of you to see which could bruise me the most."

She saw Ashtyn flinch at her words.

"It was unfortunate I had to recapture you in such a way, and I ask your pardon. Know this—I would never strike you," Ashtyn said, his silver gaze sweeping her face. "The next time Turk and I meet, one of us will die."

Thalia knew she had just caught a true glimpse of the Destroyer, the man whose name struck fear into the hearts of his enemies.

She was startled when she caught the eye of one of the older boatmen, and he immediately went to his knees and bowed his head.

"Make them stop," she said, stepping back quickly. "I do not want to be worshiped like some goddess. I am not someone on whom that man can place his hopes."

"But you are his only hope," Ashtyn said, then snapped his fingers at the boatman and sent him away.

Thalia still wore Ashtyn's robe over her short tunic, and she had to hold it up to keep from tripping over it. Her hair was tangled, and she could still feel sand and grit on her face. "You know full well I look more like a guttersnipe than a princess of Bal Forea."

He placed his hand on the railing of the ship and stared down at her. "It is not the clothing we see—it is the woman inside."

Her chin went up. "Not me!"

"You are everything we could hope for." He smiled. "That little dimple in your chin, the bright blue eyes, the gold in your hair. We see in you our future queen."

He was using that seductive tone again, and it twisted Thalia's insides. Drawing two quick breaths, she felt a quiver deep inside her. "I have no knowledge of signing treaties or ending wars. Your island needs someone well-versed in political relations between countries." Her gaze found and locked with Ashtyn's. "You should know this about me—I was once a thief and pickpocket. Not a commonplace thief—I was good at it."

Thalia had intended to shock Ashtyn, but she saw him smile. "There is very little of your past that is unknown to me. I have been informed about your life on the streets of Rome."

"Then you should realize I am unworthy. I know what it means to see someone worthy sit on a mighty throne, because I have observed Queen Cleopatra. She is wise and learned. I am not like her."

"You will be surrounded by men of great knowledge, and they will advise you. And you will have—"

Suddenly he wouldn't meet her eyes, and he seemed nervous. "There is something you are not telling me," she said suspiciously.

"Nay."

"If you want me to trust you, Count Ashtyn, you must be truthful with me. Else I will not believe anything you say."

"What would you have me tell you?"

"What you are keeping from me."

Ashtyn realized Thalia was astute like her grandfather, and not easily misled. "The king will explain everything you need to know."

"I say, nay. You answer my questions since your king is not here," she demanded. "What more should I know?"

Ashtyn looked away as he spoke, "A husband has been chosen for you."

Thalia's eyes widened, and she grabbed his sleeve. "You have taken me away from my country by force, you dragged me across the desert and put me on this ship, and now you tell me I will be forced to marry someone I do not know?" She shook her head. "I will not!"

Guilt settled on Ashtyn's shoulders. "You must take this matter up with the king."

"Did your king not learn anything by trying to force his daughter to marry against her will?"

Ashtyn said nothing.

But Thalia was unrelenting. "Who is this man that has been chosen for me?" she demanded.

"That is for the king to say."

"Are you telling me you don't know who he is?"

"Nay, I know."

Thalia took a step backward, feeling sick inside. Count Ashtyn was not going to say anything more. Her chest tightened and she shook her head. "I want to be taken to my cabin."

He swept her a bow, and she did not see the relief in his eyes. "As you wish, Highness."

Ashtyn escorted Thalia across the deck, and she kept her eyes downcast so she wouldn't see the men dropping to their knees as she passed. Feeling angry and helpless, she followed Ashtyn down several steps and waited with him as he opened a door. When Thalia stepped inside, the luxury of the cabin took her by surprise. As she turned around slowly, her mouth opened in astonishment. The walls were covered with beaten silver, and the floors were covered by a red silken rug with the image of a black hawk woven into the middle.

When Thalia noticed the woman who stood silently with her head lowered, waiting to be presented, she looked inquiringly at Ashtyn.

"Princess Thalia, this is Eleni. She has been chosen to serve you. Should you wish to learn our language, she has knowledge of Greek, which is spoken on Bal Forea."

Thalia's eyes burned with indignation. "Were you so certain you would capture me that you brought this woman to serve me?"

He stared into her eyes without blinking. "I had no doubt you would be sailing home on this ship."

Before Thalia could reply, Ashtyn bowed and left, closing the door behind him.

Slowly Thalia turned to the woman. "Do you speak Egyptian or Latin? I know very little Greek, certainly not enough to converse with you in that language."

The servant appeared to be in her thirties. Her blonde hair was braided and clipped to the top of her head with an onyx clasp. There was a serenity about her, a calmness that showed in the smoothness of her smile. She seemed hesitant to speak, and Thalia thought she must not understand Egyptian.

"Did you not understand my words?"

"Aye, gracious Highness," she replied in stilted Egyptian. "I speak both, which is why I was chosen to serve you on this voyage. If I hesitate, it is merely because of the honor I feel in standing before you. We of Bal Forea were not sure if you were our hope or merely a myth."

"I am neither—I am Egyptian."

Eleni looked confused.

Trying to rid herself of her frustration, Thalia paced across the rug, pausing when she came to a shelf filled with sheepskin scrolls. At any other time she would have been tempted to read every one of them, but they were probably written in Greek.

"Highness, shall I prepare your bath?" Eleni asked shyly. "The trunks along the wall are filled with clothing and shoes for you."

Thalia wanted to say no, but a bath sounded wondrous. She nodded, moving to one of the trunks and lifting the lid. She drew in her breath at what she saw. There were gowns of the most brilliant colors she had ever seen: blues darker than the sky on a cloudless day, reds that rivaled the sunset, and the deep purple worn only by royalty. She ran her hand across the material of a green silk, wanting very much to feel it against her skin.

Thalia stared at the filthy robe that covered her short tunic. She quickly lifted it over her head and tossed it aside. She certainly could not confront her enemies if she looked like a peasant.

❧CHAPTER FOURTEEN

For two days Thalia remained in her cabin, seeing no one but Eleni. She had many questions, and the young woman seemed to be knowledgeable, but stubbornness and pride prevented Thalia from asking anything about Bal Forea.

Succumbing to boredom, Thalia removed one of the sheepskin scrolls from the shelf and was delighted to discover it was written in Latin, a language she read as well as Egyptian. She spread it before her on a table and began to read.

She went from one scroll to another, devouring the history of Bal Forea. She frowned when she came to the part where the ancient ancestors of the present-day Bal Foreans had survived a great catastrophe from a massive volcano eruption. The volcano had buried the entire landmass, and it sunk into the sea, killing tens of thousands. According to the scrolls, those few who lived made their way to an uninhabited island where the only survivor of the royal family was the youngest son, who named the island Bal Forea.

Their homeland that had sunk into the ocean was called "Atlantis"!

With renewed fervor, Thalia bent her head to another scroll. She recalled reading a translation of the works of the Greek philosopher Plato, where he mentioned a cataclysmic eruption that had devoured all signs of Atlantis. Could the Bal Foreans actually be descended from the people of that doomed land?

After reading for hours, Thalia's eyes were stinging, and she realized the light was fading. But she was too excited to stop. The ever-observant Eleni lit a lantern, and Thalia continued to read.

Eleni brought her a meal of cheese and fruit, and still Thalia read.

"Will you not rest now?" Eleni asked timidly.

"Nay. I have too much to learn in so little time. It will be better for me if I know something of your people's history when I face your king." Thalia bent her head back to the fascinating chronicles.

Long into the night the lantern burned low as Thalia rubbed her tired eyes, still too excited to stop reading.

Standing high upon the deck, Ashtyn watched Eleni cross to him as she had every day to make her report on the progress of the princess.

"How does your lady fare?" he asked, his gaze sweeping to the stern and the small island to the west.

"She is well, Lord. She continues to read the scrolls, and she will not be stopped."

Ashtyn took a deep breath. It had been the king's hope that Thalia would want to learn about Bal Forea. Ashtyn had thought it was a futile undertaking since it had taken seven scholars three years to complete the task of translating the work into Latin, and they had not been certain the princess would even be able to read.

Ashtyn glanced down at the woman. "What do you think of her highness?"

Eleni's eyes rounded. She had not expected the great lord to be interested in her opinion. "There is kindness in the princess, but she is sad, missing her family. And she is angry because she does not want to believe she is the princess."

Ashtyn met the woman's gaze, but he did not actually see her. It saddened him that Thalia still suffered. "Return to her and serve her well."

The ship was riding the waves, and Thalia stared at the ceiling of her cabin, feeling as if she was being gently rocked to sleep. Her eyes drifted shut, and she lost herself in a dream. But there was something different about this dream: there was a man standing between Thalia and danger. The man had piercing eyes and a mighty sword arm.

He stepped out of the shadows and stared at her as if he wanted something, but his eyes gave nothing away.

"I have been waiting," she stated. Suddenly he came to her and crushed her against his breastplate. "What is happening to me?" she asked.

His mouth was near hers, but he did not bend to touch her lips. "I will answer you thus," he said in a deep, mesmerizing voice. "What is happening to you is also happening to me. We were destined to be together."

Disappointment assailed Thalia when he held her away

from him. She felt a yearning so deep it was like a ripping pain in her heart.

"You must find your way to me," *he told her softly.*

Thalia felt the dream fading, although she tried to hold on to it. Her eyes flew open, and she found herself sitting up in bed. Her heart was pounding, and it took her a moment to realize where she was. But the sway of the ship brought her back to the present, and she knew well the man who had walked in her dream.

Ashtyn.

Her gaze swept the darkened cabin and she could barely see Eleni where she slept near the door. Thalia eased her body back onto the bed, wide awake. In her dream she had wanted Ashtyn as a woman wants a man.

Thalia reminded herself that dreams were not real. She wanted more than anything to be rid of Ashtyn, the Destroyer.

As sunlight advanced across the rug, there was a pounding on the door. Eleni opened it a crack and spoke quietly to whoever was on the other side. When they left, she turned woefully to the princess.

"The master says you will become ill if you continue to remain in the cabin. He wants you dressed and on deck before the noon hour."

"Who is he to issue me orders? I am not bound to obey him. Go and tell him I shall do as I please."

"But Highness, I dare not," Eleni said, looking distressed. "Next to the king, he is the most important man in Bal Forea."

Thalia glared at the door, then her head snapped

around in the maid's direction. "Do you believe me to be your princess?"

"Aye, Highness."

"Then you should have no trouble obeying my orders over Count Ashtyn's."

Eleni paused before she spoke. "I will obey you over Count Ashtyn."

"It is distasteful to have the ship's crew bowing to me. Nay, I shall not leave this cabin, and you may tell him I said so."

"As you wish, Highness. Shall I not bring your food and help you dress before I approach Count Ashtyn?"

"Aye. I want to be dressed should he decide to storm this cabin."

When Eleni told the count what Thalia had said, storm the cabin was precisely what he did. Not bothering to knock, he thrust the door open with such force, it banged against the wall.

Thalia had been expecting him. Taking her time in rolling a scroll and reaching for another from the shelf, she didn't look up as he stood seething before her. At last she met his angry gaze. "What is the meaning of this intrusion?" she asked, while Eleni cringed in a corner.

"You will accompany me on deck and take the air. I have no intention of delivering you to your grandfather in an unhealthy condition."

"I shall not!"

Without ceremony, he swept her into his arms. "I think you will, Highness."

She kicked her legs and twisted her body, trying to be free of him, but he held her tightly.

"Put me down!"

Ashtyn's jaw clenched. "Only if you accompany me of your own will."

"Nay!"

Without a word he carried Thalia out of the cabin, not stopping until he reached the steps that led to the deck. "Shall I carry you all the way, or will you walk?"

She was so angry she wanted to hit him. But when her gaze settled on his piercing eyes, she saw no yielding reflected in the silver-blue depths. After struggling with her own anger, she finally nodded. He had won this battle, but she was determined she would win the final one. Just when she was about to tell him so, the oddest thing happened.

He dipped his head, his long unbound hair sweeping against Thalia's cheek. He said in a deep voice, almost as if the words were being forced from him, "Since meeting you, my dreams have been disturbing."

Thalia could not find her voice, as she remembered her own dream.

Their gazes locked. "You have beguiled me, Highness."

His mouth was so near her own that if she moved the merest bit their lips would touch. "Nay," she whispered, wanting to touch his lips, to tangle her fingers in his dark hair. "I am no caster of spells. And why would I want to draw you to me?"

With an abruptness that took her by surprise, Ashtyn set her on her feet. "I expect you to spend part of each day in the fresh air."

Thalia stood on the first step, her anger returning. "However can I resist such a charming invitation?"

A sudden smile lurked at the corner of Ashtyn's

mouth. "We are within sight of the isle of Capreae, and I thought you might like to see it."

"I can't think of anything I would like better," she said with a bite to her tone, "unless it would be to look upon the coastline of Egypt." In a swirl of green silk, she stepped on deck. She cried out in alarm and stepped back when one of the helmsmen dropped to his knees before her.

"Get up!" she ordered him. But the man did not understand Egyptian and, of course, he did not move.

She glanced back at Ashtyn, pointing to the man. "Tell him to rise."

Ashtyn laughed as he tapped the man on the shoulder and nodded for him to move away. "I cannot order the whole crew not to worship at the feet of their future queen."

"There is no truth to what you say," she said, gingerly stepping around the still-prostrate figure. With measured steps she moved to the railing, her gaze on the landmass in the distance. "I have heard about Capreae. It is not a very important island, and Egypt does not bother to trade with its people."

"Bal Forea, on the other hand, does trade with Capreae. Most probably, Egypt would find our island too insignificant to bother with as well."

She looked up at him. "When my family discovers where you've taken me, I expect Egypt will *not* find Bal Forea too insignificant to bother with."

"You are probably right," he agreed. "We have considered that possibility since discovering how close your ties are to Queen Cleopatra."

Thalia glanced back over her shoulder and noticed some of the crewmen were leaning against the railing and staring at her. "I wish they would not treat me in such a manner. It's very disconcerting."

"You have to understand that the poor man who fell on his knees before you was struck dumb by the honor. It is not every day one of your subjects comes face-to-face with the real, live woman they thought was a legend."

In disgust, she turned back toward the railing. The air was hot and moist, but not unpleasant. "I am but a few short years from my childhood. How can I be their rescuer, when I cannot even save myself?"

"'Tis a daunting task that is set before you." He turned her to face him and said with sincerity, "I stand ready to help you in any way I am able."

She was quiet for a moment as she watched the wind sift through his long black hair. He was dressed in magnificent red and silver armor with the black hawk of Bal Forea engraved on the breastplate. "I have been reading the history of Bal Forea and it is quite fascinating. Since Greek is the language of the island, I was surprised to find the history was in Latin."

"Your grandfather had that done for you. Of course, at the time he thought you were in Rome, thus the Latin translation."

Thalia let out her breath, secretly pleased.

"Your grandfather hoped you would arrive at Bal Forea knowing something about its people."

She was coming to the conclusion that she could not rail against everyone who called her 'highness', or those who referred to their king as her grandfather. "I am curious about something, Count. If the history is a true one, the people of your island are supposedly descendants of Atlantis."

"That is fact."

"There are scholars in Egypt who argue that Plato's account of Atlantis is fiction." The ship was sailing out of sight of Capreae, but Thalia hardly noticed. "I always believed his account was true. I don't know why."

Ashtyn studied her face for a long moment. "You are more than we thought you would be. There is no woman on Bal Forea who can read both Egyptian and Latin. It is rare to find a woman who can read at all. No doubt you have already discovered that your maid Eleni speaks many languages but does not read."

"All in my family read, be they male or female."

"The Tausrat family is truly admirable."

"I have turned my attention to learning Greek. Eleni has been most helpful." Thalia stared at the disappearing landmass. "And I have enjoyed the history of Bal Forea, but I know little of the present. Can you tell me about the island?"

He gave her a charming smile that melted her heart.

"It would be my pleasure. Shall I begin with our ancestors who survived the destruction of Atlantis?"

"Please."

Ashtyn was watching the way the sun played across her golden hair, and almost became distracted. "Try to imagine a people who had lost everything. Then think of them washing up on the shores of an inhospitable and uninhabited island. Imagine their grief at their loss, and how they were forced to make a life for themselves. They had no tools and had to dig with their hands to plant crops. King Talystar, who had been the youngest and was the only survivor of the royal family, united the people and guided them through many hardships. Because of his bravery and courage, most of them survived."

Thalia was silent as she pondered what Ashtyn had told her. "It would be wonderful if it was true. But your people seem to fabricate royals where there are none."

"But suppose for a moment you have been chosen to save your people, just as King Talystar was."

"Do not make that comparison." Thalia clamped her hands over her ears. "I will not hear of it."

"Very well. What would you like to speak of?"

"Tell me what you know of the woman who is supposed to be my mother."

He let out his breath. "There is a fountain room at the palace with a statue of Princess Jiesa. I have oft been drawn to that room to stare at her likeness."

"Why would you do that?"

He glanced down at her and frowned. "How can a man say what draws him to a woman?"

"Surely you were not drawn to my mother."

His gaze swept over her face, resting on her lips. "Nay, not her—she is carved out of cold marble." His voice grew deep. "It was a flesh-and-blood woman I thought of."

Thalia felt a catch in her throat. Suppose this *was* her mother. "Describe her to me."

Ashtyn's hooded gaze pierced hers, and he spoke so low Thalia wasn't sure she had heard him correctly. "She is you."

"What do you mean?"

"When I saw you that night in the garden, I thought the statue of your mother had come to life."

Suddenly, a strange mood washed over Thalia, and she smiled up at him flirtatiously. "It is difficult to gather an image of a man who commands armies staring at a statue and believing it came to life in far-off Egypt."

He did not smile as he studied her face. "I saw how you beguiled those men the night I slipped into your garden. Is it not possible you did the same to me?"

Thalia felt she was walking into trouble. "I beguiled no one, and least of all you. No doubt you are an important man on Bal Forea, but to me, you are merely my prison guard."

Their gazes locked, her eyes fiery with anger, his seeking and piercing.

"Stand aside," she said.

And he did.

Once in her cabin, Thalia kicked at a stool and sent it careening across the floor. "That man infuriates me!"

Eleni was folding clothing and looked at Thalia inquiringly. "Do you speak of Count Ashtyn?"

"Aye. If all your men on Bal Forea are like him, it must be a miserable place for your women."

"But, Highness, Count Ashtyn is considered the best of men. He has won many battles and brought glory to his name. So many of our women wish he would take notice of them."

"I can well imagine," Thalia remarked sourly. "And most probably he gives them all a try."

"Nay, dear lady, he is too often leading our men into battle. He is a dedicated general who rides at the front of his men, not at the rear like others before him."

"You are one of his admirers."

"Who would not be?"

Thalia nodded. "Indeed. Who would not?"

❧ CHAPTER FIFTEEN

As the days passed, Thalia began to look forward to the hours she spent on deck. The *War Bird* was swift and sleek, and she loved the feel of the wind in her hair and the tangy taste of salt on her tongue.

She'd been told poor Captain Darius spent most of his time below deck, too ill leave his bunk. Thalia was spending more time with Ashtyn and discovering he had a sense of humor. She learned he had no family, and it saddened her when he spoke of how his mother and sister had died in a siege on their villa. His father had been killed at the head of the king's army, and Ashtyn had taken his father's place.

That particular day, Thalia was seated in the shade while Ashtyn sat with his back braced against the stern.

"How does your island differ from my Egypt?" she asked, as she rolled a scroll she'd been reading.

Ashtyn's laughter was warm and sent shivers across her skin. "As you already know, I was not prepared for your desert. You recall very well how you had to save Captain Darius and myself from dying of thirst. We have no arid land."

Thalia smiled with gratification. "So you admit you made a mistake?"

He nodded with good grace. "Utterly."

Ashtyn wore his black hair loose about his handsome face, and Thalia could only stare at him. She had little doubt he'd set out to charm her, and for the most part, had succeeded better than he knew. She found herself fascinated by his hands—his fingers were long and lean, and she had already felt the strength of them. They were not the hands of a courtier, but of a man who wielded a sword in defense of his country. Earlier that morning, when he'd handed her the scroll, their fingertips had accidently touched, and they both quickly withdrew their hands.

For the moment, Ashtyn was staring across the deck, watching a man scrub the wood until it gleamed. Thalia watched his lips compress, and she felt weak all over just thinking what it would feel like to have that mouth touch hers. The thought of it made her feel giddy. There were times when she wanted to lay her head against those broad shoulders and have him hold her close and tell her everything was going to be all right, that she would one day see her family again.

She lowered her head, distressed that she should have such longings for Ashtyn. "Insomuch," she said, bringing the conversation back to the island, "as you have no desert on Bal Forea, it is no wonder you did not know how dangerous it can be for those without water."

He swung his head back to her. "There is beauty on Bal Forea. You will see enclaves that sweep inward from a sea that is as blue as your eyes." He studied her eyes for a moment before continuing. "On the side of the island where we will go ashore, the capital city, Harjah, shines like a red jewel in the sun. That is, if you don't look too close and see the scars left by years of war."

"Tell me of the palace."

He smiled. "It stands on raised ground and is surrounded by two courtyards with high walls. I noticed many of the houses in Egypt are built of mud-brick. On Bal Forea the houses are build of red stone because the quarries on the island are red. There are high mountains that have snow on their peaks even in the hottest season. It is an island of contrast, for there are also date palms, orange groves and farms. The capital city produces the finest date wine in all the world, and the most succulent oranges you will ever taste. I will ask you if my boast is true when you have tasted them." His brow knitted. "Of course, there is no one to tend the crops, and many of the trees have died. Most of our fields have gone untended since the beginning of the war."

"How can this be? Do the people not know that armies need food to win victories?"

She watched his silver-blue gaze sharpen.

"The fields are barren because Sevilin's troops have been particularly brutal in their attacks on the farmers. The rebels indiscriminately burn crops and kill whole families. Sevilin sent men to burn our fishing fleet, and warned both the fishermen and the farmers that if any took up the hoe or the fishnet, they would be the first to die."

Unexpectedly, tears stung the back of Thalia's eyes, and a tight knot formed in her throat. She felt anger growing inside her. "That is monstrous! It is one thing to make war on trained soldiers, but to wage war on helpless citizens is an abomination. That man could not care for the people if he is willing to see them die."

"He came close to realizing his plan. The people were hungry and ready to give up until the king intervened." Ashtyn looked down at her. "Whatever you may think of your grandfather, he has always put the good of his people before his own. He sent men he could not spare to guard the farms. His Majesty opened his treasury and sent ships to buy grain and foodstuff from other countries." Ashtyn closed his eyes as if he were remembering the horror of that time. "Our citizens came close to being wiped out completely."

Thalia stared at him for a long moment, trying to imagine the hopelessness the citizens must have felt. "And did the king's gold save them?"

"Aye, it did, but only for a time. Those who were ill or old or too young did not survive. Our men mustered beneath Bal Forea's banner and sought the enemy in their fortresses. We flushed them out of caves, burned their hideouts and had them on the run."

Thalia leaned forward, not realizing she'd placed her hand on his arm. "And who is winning the war at this time?"

"When I left, the king. But it is far from over. The palace is filled with a network of spies, and the streets are dangerous at night." He placed his hand over hers. "That is why we are in desperate need and hold you as our hope. Sevilin knows this as well."

Thalia was silent as she considered all he had told her, not realizing she had laced her fingers through his.

"May the gods come to the aid of the citizens. Kings wage war, and it is the common man who suffers."

He raised her hand and pressed his mouth to it. "The wisdom of your grandfather is in you." His voice whispered through the air. "There are many who already love you."

Thalia drew in her breath, her fingers tingling. Reluctantly, she withdrew her hand from his clasp. "I am but a young woman. The problems you described must be left to wiser heads than mine."

Ashtyn stood, offering Thalia his hand. "I believe that concludes your lesson for today."

Thalia was learning that Ashtyn could be two different men: He was the soldier honed hard with a merciless will of stone, but he could also be soft-spoken, fascinating—capable of entrapping his victim with words. Each hour she spent with him served to break down the wall she had built. The king had chosen well when he sent his general after her.

As they strolled toward the companionway, she said, "While I understand the troubles your people face, it does not fall to me to help them. I still want to go home."

His jaw tightened, and he turned away from her. "You have said this all too many times," he muttered.

"Then you should listen to me."

Ashtyn watched her walk away, knowing his heart cried out for her, and that her heart did not answer.

Captain Normah approached Ashtyn, and they both watched Thalia disappear down the companionway.

The captain breathed a sigh. "It grieves me to see her so unhappy. She reminds me so of her mother."

Ashtyn was curious. "You knew her mother?"

Captain Normah rubbed his chin in thoughtfulness. "Aye. She was always happy and smiling. Then the day came when her heart turned to the captain of the guard, and tragedy followed. I do not like to mention this, but the people were in dire need when she fled the island with her lover. Many say she thought only of herself. But what will a woman not do when she loses her heart?"

Ashtyn shook his head. "I don't believe her daughter will easily succumb to matters of the heart."

The captain solemnly stared at the gathering clouds in the east. "She is even more comely than her mother. Men will love her for her beauty, but I have watched her," Captain Normah said, nodding to himself. "She has beauty of the heart—is that not right?"

"I have never known a woman who equals our Princess Thalia," Ashtyn remarked, as Captain Darius joined their group.

"Does she not know King Melik has chosen you for her husband?" Darius asked.

Ashtyn gripped the railing until his knuckles were white. "Nay, she does not. I would have you say nothing more on that subject lest you be overheard, and word reach her ears. The princess barely tolerates me as it is. Let her grandfather tell her. She will refuse the marriage, and there will be an end to it."

Darius gave a great belly laugh. "How are you going to let the princess go when you cannot keep your eyes from her?"

"She will not be allowed to reject the marriage," Captain Normah observed. "The king will see to that."

Ashtyn paused for a moment and put in words what the others may have suspected: "The king is dying."

"Then the rumors are true," the captain remarked, lowering his voice. "Pray Sevilin does not hear of it."

Ashtyn agreed with a nod. "Ask the gods to give us fair wind and a full sail so we can reach Bal Forea while his majesty yet lives." He walked away, seeking solitude.

For so long his attention had been centered on war and the survival of Bal Forea. But of late, those blue eyes of Thalia's kept creeping into his thoughts at the oddest moments. He had no time to think of a woman, especially not this one. She had accomplished something no other woman ever had—she made him want her with an ache that stayed with him day and night.

Doubtless trouble would fly in his face when the king informed Thalia he expected her to marry his general.

By the gods, he dreaded that day.

Ashtyn was playing a game of jackals and hounds with Captain Normah when Thalia approached him the next morning. Both men quickly rose to their feet and bowed.

"Excuse me Count Ashtyn, may I have a word with you?"

"Of course," he said, nodding at the captain, who was already scooping the game pieces into a case.

Ashtyn took Thalia's arm and led her toward the bulkhead, where they could speak in private. "How may I serve you?"

"Will you help me with my Greek?"

He hid his smile. "It would be my honor. Your grandfather will be happy if you can greet him in his own language."

"It's just that . . . I do not . . . it will be awkward to be in a country where I do not speak the language." She gnawed at her lower lip. "And it is as if somewhere in my past, Greek was not unknown to me."

He was surprised at her admission. "That is probably because you spoke it as a child."

"You were playing a game with the captain when I disturbed you."

"I was losing when you came to my rescue. Let us find a comfortable place and begin now."

A shade was erected near the bulkhead, and Thalia met Ashtyn there each day for her lessons. Amazingly, the language came to her easily. There were times when Thalia would know the word before Ashtyn spoke it.

As the days and weeks slipped by, Thalia found herself more relaxed in Ashtyn's company. He was a patient teacher, and they were soon holding conversations in Greek.

In the back of her mind she could hear a voice, the old nurse, speaking to her in the same language.

Another clue to her past.

Even though the notion grew in her mind that she might indeed be the missing princess, she would never admit it to Ashtyn.

It seemed to Thalia that everyone onboard was becoming tense. She could feel it in the air, and she wondered if it was because they were nearing their destination.

Eleni was already packing Thalia's trunks.

"Let us hope the wind holds so we can soon make landfall."

Eleni looked guarded. "I am not ready to reach Bal Forea. On this voyage I have been allowed to feel important for the first time in my life."

Thalia frowned. "Will you not be happy to see your family, Eleni?"

The woman, who was usually so charming, said in a harsh voice, "I no longer have family. There were five of us children, and we were poor. Often we went hungry because there was not enough food to go around."

"I know what it is to be hungry," Thalia said.

Eleni's dark eyes grew even darker. "Forgive me for saying so, Highness, but how can you know what hunger is like?"

Thalia remembered her childhood in Rome, where more often than not, she went to sleep without enough to eat. "Then tell me."

Eleni avoided Thalia's eyes. "My four brothers died in the war, and soon after, my mother and father died."

"I am sorry for your loss," Thalia said gently.

Eleni shrugged. "It was not so bad after I was sent to live with my aunt, who held the post of royal interpreter at the palace. She instructed me in Latin and Egyptian. Although I was not born into a noble family, I had the honor of being chosen to serve you. I believe it was because his majesty remembered my aunt with affection."

Thalia imagined there were many sad stories on Bal

Forea, but she sensed a change in Eleni, and it was deeply disturbing. In the past few days, the maidservant had become silent and distant, and she wondered why.

With a sigh, Thalia stretched out on the bed and closed her eyes. Each day took her closer to her destination and her confrontation with the king.

❦Chapter Sixteen

A heavy mist shrouded the ship, and Thalia could not see past the small window in her cabin. She remained below deck reading the last of the scrolls.

By mid-afternoon the sun broke through, and Ashtyn sent Darius to request that Thalia come topside.

When Thalia stepped on deck, she was immediately bathed in golden sunlight. She stepped to the railing and stared at the green mountainous landmass where waves washed onto sandy beaches and the air was warm and moist.

The sails unfurled, taking them closer to land. Thalia could clearly see palm trees lining a winding road that swept upward and away from the beach to disappear somewhere in the mountainous terrain.

"Bal Forea?" she asked, glancing up at Ashtyn.

"Aye, Highness. The shoreline is deep, so the ship is able to dock at the wharf you see jutting out into the ocean."

The water was so calm it looked like aqua-colored glass. "'Tis lovely to behold."

"Aye, so lovely it takes my breath." Ashtyn said, looking not at the scenery, but at Thalia. Then he looked away. "I have a request."

She arched her brow at him.

"Eleni tells me she packed a breastplate for you at the king's request. Would you mind being buckled into it before we make landfall?"

Knowing a breastplate fit snugly and was usually made for the person who would wear it, she was curious. "Perhaps it is too small or too large. How could anyone have known my size?"

His lips twitched in a smile. "I am told it was your mother's. It will not matter that it is not a perfect fit— the reason I ask you to wear it is for the benefit of the people."

"My mother's?" She examined the island more closely. It didn't feel like home to her. She felt no kinship with the citizens that dwelled there.

Ashtyn touched her sleeve. "Will you do this for them, Highness?"

She reached up and re-fastened the golden clasp that kept her hair pulled away from her face. "I will do as you request, although I think it will be of little matter."

Ashtyn watched her walk toward the companionway. His heart felt heavy. As long as they were on this ship, Thalia was under his protection, and he could be near her daily. Once they reached the island, she would belong to the people, and he would be forced to step aside.

Or worse. When the king told her about the betrothal, she would never want to see him again.

The gown Eleni chose for Thalia was a lovely royal purple linen. On Thalia's feet were a pair of golden sandals, and her hair had been released from its clasp and hung down her back to her waist. Her eyes were not outlined with kohl because Eleni had informed her it was not the custom on Bal Forea.

The maid reverently uncovered the breastplate that had been wrapped in a thick layer of lamb's wool. Shyly she held it out for Thalia's inspection. It was crafted of beaten gold, with a winged hawk etched in black enamel.

"Highness, the leather straps were worn from age so they were replaced before we sailed for Egypt. The last person to wear this was your blessed mother, Princess Jiesa."

Thalia could not speak because her throat had closed off.

"Will you wear your mother's armor, Highness?" Eleni asked, worriedly.

Thalia nodded. When Eleni slid the breastplate around Thalia's torso, it fit as if it had been crafted for her. Thalia tried to breathe while Eleni fastened the straps in place, wondering why she wanted to cry.

When Eleni stepped back to look at Thalia, she fell to her knees with tears streaming down her face. "This is a glorious day, Highness. How happy the people will be to see you!"

Thalia steeled herself for what was to come. Drawing in a deep breath, she knew she could not delay the moment any longer. Slowly she climbed the steps and stood on deck. At first no one noticed her since the crewmen were busy bringing the ship into port.

Captain Darius was the first to see her. For a moment the giant man stood stock still, then fell to his knees before her, bowing his head. Next Captain Normah left his wheel and came to kneel before Thalia.

Ashtyn was standing at the railing with his back to

her. When he heard the commotion, he turned slowly. For a long moment he could not move. The sun struck Thalia's golden breastplate, and with her wheat-colored hair rippling in the wind, it was as if she stood in a halo of gold. Slowly he approached her, but he did not kneel to her as the others had done, because he knew it would not please her. Instead he took her hand and raised it to his lips.

"Gracious Highness, if ever you had doubt that you are your mother's daughter, you should now know the truth."

Thalia fought against the tears that were gathering behind her eyes. With effort she glanced across the deck, where every man was on his knees. There was such devotion on their faces, she almost wished she was the princess they believed her to be.

"Please," she said to one and all in flawless Greek, "I beg of you, rise."

One by one they stood but continued to stare at her. She reached out for Ashtyn's arm and laced her hand around it, staring into his steady gaze. "I am frightened," she said so only he could hear.

His throat had closed off, and he could do no more than whisper, "You will find only those who love you here."

She was still gripping his arm as if it was her life-line. "I want the ordinary life I left behind in Egypt."

There was sadness in his eyes when he looked at her, but it was quickly gone. "I fear there is no going back."

She gave her head a small shake. "If only . . ."

His tone was decisive. "'Tis too late."

"I know why you asked me to wear my mother's breastplate."

"I told you why. For the people."

"You only told me half the reason. You want word to reach Lord Sevilin that I have arrived in all my splendor."

He did not deny it. Leading her toward the gangplank that was now being lowered into place, he compressed his mouth.

Thalia stepped away from him and raised her head to a proud tilt. If she was being used to bring the people hope, she would walk ashore on her own. Glancing toward the crowd that had gathered and others who were running forward to join them, she almost reconsidered. The cobbled streets that led through the village were lined with silent watchers.

With her courage in hand, Thalia moved down the gangplank, reminding herself to put one foot in front of the other and not to trip. Head held high, she took her first step onto Bal Forean soil.

A stately-looking gentleman dressed in somber black with a wide golden chain about his neck came forward. His face was aged, the wrinkles as brittle as old parchment. He tried to present a dignified figure, but Thalia saw his lips tremble as he searched her face. He must have been satisfied with what he saw there, because he went to his knees and dipped his head. "May I welcome you home, Most Royal Highness?"

In that very moment the roar from the crowd was deafening. Flowers quickly littered the roadway, and there was happiness on every face.

Seeing Thalia's unease, Ashtyn came forward and

presented the stately-looking man to her. "Your Highness, this is the Lord High Chamberlain, Lord Parinez."

The elder statesman, bent with age, bobbed his head awkwardly. "Long have I waited for this day, Highness."

"I beg you rise, Lord Parinez," Thalia said with growing unease. "There is no need for you to kneel to me."

She watched the poor man rise with difficulty and lean heavily on an ebony- handled cane. She saw Ashtyn exchange glances with Lord Parinez. "Her Highness has not yet grown accustomed to the honor due her."

Lord Parinez nodded. "It is understandable."

Thalia stood near Ashtyn because he was familiar to her in a world whirling out of control. Several horses were led forward, and Ashtyn lifted Thalia onto the saddle of a white mare before mounting his own horse. Two lines of guards in full red and black armor carried the royal standards of the black hawk.

As they made their way through the village, the people dropped to their knees. Some reached out to touch Thalia's gown—one young woman even lifted the hem and kissed it. Thalia saw hope mixed with tears on upturned faces, and she saw joy. Unlike in her beloved Egypt, where most of the populace had black hair, most of these people had hair near her own color. But all the eyes she gazed into were brown, not blue like her own.

Thalia was unaware she was crying until she felt the wetness on her cheeks. These people had found their way to her heart. They had lived with war for so long, they saw her as their savior. The pity of it was they would be disillusioned when they learned that, royal or not, she was but a girl and every bit as frightened as they were.

She fastened her gaze on the grand houses that sat against the distant hills. The houses that lined the road were little more than crumbling red-brick huts. The sight Thalia feared most was the palace atop the winding cobbled street, and the man who waited for her there.

Her grandfather, the king.

The palace gleamed in the sun like a red jewel. The gates were thrown open and guards, wearing red and black armor, stood at attention with hardly a flicker in their eyes as she drew near. But as the procession passed in front of them, they dropped to one knee and bowed their heads.

It was strange, but Thalia could feel the love of these people wash over her. She thought her arrival would have been very different if Turk had brought her to the island. As if thinking about him conjured him up, she gasped when she saw him among the crowd. With a slight bow, he lifted his hand in salute and disappeared among the multitude.

Thalia glanced quickly at Ashtyn, but he had not seen Turk—he'd been watching her. Tightening her fingers on the reins, she trembled with fear. Turk was letting her know he was still watching her. As she rode beneath the wide archway to the outer courtyard of the palace, she remembered Ashtyn's warning that the palace was peopled with Lord Sevilin's spies.

Her gaze moved over the charred bastion, seeing the first signs of war. There were blackened walls where enemy catapults had flung fireballs, in places the walls were chipped, and there were even gaping holes where the bricks had fallen away. It was in that moment she clearly understood that the palace fortress was all that stood between victory and defeat for the villagers below.

As the procession entered another courtyard, Ashtyn held up his hand to halt. Dismounting, he moved toward Thalia and lifted her from her horse. With his hand on her arm, he guided her toward the entrance of the palace.

The moment Thalia entered the great room, servants went to their knees, and she felt even more wretched. She had been brought into a situation that was most dire, and there seemed no way out of it.

Her frightened glance met Ashtyn's, and he mouthed the word "courage."

Lord Parinez stood at Thalia's right hand, and now spoke in a soft voice. "I had my doubts when Count Ashtyn set out to find you. But now that I have looked upon your face, I know you are indeed our Princess Thalia."

She looked into his damp eyes. "Then you are more certain than I, Lord Chamberlain. Pray you do not pin your hopes on a myth that will soon fade into nothingness."

The old man laughed, his eyes filled with mirth. "Even if I had doubts who you were, the words you speak would have convinced me. Highness, those words could easily have been spoken by your grandfather, the king."

Ashtyn reached out to Lord Parinez. "How fares the king?"

Pain flashed across the creased brow, and Lord Parinez lowered his voice. "Poorly. He clings to life so he can set eyes on his granddaughter. It is good you arrived today. He refuses to allow the physicians to give him medicine to ease his pain until he has seen the princess."

"Then let us go directly to him," Ashtyn said, taking Thalia's arm and leading her down a long, dark corridor.

The palace was a maze of chambers, and Thalia was sure she would never learn her way around. She saw dark places on the walls where tapestries had been removed, no doubt sold to pay for the war.

They walked through a garden choked with weeds, the flowering plants dying from neglect. The family suites revealed more evidence that precious treasures were missing, for the marble tables along the walls were bare of decoration.

Ashtyn paused before wide double doors that swept upward to a high, domed ceiling. "These are the king's chambers," he informed Thalia.

She nodded, gathering her courage. "Take me to him."

Chapter Seventeen

Flickering lanterns cast dim light on the middle of the huge room but left the far corners in darkness. The chamber was cluttered with mementoes: a favorite chair, a desk piled with scrolls, couches that were worn and tattered—a lifetime of living was collected in this room. The marble floors were dull from lack of polishing. The smell of herbs and spices filled the air, but Thalia's gaze was fastened on the bed half-hidden by filmy white curtains. A scribe sat on a rush mat, his legs folded, his stylus poised and ready to take down any words the king might utter.

Two men bowed to Thalia as Ashtyn led her forward. She assumed they were the physicians who attended the king. One of them pulled the curtain aside and attached it to a hook.

The room was so quiet, Thalia could hear her own breathing. Her only comfort was knowing Ashtyn stood at her side.

"Gracious Majesty," the lord chamberlain said, "Princess Thalia has arrived."

Thalia heard movement on the bed and a disgruntled voice issuing orders.

Lift me up. Plump the pillows. I will not receive my granddaughter like a man going to his tomb!"

Thalia's first glimpse of the king filled her heart with pity. He was gaunt and pale, his lips parched, his long white hair tangled about his face. Blue eyes, the color of her own, stared back at her.

She stood stiffly while he examined every detail of her face. Then he did something unexpected that wrenched Thalia's heart: tears welled in his eyes and rolled down his hollow cheeks.

His seeking blue eyes perused her face. "You are the image of my Jiesa. You could be her returning in the flesh. Let everyone within the hearing of my voice know that I proclaim this young woman to be blood of my blood, my granddaughter, and your future queen!"

His words struck Thalia like a lightning bolt. Was it as simple as that? A few words spoken, and her life would change forever? Her eyes locked with the king's as she stated, "Majesty, you are mistaken."

"Nay," his voice cracked, "I am not mistaken. Would you question a sick man who has taken to his bed?"

She shook her head, thinking he had paled a bit more. "I am saddened to find you unwell. Please accept my good wishes for your recovery."

He waved an agitated hand at the scribe. "Bring the princess a stool. I'll not have her standing over me." His bushy white brows arched. "Soon enough she will be raised above me, but not until I leave this world."

In confusion, Thalia lowered herself onto the stool that had been hastily provided for her, wishing she could loosen the tight straps of the breastplate. She felt no kinship with the sick old man, but she did pity him. "If you are my grandfather, would you tell me of the woman you call my mother?"

King Melik's jaw clenched. "Your mother was as frivolous as she was beautiful. She put her own needs ahead of those of her people. Had she remained and tended to her duty, we would not be at war."

"As I understand it, she left so she could marry the man she loved."

He nodded, all the while searching her eyes with a placid expression. "And forgot about her obligations. Let us hope you are not the romantic fool Jiesa was and are ready to accept your responsibility." His hard gaze softened. "But then, you are only a woman. What do women really know about duty?"

Thalia was offended by his assessment. "Majesty, as a woman I was brought up to run a household, to manage servants and slaves. I was taught that a wife must see to her husband's comforts and render him her loyalty. I know naught of the kind of duty of which you speak." She stared at his blue-veined hands without seeing them. "My brother Ramtat could tell you of duty. I have seen Queen Cleopatra break her heart as she rendered sound judgment on a wrong committed by those she trusted. This is the only way I can answer you."

He gave a slight smile that softened his expression. "Answered like one of my blood. By the gods, with the right instruction, you will fare well." Cunning, intelligent eyes watched her as he asked, "Would you say duty should outweigh matters of the heart?"

"I know not, since I have never been tested in the matter."

The king's gaze probed harder. "Let us hope you are not yearning for some man back in Egypt."

"There is no one," Thalia admitted, realizing how easily he could pull secrets from her.

"Understand this—as ruler of Bal Forea, the country's interests must always take precedence over that puny emotion the very young call 'love.' I tell you this because young women are apt to look for love and overlook a worthy husband."

Thalia thought of Queen Cleopatra, and how her love of Marc Antony had not conflicted with her ability to rule. "Although Cleopatra is a woman, she is one of the strongest rulers in the world. So let there be no doubt that a woman's love of her country is no different from a man's love of his duty."

"Bal Forea is at war and in need of a leader with strength to pull us through."

Thalia shifted uncomfortably on the stool. "I have observed some of what war has done to this island, and I am told there is yet worse to see. "

"So what would you do if you were queen?" He watched her closely, not giving her time to think. "What *would* you do?"

"Seek every path to end the war so the people could know peace."

"But you are a woman," he pressed. "What can a woman do?"

Thalia realized the crafty old fox was trying to trap her, and she took up the challenge. "I would look for a solution that you have failed to find. You are a man, and the war still rages."

Laughter crackled from the king, and he met

Ashtyn's gaze. "By the gods, is there another such woman in this world?"

"Do not speak about me as if I am not here," Thalia said, her jaw clamped in such a way it brought a smile to Lord Parinez's lips. Many's the time he'd seen that same expression on the king's face.

"You have not said how you would approach the responsibility of being a queen," the king told Thalia.

"I do not want the responsibility. I leave that to men like you, to write your peace treaties or continue with your war."

The king choked on a laugh and waved for Ashtyn to come forward. "My granddaughter is not a frivolous lass with naught on her mind but her own needs. I challenge anyone within my hearing to produce such a rarity in a woman. What say you, Count Ashtyn, will she suit?"

"The princess is everything you had hoped," Ashtyn replied, knowing he was about to be pulled into the old fox's trap along with Thalia, and wishing he could postpone it as long as possible. "But we have tired you, Majesty. Let us withdraw so you can rest."

King Melik gave Ashtyn a guarded look and then nodded, a smile playing on his thin lips. "Both of you come to me at the hour of sundown. I have much to discuss with you."

"Your Majesty, have I your permission to rejoin my troops?" Ashtyn queried, wanting to escape the inevitable.

The king stared at his most trusted general, knowing he needed him in the palace more than the battlefield for the foreseeable future. But he waved his hand in dismissal. "See that my granddaughter is settled. Then return with her at the appointed time."

Thalia had not wanted to be acknowledged by the king. She felt his trap closing around her, and there was no escape.

The lord high chamberlain closed the curtains. "His majesty will need his rest."

Ashtyn nodded at Thalia, and they both backed away, bowing. At the door, they turned into the corridor.

"I have no feeling for him other than pity," Thalia said, searching Ashtyn's eyes for answers. "Should I not feel something more?"

His brow lifted, and he seemed agitated. "How could you be expected to love a man—any man—who is but a stranger to you?"

"Now that I have seen him, and the people have seen me, can I not return to my home in Egypt? How many times must I tell you I do not belong here?"

Ashtyn's jaw clenched in sudden anger. "Don't be such a child." He nodded to Eleni, who had just appeared beside them. "Show your mistress to the suite that has been made ready for her." To Thalia he said, without looking at her, "Make yourself ready and return to his majesty at sunset." Without another word, he turned and left.

Eleni watched him leave and then turned to Thalia. "Princess, shall I show you to your quarters?"

Wordlessly, Thalia followed the woman across dull granite floors, her sandals making a whispering sound. A group of servants were standing in a circle, their tense voices murmuring through the room. When they saw Thalia, they dropped to their knees and lowered their heads.

Thalia walked down a wide corridor past a garden

room until Eleni paused at the door to bow. "I will be leaving you here, Highness," she said, thrusting wide the tall copper doors. "But . . . if you ever have need of me, the mistress of servants will know where to find me."

Eleni was the one person who was familiar to Thalia in this awful place. "Why must you leave?"

There were angry tears swimming in the woman's eyes. "Your personal handmaiden is a woman of high birth. I am common born and unworthy of the honor of serving you."

Thalia detected bitterness in Eleni's tone, and who could blame her? She wanted to object to Eleni being sent away, but was unaccustomed to the protocol of the palace. "I wish you could stay with me."

"Surely you have noticed I have no great skill at dressing hair or tending your wardrobe." Eleni dropped her gaze. "It is the custom, Highness."

Thalia had no time to say more before a reed-thin woman with piercing dark eyes smiled and bowed. "Gracious Highness, long have been the days we have looked for your coming."

Eleni had already scurried away, so Thalia turned her attention to the handmaiden. "Who are you?" she asked in a stilted voice, her mind still on the unhappy woman who had served her so well on the voyage.

The dark head bowed. "I am called Uzza, Highness. It is my pleasure to serve you."

Thalia swept past the woman, taking no notice of the rooms. Her steps took her through an ornately carved archway that led into a small garden. Angry tears she had held back until now blinded her. With quick steps she moved around the walled area, frantically searching for a gate—an escape.

There was none. Thalia was as much a prisoner now as she'd been on the *War Bird*. She had worn her mother's armor as she had been told, shown herself to the citizens on the way to the palace and silently endured the humiliation of their homage to her.

"Highness, is something the matter?" Uzza asked with concern in her tone. "How can I serve you?"

"You can serve me best by leaving me alone!"

The woman bowed, looking distressed. "As you wish."

Thalia heard footsteps retreating down the gravel path and turned to the poor woman who had done nothing to earn her wrath. "Wait. Forgive me if I was sharp with you. It's just that I am not who everyone believes me to be, and I want to go home."

"I do not believe such a thing is possible, Highness," the woman remarked. "Are you not soon to be anointed queen?"

Thalia glanced up at a yellow bird perched on a low branch that hung halfway over the garden wall. "So I have been told. And yet, I had hoped—" Thalia shook her head and re-entered the chamber. "Who do you serve, Uzza—me or the king?"

The poor woman looked taken aback for a moment, her complexion ashen. "One is the same as the other. Do I not serve you both?"

There was no more time for conversation. A rap on the door brought in seven young maidens, their eyes wide with wonder. "Highness, these are your handmaidens," Uzza said. "Each is well-versed in a different function. They are here to take your measurements."

Before Thalia knew what was happening, the servants had measured her from head to foot, even the size of her head.

After they had gone, Thalia let out her breath and sat back onto the softness of a bed that was carved in the shape of a hawk in flight. Staring up at the light green bed hangings, she noticed the coverlet was the same color green, only it was edged in gold.

Someone had taken a lot of trouble to make the chamber worthy of a princess, or a future queen. Thalia derived no pleasure from the richness of the room—it was still a prison. She thought of her bed-chamber at home, where she had been surrounded by all the items she treasured. Even with gilded chairs, shelves filled with scrolls, and the cushioned couches scattered about, this room was cold and impersonal, and she could not imagine ever feeling at home in it.

. "The seamstresses have been busy making your clothing," Uzza said softly. "Would you like to see the robes? They are quite magnificent."

"I would like a bath and a change of clothing."

Uzza nodded and clapped her hands. Almost immediately two young handmaidens scurried into the chamber. Uzza gave them instructions, and they hurriedly left to obey, bowing to Thalia and backing out the door.

"Highness," Uzza said, "may I ask a question?"

"Of course."

"Is it true that highborn Egyptian women bathe twice a day?"

"That is the custom. Is it not the same here?"

"Nay, Highness, once a day is the custom here, but I will be certain your bath is brought twice daily."

Thalia lay back on the bed, weary from the long journey.

For better or worse, she must accept her captivity.

* * *

Ashtyn was seated in the sparse quarters that were as-
signed to him whenever he stayed in the palace. The
furnishings consisted of nothing but a cot and a desk
cluttered with maps and scrolls. A low table had been
set before him with fruit and cheese, but he had no ap-
petite and shoved it away.

He had felt Thalia's confusion today, and her anger.
He reached for the wine goblet and raised it to his lips,
then set it back on the table without taking a drink.
At the moment, he wished Thalia were a commoner;
then if they wed it would be by her choice.

"Thalia, my heart," he whispered, leaning his head
back against the chair rest. "How my body hungers for
yours."

He brought his fist down on the arm of the chair.
"I shall overcome this weakness. I will think no more
of her soft, sweet body, or the smile that yanks at my
heart."

Captain Darius had just entered the room carrying
Ashtyn's armor. "Begging your pardon, Commander—
did you ask something of me?"

Ashtyn rose. "Nay. I was merely clearing my mind
of cobwebs."

The sun was low in the west as Ashtyn stood on the pa-
rade grounds, glancing at the double row of barracks
that lined the outer courtyard. With a grim expression,
he confronted the soldier at the end of the line who
stood nervously awaiting his inspection. Withdrawing
the man's sword from its scabbard, Ashtyn frowned and
nodded at Sergeant Komondor, who quickly ducked his
head.

"Look to this weapon—rust on the blade. You have done slovenly work in my absence." Ashtyn glared at the man whose ruddy complexion had paled. "Explain this to me!"

"Commander, I . . . the—"

Ashtyn held his hand up to silence the man. "Every apprentice recruit knows that his first duty is to his weapon, since it is all that stands between him and death."

"Aye, Commander," the sergeant answered.

Captain Darius stepped forward, his eyes locking with those of the luckless sergeant who had allowed the recruits to neglect their weapons. "They will all learn the folly of carelessness, Commander."

Ashtyn glared down the row of nervous soldiers, who were having a difficult time meeting his hard gaze. "Have you all lounged about the barracks too long with nothing to occupy your time? That will change." He turned to Darius. "Examine all the weapons, Captain, and if there is rust on any blade or spear, you know what to do. Take the rank away from this sergeant and send him to the front lines."

Ashtyn mounted his horse and glanced down at the men who still could not meet his gaze. He heard Captain Darius call out to them, "Clean the place, polish your swords! No man will sleep this night!"

Spinning his horse around, Ashtyn rode back toward the palace. Dismounting, he hurried inside. It was almost sundown, and he dared not be late for his audience with the king.

CHAPTER EIGHTEEN

Fool! Imbecile!" Lord Sevilin glared at Turk. "Once again you return without the princess. Explain to me how such a thing can happen."

Turk lowered his head. "Lord, I had her in my grasp, and even managed to sneak her out of Alexandria. How could I have known my every move was being watched by the Destroyer?"

Lady Vistah paced in front of the big man, clutching her robe, her hair disheveled because her son had awakened her from a deep sleep. "Explain!" she screeched.

Turk glanced at the floor. "He's a clever one. Slipped right into my camp and whisked the princess away in the middle of the night—stampeded our horses so we couldn't follow."

Lady Vistah's face contorted with anger as she ranted at Turk. "We cannot control the people if we do not have her!" She cast an appraising glance at her son. "With Princess Thalia we could have had everything we wanted." She whirled around and shook her fist in Turk's face. "When I married into the royal family, I expected to get a child by my husband. Who would have thought he'd die before giving me a son?

With his death, the king no longer had an interest in me or my own son. I was left to raise Sevilin on what meager handouts his majesty allowed us. I vowed revenge on his house then, but I now taste the bitterness of defeat!"

Turk saw something that had eluded him before: Lady Vistah cared nothing for the citizens of the island. She was eaten up with hatred and ambition. He turned his gaze to Lord Sevilin, wondering if he'd been duped by the son as well.

"I will have that girl," Lady Vistah continued. "If we have to attack the palace to get her, then so be it."

"Mother," Lord Sevilin said soothingly. "You know that's impossible. We must find another way."

"What we don't have is time," Lady Vistah stated. "King Melik will marry the girl off as soon as he can, but not before he sees her crowned queen." Her black dressing robe swirled about her as she continued to pace the room. "I curse the royal bloodline—if not for that, you, my son, would already have ascended the throne."

"Since I'm not of royal blood, and we don't have the girl, all is lost."

Lady Vistah whirled on her son. "You give up too easily. It is a weakness your own father possessed. If I had not been the driving force in your life, where would we be now?"

Lord Sevilin's face was red when he ducked his head and stared at his feet. "I know defeat when I see it," he remarked sullenly.

His mother shook her head in disgust. "All is not

lost. Not yet. I have spies in the palace. One I placed close to the princess. Let us wait and see what comes of that."

Turk looked from mother to son, seeing what had eluded him in the past. The son was driven by his mother, and it was not for any noble cause.

"We must strike fast and hard!" Lady Vistah said, smacking her fist against her open palm. "Because of this man's blundering, it just became more difficult. If the king has chosen Count Ashtyn for the husband of Princess Thalia, one—or both—must die." Her eyes narrowed on Turk. "Unless there is a chance she is not the princess."

Turk met her eyes. "There is no doubt she is King Melik's granddaughter."

"Then she will have to be dealt with."

Lord Sevilin glanced at Turk. "Tell me what she looks like."

"She is the image of her mother, only more intelligent and with more spirit. Over the years I have come to admire her."

Lady Vistah paced to Turk. "Think you we care about your opinions on this girl?"

Lord Sevilin held up his hand to silence his mother. "I asked for his opinion and he gave it." He smiled slightly and leaned back against his chair. "I will see this beauty for myself." His eyes hardened when he pointed to the big man. "Find a way to get her here, and this time you must not fail me."

Turk saw the spark of anger in his lord's eyes. There was fire in the son if the mother didn't smother it with her own vain ambitions. "Tell me of the spies you set in the palace so I can work with them to capture the princess."

"Foolish, foolish man. Why should we trust you when you have failed us so many times in the past?" Lady Vistah muttered.

"Leave him to his task, Mother. For now, he's our only hope."

Cleopatra paced from the edge of her bed and back to the steps that led into the pool garden. Marc Antony caught her hand and stilled her.

"Share with me what is troubling you."

"Thoughts of my little Thalia rob me of sleep. I had no knowledge of a country with a flag of a winged hawk perched on a crown. But my scholars have discovered an island called Bal Forea with such a flag. Why would they have taken Thalia?"

"Bal Forea," he said, his brow furrowed in thought. "I recall Caesar once mentioned such a place to me." His frown deepened. "I shall find out more about this mysterious island in the morning." He tugged on her hand. "Come to bed with me. We cannot solve the puzzle tonight."

Her shimmering black hair slid across her shoulders as she nestled against his broad chest. "Surely whoever took her cannot mean her harm." She raised troubled green eyes to Antony. "Surely they do not mean to sell her as a slave?"

He touched his mouth to her cheek. "Nay. There are other reasons they went to so much trouble to capture her. We will soon have the why of it, then gather our forces and strike!"

She slid her arms about his waist. "Whoever did this to her will feel the full might of my wrath. I will not rest until I see her safely back on Egyptian soil."

Antony nodded. "Pity the poor fool who dared take Lady Thalia. Lord Ramtat is amassing an army. Even I would hesitate to go against his fierce Badari."

"Lady Larania is doing poorly. This morning I shall send my own physicians to tend her. Lord Ramtat believes she is suffering more from melancholy than any real illness." Cleopatra glanced into Antony's eyes. "Have you sent word to Lady Adhaniá to return to Egypt?"

"Aye. General Marcellus and Lady Adhaniá had already taken a ship before my messenger reached them. They were on their way here for a family gathering. Unfortunately, it will not be the happy event they expected."

"Hold me," Cleopatra said, burying her face in his tunic. "I am afraid."

He clasped her to him. "You, love? What can concern you when I hold you thus?"

"I don't know. I have always thought my country was safe, and my children would grow up healthy and happy. But some shadow troubles my mind. The gods may be jealous because I have found such happiness."

"Then I shall hold you until the fear leaves you, and you see only happiness."

"Antony, tell me we will find Thalia safe."

"Hush, now. All will be well."

But fear for Thalia still lingered at the edge of the queen's mind, and she could not be rid of it. Her husband's lips touched hers, and her unease began to fade. When he lifted her in his strong arms and carried her to bed, she thought only of him.

Thalia was surprised when she entered her grandfather's chamber and found him sitting in a chair with Ashtyn standing behind him. The scribe was seated silently on his reed mat and two physicians stood across the room, huddled in quiet conversation, no doubt discussing the king's health.

Thalia could feel the men's gazes follow her as she advanced toward the king. He reached for her hand when she swept into a bow.

"Sit beside me, Thalia," he indicated the empty chair. "We have much to discuss."

Thalia saw the king was pale, and his hand trembled. "How are you feeling, Your Majesty?"

He looked into her eyes with an expression akin to sorrow. "Can you not call me 'grandfather'? For so long I thought myself without family, and now I have you."

Thalia twisted on the cushioned chair, glancing down at her hands folded in her lap, determined not to be affected by his words. "Like you, there was a time when I was alone. Now I have a brother and sister, and nieces and nephews. My mother is very dear to me, and I want to return to her as soon as it can be arranged."

His head snapped toward Ashtyn. "Surely you explained to her that this is her home, and she has no other?"

Ashtyn reluctantly looked at Thalia. "I did not put it quite as bluntly, but aye, Majesty, she has been informed that Bal Forea is her home."

The king put a trembling hand to his brow, causing one of the physicians to rush forward, handing him a goblet of wine. King Melik observed Thalia over the rim. Pushing the physician's hand away, he asked Ashtyn, "What else did you not tell her?"

Thalia noticed that Ashtyn looked somewhat uncomfortable, and she wondered at the reason for it.

"I spoke to her only of what I was instructed to say," Ashtyn replied, as if the words had been forced through his lips.

King Melik was grim as he turned his attention back to his granddaughter. "I would have you see for yourself the sadness of a country with no hope. The real sorrow in all this is that we slay our own brethren. I am daily growing weaker and can no longer hold back the tide of war or stave back the curtain of death. You must take up my scepter and care for the people of Bal Forea."

Thalia frowned. "But I am neither warrior nor diplomat. I am but a woman."

"And as you pointed out to me only this morning, so, too, is the queen of Egypt. I have heard it said that men would gladly follow her to their deaths if she required it of them. It will be the same with you. Rally my people, let them see they have a future without war."

She quickly dipped her head, biting her lip. "I am afraid of what you expect of me."

"Granddaughter," he said in a gentle voice, "you must never show that fear." His hopeful gaze settled on hers. "You shall be crowned queen before the sun sets tomorrow, and at that time you must exhibit courage to inspire your people."

She dropped to her knees before him, grasping his hands. "You dare not place your power or your hope in untrained hands! It takes a king to rule during a war, not someone untried such as me."

King Melik met her gaze. "Stand up, Princess Thalia. From this day forward, you bend your knee to no man or woman."

"But I—"

King Melik held his hand up, catching his breath with difficulty. "By the gods, if I had the time I would instruct you in the ways of a queen. But I have no time." He pinned her with a sharp glance. "My dear girl, a crown does not make a queen, nor does wisdom. Nay, it does not. The blood-right to rule creates a monarch. It will be up to you to decide if you will rule with wisdom, or allow others less worthy to steal your crown."

"How can I be expected to do that?"

"You will not be alone—you will be a wife just after sunrise the day after you become queen, with trusted advisers to help you."

Thalia sprang to her feet and backed away from him. "I will do no such thing! I have already told Lord Ashtyn I would not marry a man unless he is of my own choosing. As far as being queen, you must find someone more qualified than I."

"Child, child, I know I cannot just thrust the title of queen on you and expect you to know how to rule. That is why I have chosen a suitable husband who has been trained in his duties toward you."

Thalia's gaze flew to Ashtyn, hoping he would help her, but he did not meet her eyes. "Grandfather, do not do this to me."

"Now you call me grandfather? Perhaps you think it will soften my heart—it will not. I cannot think of your needs while there are so many with greater needs."

Fury boiled inside her, and she almost choked on her words. "I will be neither a queen nor a wife!"

"Oh, aye, my dear girl, you shall be both."

"I shall never marry a stranger!"

"Nay, you shall not," the king agreed. "Lord Ashtyn is your chosen husband. You became acquainted with him on the voyage, so he is no stranger to you."

Thalia whipped around, her hardened gaze on Ashtyn, feeling betrayal in the very depths of her heart.

"So the truth comes out at last! You, who took me away from the life I love, think to become king through me." Words tumbled from her mouth. What a fool she had been not to see the plan all along! "You deceived me, and I will never trust you again."

"Blame him not, 'twas my doing," the king told her. "Count Ashtyn was formally betrothed to you when he was but a boy—the moment I learned you existed. Why else would a man such as he still be without a wife?"

Thalia backed away, feeling as if she had been ripped apart inside. "You cannot expect me to marry him," she whispered. "I had come to think of him as a friend, but I do not care for him."

"What does that matter?" her grandfather asked, his voice as hard as nails, his face as red as a ripe pomegranate. "Depend on it, you will take the crown, and you will take Count Ashtyn. And if he is the man I believe him to be, he will have you with child before he rejoins his troops."

Thalia was horrified, wishing she could flee the room. But she planted her feet and stood her ground, her hands fisted at her side.

"And you, Lord Ashtyn," she asked, glancing into stoic silver-blue eyes, "what are your views on such a marriage?" She wanted him to reject her. She prayed he would.

"I will always do what I must to save Bal Forea. If marriage with you is the only path to peace, I shall marry you."

"You knew about this betrothal all along. I recall you telling me I would have to marry, but you failed to tell me *you* were the intended bridegroom."

Ashtyn took a step toward her. "Thalia—"

His treachery hit her like a knife to the heart. "I will never forgive you."

"Thalia, you will conduct yourself as befitting a princess," her grandfather ordered in a hard voice. "You can save many lives if you will but reach out your hand and take what is offered to you."

Tears stung her eyes, but she would not cry in front of either of these men. Her body shook as she backed toward the door. "I will conduct myself as pleases *me*. You are a cruel old man who wants his own way and will sacrifice anyone to get it. No one, not even you, can make me marry that man."

Her grandfather leaned heavily against the back of his chair, his face as pale as Egyptian linen. "You have no choice."

She glared at the guard who blocked her way, and he moved out of her path.

"Thalia, wait. It is not what you think," Ashtyn said, taking a step in her direction.

She held up her hand. "I have nothing to say to you."

"Leave her be, Count," the king cautioned. "Allow her to think on what I have told her."

Thalia rushed out of the chamber, hurrying down half-lit corridors, not caring in what direction she ran. Soon she was lost in the maze of twisting hallways, and still she ran.

She had to find some way to escape!

❦Chapter Nineteen

Thalia had passed a restless night, feeling battered, overwhelmed by betrayal. She was out of bed and dressed before sunrise. She'd ignored the meal of sweetmeats and melons that had been set before her, seeking instead the solitude of the small walled garden off her bedchamber.

A stubborn calm settled over her as she began to plan her escape from the palace. Perhaps she could convince Lord Sevilin to help her get back to Egypt. Once he understood she had no intention of accepting the crown, he would be as anxious to have her gone from Bal Forea as she was to leave.

She had serious misgivings about her half-cousin, but surely he wasn't as bad as Ashtyn had painted him. Thalia's problem would be finding a way out of the castle and locating the rebel camp. She was surely being watched.

Thalia paced around the small courtyard and had just decided to return to her chamber when she heard a commotion at the door. As soon as she recognized Count Ashtyn's voice, she spun around savagely. Ashtyn wore bronze and black armor with the black hawk on the breastplate. His dark hair was tied back with a leather band, his winged helmet tucked under his arm. He moved toward her with a grace that drew her unbridled attention, and she hated him for it.

She glared at him when he bowed low to her. "Highness."

As always, Thalia was unable to discern what he was thinking. The man was a master at disguising his feelings.

She realized that she had been secretly hoping he'd come to her and explain why he had kept secrets from her.

Thalia ignored her heart fluttering inside her and thought instead of his deception.

"I have no wish to see you, now or ever," she told him petulantly.

He gazed at her with growing intensity. "I fear it cannot be avoided. I have come by order of the king."

"If I am to be anointed queen, is my word not law? If I order you from my sight, are you not compelled to leave?"

"When you wear the crown of Bal Forea, I will obey your every command."

Thalia stood her ground as he moved toward her.

"I have something to say to you, and then you can send me away if it is your wish."

Just seeing him again stirred heat within her body, and Thalia leaned heavily against a marble bench. "You have nothing to say I want to hear."

Ashtyn stared at her soberly. "I understand how you feel. You have had so much thrown at you, I can imagine you want nothing to do with any of us."

Thalia tried to ignore the calming effect his voice had on her. "Say what you will and leave."

Ashtyn took a step toward her. "Thalia, I would have told you about the betrothal on the voyage, but the time was never right. You must believe me."

There was no sign of penitence in those mesmerizing eyes. "Just because the king had you betrothed to me does not mean I feel bound to marry you."

He took another step in her direction and stood in front of her. "Thalia, here on Bal Forea your grandfather's word is law."

"Except in the rebel camps," she reminded him.

He nodded. "That much is true. I wanted to tell you word reached me this morning that the rebels are deserting Sevilin in high numbers."

Thalia did not know whether to be happy or more concerned. She turned away from Ashtyn and glanced about the courtyard, watching a gentle breeze sway the branches of a tamarisk tree. "What would happen should I go over to Sevilin's side?"

Ashtyn reached out and gripped her shoulders, spinning her to face him. "Do not dare consider such a thing! Have you not been warned about Sevilin? If he had you in his power, the island would fall into chaos. Do you not understand he sends out warriors to rape and murder innocent women and children if their men refuse to fight for him? Is he the kind of man you would have guiding your people? Is he the kind of man you want to stand at your side?"

His eyes were hard and cold, but she was not afraid. "I have only your word that he commits such atrocities. And your word means nothing to me."

He glanced down at her. "One of the reasons I'm here is to explain to you about our betrothal."

Her gaze fell to his mouth, and she melted inside. "I am listening." She wondered if he'd heard the tremor in her voice.

He glanced up at the sky as if trying to remember a moment out of his youth. "I was but a young boy when I was told by my father that my future wife had been chosen for me. At that time it meant nothing to me. I was more concerned about swinging the small sword my father had given me, and thoughts of females had not entered my mind, much less thoughts of a wife."

"How could they betroth us when they could not be sure I would ever be found?"

"No one doubted you would be found. Already you had been sighted in Rome. Turk was after you, but so was the king's man. Did you never see them?"

"I only knew about Turk."

"The king's man almost caught you one day when he saw you stealing from a vendor in the market. Later he learned that a noblewoman had taken you away with her."

Thalia's mouth flew open. "I recall that day. I thought those men were after me because I was a thief. It is the day Adhaniá found me."

She saw his chest rise and fall as he took a deep breath, and she realized for the first time that he was nervous.

"It was not until my seventeenth summer that I first asked my father about you. He explained the importance of uniting the island and told me that when you were brought home, I was to be your husband."

That caught her attention. "What made you ask about the betrothal then?"

He met her gaze. "I thought I had lost my heart to a young woman of good family, and her parents were not opposed to considering me as her husband."

The thought of him loving another made her ache inside. She wanted to ask if he still loved the woman. Instead she said, "You are now free to marry where you will. If you will help me escape, nothing will come between you and your lady."

"That I cannot do. My word was pledged to the king, who renewed the betrothal vows before I sailed for Egypt. It is a sacred oath, and I will not break it."

"But I gave no oath." She glared up at him. "You are the last man I would ever have for my husband."

Thalia watched as his silver eyes closed for the briefest moment, and his mouth compressed.

"You have the right not to marry me. If that is your wish, a different husband will be chosen for you. But marry you must."

"Are you saying I will be forced to marry against my will? That there is a list of suitors waiting to be chosen if you do not meet with my approval?"

"Nay, it is not like that. I beg you to understand this: if you are not wed and with child, Sevilin will still hold out hope of capturing you. And no matter what you think of me, you do not want to be under his power, or that of his mother."

Thalia stalked away from him. "Nor do I want to be under *your* power. I will not marry you, and I will never stop trying to escape."

His lips curved into a slow grin, taking her by surprise. "Let us put that aside for now. How would you like to go for a ride and see more of the island?"

Thalia's first instinct was to refuse, but she reconsidered. To get out of the palace she would endure even this man's companionship. "Is it safe?"

Ashtyn looked deeply into her eyes. "At the risk of my own life, I shall keep you safe."

"Then I shall go with you. When?"

"As soon as you are properly dressed."

Ashtyn bowed and departed, leaving Thalia to puzzle through their conversation. She walked inside and sank onto a chair, leaning back against the headrest. Perhaps she had been wrong about him wanting to marry her. Clearly he had been expecting her to refuse him—he must still love the woman of whom he'd spoken.

Wearing her mother's breastplate, Thalia was delighted with the beautifully crafted helmet Ashtyn handed her when she was about to mount a horse. Like everything else that had been given to her to wear, it was a perfect fit. "My mother's?" she asked.

"It was made for you alone at your grandfather's insistence. The goldsmith stayed at his table all night so it would be ready for you this morning."

She slid it on her head and snapped the strap beneath her chin. She'd thought it would be heavy, but it was of little weight. "I would like to reward the goldsmith for his kindness. You must tell me where he can be found," she said, smiling.

Ashtyn's laughter danced on the wind. "His true reward is in everyone knowing he was chosen to craft the helm for his future queen. You can be certain he lost no time in bragging to any who would listen."

As they rode away from the palace, the morning sun was high. Galloping toward the distant mountains on a fine black stallion, Thalia felt her heart lighten.

A column of twenty armed warriors rode behind them with Captain Darius at their head. There had been an early shower, and the air smelled fresh and clean.

Thalia was smiling as she glanced over at Ashtyn, but the smile was soon replaced by a strong ache in her breast. He looked so noble, and it was easy to see he was revered by those who served under him. Citizens poured out of their huts as they heard the cavalcade approach—when they saw Thalia attired in her mother's breastplate and bedecked in gold and red, they dropped to their knees and bowed their heads.

"I will never grow accustomed to such deference," she said, feeling uncomfortable and embarrassed.

"There will come a time when you will accept it as your right," Ashtyn told her.

"I have done nothing to deserve such devotion."

"It matters not what you have done, it is who you are."

Thalia jabbed her horse in the flanks, pressing the others to follow.

At midday they stopped at the ruins of an old fort. Thalia walked around the crumbling edifice and glanced at stone stairs leading nowhere. The once high ramparts now sagged to the ground. She stepped over broken pottery and other remnants of shattered lives. Anger was beginning to grow in her, and it took her by surprise. "This was done by the rebels?"

Ashtyn nodded.

Thalia glanced toward a nearby field, overgrown and abandoned. Her gaze fastened on a flowering juniper that perfumed the air. "Yet, even among this devastation, flowers manage to grow thick and fragrant like a promise of life renewed."

He nodded down at her with a smile that tightened her insides. Just the sight of him still sent her heart pounding.

"I have to believe there will always be hope, Highness."

She stared into the distance and thought to herself, I have gone from street urchin to queen in the span of a few short years.

After they had dined on cheese and fruit, they continued their ride. By late afternoon, Thalia noticed they had been joined by at least fifty more mounted men who closed around them, forming a protective barrier.

They had not ridden much farther when Ashtyn called a halt and glanced at Thalia. "Just ahead is what your grandfather wanted you to see."

At first, her gaze was drawn to the lush valley with its jagged cliffs and rugged beauty. Off to the left, rounded hills eventually rolled into snow-capped mountains that dominated the sky. There were woods and thick foliage that abutted a clear mountain stream. Her gaze ran along wide gullies that changed into low craggy hills. Something caught in her throat, and she wondered how her mother could have left such a place.

But Thalia did not know her mother's side of the story. Now that she'd met Ashtyn, she understood that a woman might do desperate things for the man she loved. She frowned. But no matter how much a woman loved a man, if she was a princess, she should never turn her back on her duty. Thalia certainly wouldn't.

"If there is a more beautiful place in this world," she said, turning to Ashtyn, "I have yet to see it."

He pointed to his left. "Aye, but *there* is what your grandfather wanted you to see. Rapolt."

"The ruins of a village," she said, frowning.

"Nay, not a village, a once thriving city with over two thousand citizens. Look at the ruins and imagine it as it was before most of its inhabitants were either slain or fled for their lives. Imagine the great battle that took place here, and the blood that soaked into the earth."

Thalia gasped.

Ashtyn nodded to what had once been the outer wall but was now only crumbling stones. "At first we fought until our swords were broken, then we used our daggers—after they were broken, we fought hand-to-hand." He closed his eyes, momentarily reliving those awful days. "Even now I can hear the cries of the innocents who died here."

Thalia's lips quivered, and she could almost imagine the battle, for the stench of blood and death still clung to the air. "How many perished in this tragic place?"

"We counted over nine hundred dead. Over half were women and children. There are very few people on the island who could not claim kin to someone who died here."

Anger seethed inside Thalia, along with heavy sadness that twisted in her heart. "I understand the destruction of a fort, for it would be manned by soldiers. But why destroy a city filled with women and children?" Thalia looked into his eyes. "Why?"

"You would have to ask Sevilin that question—it was his orders that brought down Rapolt. I still dream of this battle. Sometimes at night I can hear the cries of the children." Ashtyn stared into the distance, and Thalia could feel the anger in him, and she understood it.

"You blame yourself. Why?"

"Sevilin had planned it well. Most of my men were defending the fort I showed you earlier. I had not considered Sevilin would strike hardest here. When I discovered his intentions, we rode with all haste to the city's defense, but it was too late to turn the tide of battle. After a while, those of us who survived knew we were fighting simply to hold the ground, for most of the people were dead by then."

"You lost someone in the city."

"My mother and two young sisters."

She cried out and placed her hand on his arm. "'Twas not your doing. How could you have known?"

"I was in command, thus I must bear the guilt until I draw my last breath."

"What must we do to stop this?" she asked.

"Win this war and drive Sevilin and his evil mother into the sea."

"How can this be done?" She met his gaze. "Tell me, and I shall do it."

"Be anointed queen. Take up the war, and the people will follow you."

She lowered her head in contemplation.

"We are a wounded country, bleeding unto death. We have mothers with no children, and children with no mothers—a country of orphans and widows. Give the people someone to rally around. Be their queen."

Ashtyn's eyes were glowing, and Thalia was almost certain she caught a glint of tears.

" 'Tis a tragedy that so many died here."

"Aye," he said without looking at her.

"Sadness may leave scars on the land, but they will heal."

He looked down at her. "Not as long as war continues to leave fresh scars."

As Thalia watched the setting sun, a strong sensation of strength poured through her. She did not know from whence the strength came, but she felt it in her heart, and then throughout her whole body.

Perhaps it was from the blood of long-dead Bal Forean kings who cried out for justice. Perhaps it was only her anger. But no matter the cause, these were her people, and they needed something to believe in.

"Take me to my grandfather."

❦CHAPTER TWENTY

Count Ashtyn left Thalia at the door to her grandfather's quarters and disappeared down the corridor. The door swung open, and Lord Parinez bowed to her. "Highness, your grandfather will be happy to see you. He has been awaiting your return."

"Lord Chamberlain," she said in greeting, taking measured steps until her eyes became accustomed to the dimness of the room.

The scribe was still sitting near the bed, and he scrambled to his feet, bowing to her, as did the physician who had been tending the king. Something had changed—she could feel it in the atmosphere of the chamber.

King Melik watched Thalia approach his bed, and she stared into blue eyes that held knowledge of the ages.

"So you have returned," he croaked in a weakened voice. "What did you think of the ruins of my once great city?"

She dropped down onto the stool next to his bed. "I was saddened by what I saw. You knew I would be."

"I hoped you would be. What you saw today was the

least of it. I could have had Count Ashtyn show you sights far worse."

"I no longer have doubts as to my true identity. Today I admit that I am truly of your blood."

His eyes flickered. "Then you will take up your rightful place?"

"I will do whatever is necessary to stop Lord Sevilin from destroying Bal Forea and its people." Her gaze dropped to the toe of her sandal. "Although I do not know how to help people in such dire need. But in doing this, I also ask something from you."

"I expected you would, and I know what it is. You want my promise that you can be free to return to Egypt when Sevilin and his mother are defeated."

Thalia nodded.

His voice was unnaturally weak, and she had to bend closer to catch his words. "I cannot give you that promise because by then I shall be dead and gone, and you will have the power in your own hands."

She lowered her head. "I am sorry for that."

"To save the people you must wed Ashtyn. Can you not do this for those who will look to you for guidance?"

She thought about it a moment, and knew he was right. "I can, if I must."

King Melik reached out his shaky hand, and Thalia placed hers in his chilling clasp. "I regret we have so little time to know one another. I find I like you very well." His mouth settled into a humorous smile. "I had little liking for my son and daughter. Neither of them had an original thought in their heads." He looked into her eyes. "You are like me. I wish I could live to see the changes you will make on Bal Forea. You shall be a glorious queen."

Thalia swallowed quickly, knowing she would speak only the truth to this man—there would no lies between them. "I had always thought a monarch could not be crowned while the true ruler lived."

"In most instances that would be true." He gave her a weak smile. "But I am king, and I give the rule over to you." He met her gaze almost desperately.

"I would like the time to know you better. There is so much you could teach me."

"Thalia," his hand tightened on hers. "I am growing weaker. There is no time."

She lowered her head. "Cannot the physician—"

"Nay. Do not look for hope of that nature. We must face this reality, you and I."

She raised her head and met his gaze. "What is the reality?"

"You shall become queen tomorrow. I would have seen you crowned this day, but it was important that you see the results of the war that ravages this land. I would like to give you more time to grow accustomed to the responsibilities you must shoulder, but I dare not."

"After visiting the ruins of the city today, I began to see the truth. I will do as you think best."

"And you will take Count Ashtyn as your husband as soon as the crown is set upon your head?"

She thought of being Ashtyn's wife, of being in his arms, having him hold her, and it made her ache inside. "I will agree to all you say, but only after I speak to him and know his true feelings on the matter. I believe you do him a great wrong in betrothing him to me, grandfather. He loves another and would wed her if he were free to do so."

The king frowned, trying to recall if he'd ever seen Ashtyn pay particular attention to any maiden. "None of that is important. Count Ashtyn will do his duty. He always has."

Thalia's gaze bore into his, and she remembered the woman Ashtyn had spoken of. "I will give him the choice that you never gave him."

"Like you, he will choose what is best for Bal Forea."

"If there is a woman he loves, I need not marry him to reap the benefits of his knowledge. I want him to marry where his heart takes him."

The king opened his mouth to speak, but Thalia held up her hand to silence him. "I will say no more about Count Ashtyn. Have Lord Parinez make whatever arrangements you deem necessary, and I will obey."

"It must be soon."

"You can rest now, grandfather."

"Aye. Because you are here, I can now loosen my grip on the crown, granddaughter."

Thalia stood and swung around with the intention of leaving, but then she turned to the physician. "How serious is my grandfather's illness?"

The man's soft brown eyes settled on her, and he bowed. "If you are asking me if he has many days left, I would have to say no. His majesty endures only so he can see the crown of Bal Forea placed on your head."

Thalia nodded to the high chamberlain. "Lord Parinez, I will need your help in the days ahead. I ask you to serve me as you served my grandfather. Instruct me on what I must do as queen."

The lord chamberlain swept her a low bow, but not before she saw his eyes glitter with tears. "I am yours to command, Most Gracious Highness."

She leaned closer to him and whispered, "I would like you to accompany me now. I do not know the way to my chambers, and there are questions I would ask of you about the ceremony."

With a twinkle in his eyes, he swept his hand toward the door. "I would be honored if you will allow me to guide you, Highness."

King Melik gazed long and hard at his young general. He had watched Ashtyn grow to manhood, and he was certain of his bravery and honor. The young man had led many hard-fought battles, and his name was legendary among his own people as well as the rebels. He had no doubt the capital city of Harjah would have fallen long ago but for Ashtyn's ingenious strategy.

"Before sundown tomorrow my granddaughter will be crowned queen."

Ashtyn drew in a relieved breath. "I hoped she would see the wisdom in ascending to the throne."

"I ask that you serve her as loyally as you served me. At the moment, she is frightened and overwhelmed, and has no real notion that her mere presence on Bal Forea will turn the tide of war." The old man looked into Ashtyn's eyes. "What do you think of my granddaughter?"

"I came to know the princess on our voyage to Bal Forea—her mind is quick, and she learns swiftly. In time, she will make a good ruler. I admire her greatly."

The king's crafty eyes fastened on Ashtyn as he asked, "Is mere admiration enough for you to be husband to her?"

"Majesty, I feel more for her than—" He looked puzzled for a moment. "The princess has already said she will not marry me, so we need not go into my feelings for her."

The king stared at the mural of constellations above his bed. "My granddaughter will need you in the days to come. Stand by her—be friend and adviser to her. Become her husband so Sevilin will no longer be a danger to her."

Ashtyn bowed. "I will always give my advice when asked. But I cannot allow you to force her to take me as a husband. There are other ways to keep Sevilin from trying to use her as a pawn."

"Such as?"

"Keeping guards about her at all times."

"Nay. Even among your guards you cannot be sure who is trustworthy. Marry Thalia and bed her. Plant your seed in her and secure the throne of Bal Forea for my bloodline."

Ashtyn shook his head. "I do not think there will be a marriage between the princess and myself."

The old man turned his head away. He was certain Thalia had feelings for his general. But she was stubborn and would have her way. "The need for sleep fogs my brain. I want to be strong enough to attend my granddaughter's coronation."

"If you will forgive me, Majesty," Ashtyn said, "I have matters that demand my attention."

"Report back to me when you have news of the last battle. I heard it did not go well."

"Aye, Majesty."

Lord Parinez accompanied Thalia back to her quarters and remained with her for a time, explaining her role in the coronation ceremony. After he left,

Thalia wearily sought her bed. Tomorrow would be a difficult day.

As she sank into the softness of the bed, her thoughts went to her family back in Egypt. What would her mother advise her to do? And Ramtat, would he approve of her actions?

With heaviness in her heart, she found no answers, and finally fell into a weary sleep.

Before the sun rose, five handmaidens swarmed around Thalia with Uzza directing them in their duties. Thalia's skin was rubbed with oil of myrrh, and her hair washed in lamb's milk. She was accustomed to dressing in fine robes to visit Cleopatra's court, but she had never worn such an ornate garment. Her gown was made of white royal linen and interwoven with threaded gold. Her hair hung down her back in golden ringlets, and her only adornment was a gold circlet crown. When Thalia stood before the beaten silver mirror, she hardly recognized herself.

Her mouth trembled, and she closed her eyes, wishing for her mother. At last, she raised her head and nodded to Uzza.

"I am ready."

When Thalia stepped out of her chamber, Ashtyn and seven other guards bowed to her. "We are your guards of honor, Highness," he said, nodding to the other soldiers behind him.

Thalia could not meet Ashtyn's eyes, lest he see her fear. As she stepped forward, the sounds of leather sandal-boots on the marble floor matched the beating of her heart.

When Thalia came to the throne chamber, she

raised her head as the lord chamberlain announced her approach to the high lords and ladies who had been called to witness the coronation. "Make way for Princess Thalia. Make way for her glory. Stand and witness the crowning of your new queen!"

She could feel many pairs of eyes on her, and all she could think about was the burden she would assume when the crown was placed on her head. With it came many responsibilities and sorrows. Her life would no longer be her own, but would belong to Bal Forea.

Thalia walked with her head held regally erect, remembering how Queen Cleopatra always looked so confident with the heavy double crown of Egypt on her head.

Lord Parinez had sent her word that the king had taken a turn for the worse during the night. Thalia was disappointed that her grandfather was unable to witness the ceremony that meant so much to him.

The guard of honor halted, and only the lord chamberlain accompanied Thalia to the steps that led to the rustic throne, which had been carved from a tamarisk tree. The only adornment was a magnificent golden hawk perched atop a crown that had been inlaid into the wood. A young boy held a red silk pillow and atop it lay a crown, glittering with precious stones.

Lord Parinez spoke decisively, but the meaning of his words did not penetrate Thalia's mind. Her heart was drumming so hard, she wondered if anyone other than herself could hear it. She was startled when Lord Parinez removed the small gold circle from her head and replaced it with the heavy crown of jewels.

Thalia raised her head to look at the people who were strangers to her. Lord Parinez's voice trembled as he announced: "Your Most High Majesty, Queen Thalia, I give you your subjects. People of Bal Forea, I give you Queen Thalia the Third!"

That came as a surprise to Thalia—she had not known she was the third queen with the same name.

The room had been silent while the ceremony was taking place, but the cheers from the crowd now echoed against the high vaulted ceilings in a deafening roar.

The lord chamberlain spoke on other matters, but Thalia did not hear anything he said. Her gaze frantically swept over the soldiers in uniform until she found Ashtyn. But that was little comfort to her when she saw his grave expression. He looked at her as one would when worshiping a goddess. Sadness struck her heart—she did not want Ashtyn to see her in such a way. She wanted him to think of her not as a queen, but as a woman.

She tilted her chin upward and stared just above everyone's head. How she wished she could call back time and walk through her mother's house, feel the desert wind on her face and live the simple life she loved—a life without war and strife.

But she could not wish she had never met the man who was standing so near, worshiping her with his eyes.

❧ CHAPTER TWENTY-ONE

Thalia felt like an imposter as she waited for the high lords and ladies of the court to swear fealty to her. Ashtyn was the first to approach. He went down on his knees and glanced up at her.

"As general of your armies, my sword and my life are in your service, Most Glorious Majesty."

Although Lord Parinez had explained it to her the day before, Thalia forgot how she was supposed to respond. It seemed every rational thought had gone out of her head. So Thalia nodded at him. "Please stand beside me," she whispered so only he could hear.

Ashtyn immediately moved to her left, for the lord chamberlain stood to her right. A long line of joyous nobles came forward one at a time, vowing loyalty. After a while, Thalia imagined herself in her chariot, racing through the streets of Alexandria. The ceremony droned on and on, and she knew she should feel something, but she was numb.

Thalia felt Ashtyn beside her, and it brought her comfort.

After a while Lord Parinez solemnly proclaimed there would be no celebration in deference to the king's illness. He bent to whisper to Thalia: "Majesty,

I ask you to come with me to see your grandfather. He will want to hear about the ceremony."

"I want Count Ashtyn to accompany us."

"Of course, Majesty, but we must go in haste. I was just informed that your grandfather's health is worse."

Fear gripped Thalia, and she found herself running toward the wide double door that led to the corridor. Her guard of honor ran behind her, with Ashtyn at her side. Murmurs filtered through the throne chamber that the queen was hurrying to her grandfather's deathbed.

Death was in the air as Thalia knelt at her grandfather's bedside. Lord Parinez had been right: even as ill as her grandfather was, he insisted on knowing every detail of the ceremony. Thalia told him what she remembered, and Lord Parinez explained the rest.

The old man smiled and closed his eyes. "The weight of the crown has left my head. May the gods proclaim I was a good king."

"You were a great king," Lord Parinez said in a trembling voice.

King Melik motioned Ashtyn forward, and the young general dropped to his knees beside Thalia. "Remember what we spoke of before," he said in a weakened voice. "Stand by your queen and be her strength when she is in need of it."

"I shall," Ashtyn assured him.

The king fixed his gaze on Thalia. "Be a good and wise queen. I die rejoicing, for I have lived to see one of my blood occupy the throne."

Thalia was grief-stricken. Her grandfather looked so gaunt, his eyes sunken, his lips parched—the shadow of death lingered on his face. "I shall try to be a wise queen, Grandfather."

"It has been a good day," he said in a barely audible voice. And with those last words, Thalia's grandfather died with a peaceful expression on his face.

Tears of grief blinded Thalia—not so much for the king, but for the grandfather she had never known. She felt a hand on her shoulder, and Ashtyn turned her into his arms. Seeing the stricken expression on his face, she realized he felt the death of his king far deeper than she.

"I am frightened," she whispered.

"Put your trust in Lord Parinez. His wisdom will see you through any trials that come your way." Ashtyn assured her.

With a last look at her grandfather, Thalia stood. "Let us leave this room of death. If I am going to do as my grandfather asks, I need time to think and prepare."

Ashtyn nodded and led her out of the bedchamber and across the corridor, pushing open the wide double doors. Thalia did not notice the grandness of the room as Ashtyn led her onto a balcony.

For a long moment she stood gazing at the night sky. "I am lost."

"Nay," he said, placing his hand on her shoulder. "You are queen."

"What am I to do?"

"First you have a king to bury. If I know Lord Parinez, he's already arranged the rites. But there will be few days for mourning—the war will not wait to bury a king."

"Should he not have a glorious funeral?" she asked, thinking of the year-long ceremonies for dead Egyptian royalty and the magnificent pyre where Caesar had been honored.

"Ordinarily there would be great mourning after the death of a king, but our sadness must be in our hearts."

Somehow his words were reassuring. "And will you be at my side?"

Ashtyn was silent for a moment, his gaze sweeping across her face. "I must soon rejoin my troops."

Thalia felt her heart lurch. "When?"

"Just before dawn." He watched her face carefully as if he was looking for something in her eyes. "If you have no more use of me."

She turned to him, grasping his hand. "But surely you do not need to leave so soon."

"If I am going to keep you safely seated on the throne of Bal Forea, I must see an end to this war."

There were so many emotions swirling through her mind: grief for the dead king, a country torn apart by war, and Ashtyn leaving her.

For the first time, she realized he could be killed.

She might never see him again.

Without thinking, she reached out and touched his face. "I have come to depend on you."

He grasped her hand and raised it to his lips while fire burned in his eyes. "I am yours in all things, Majesty. If you have need of me, you have only to send word, and I shall come to you."

"There is something I must say to you." She reached up and removed the heavy crown from her head and held it reverently in her arms. "Before you leave for battle, would you not like to wed the woman you love?"

His gaze centered on her lips. "Only if the woman who has my heart wants me for her husband."

"You must ask her." She frowned. "Unless, of course, she has wed someone else. I am sorry my grandfather made it impossible for you to wed her. Know that I release you from the betrothal he forced upon you."

Ashtyn then remembered telling Thalia about the young woman he'd been enamored with in his youth. He could hardly remember her face, and he certainly had no feelings for her. He recalled that she had married. "The woman of whom you speak is already a wife."

Thalia turned away, glancing down into the overgrown garden. "I am sorry. We are both caught in a trap we did not contrive and cannot escape."

"Have you thought that I might not want to be released from my betrothal to you?"

"I have considered that. I have weighed the possibility that you might crave the power that comes with being husband to a queen."

Ashtyn pulled back as if she had slapped him, but he took her insult without retaliating. He felt a muscle tighten in his jaw. "How does a mere general ask a queen to be his wife?"

Her heart drummed and fluttered inside her. "I have no experience in that direction."

Ashtyn was silent for a long moment.

"Lord Parinez told me it would be easier to solidify the island if we wed," Thalia said nervously.

"I have been told that as well." Ashtyn slowly turned her back to face him. "Then I humbly ask, Queen Thalia, will you consider taking me for your husband?"

Her throat closed, and her eyes burned with unshed tears. "I have come to realize that a queen must make many sacrifices for her people. Since it is in their best interest that we wed, I agree to become your wife."

Ashtyn released her hand abruptly and stepped away. "I am overwhelmed by the honor," he said, in a voice that belied his words.

She wanted him to pull her into his arms and declare an undying passion for her. But Lord Ashtyn was a man of honor and truth and would not act against his conscience. "It somehow feels wrong to celebrate a marriage with my grandfather hardly cold, but Lord Parinez advised me to marry as soon as possible. I thought tomorrow."

"I obey you in this, as in all things, Majesty," Ashtyn said stiffly.

Thalia slowly nodded. "Then make it so." She glanced out at the glorious sunset, thinking that her grandfather did not live to see the end of the day he had so long awaited. "I wish my family could be here at this time."

"You are queen now. You can send a messenger to inform your family of what has occurred and invite them to come to you."

Her heart suddenly lightened, for she had still thought of herself as a captive. "Is that possible?"

"You are queen. All Bal Forea awaits your slightest command."

She lowered her head, and her body trembled as she sobbed. Ashtyn gathered her in his arms, and she cried on his shoulder. She felt his lips touch her forehead and was comforted.

Trying to lighten the mood, for he could not bear her tears, Ashtyn said, "It never occurred to me that when I asked a woman to marry me, it would send her into tears. Is it so difficult for you to think of me as your husband?"

Her lips trembled, and she wiped her tears. "I would not want you to think of me as a real . . . wife."

Anger flared within Ashtyn. "Are you saying I should not expect to share your bed?"

"Grandfather was insistent that there be a child from our union. I know we will have to. . . ." As hard as she tried to hold back her tears, they now ran down her face. "Forgive me. This is the hardest day of my life."

"I know it is," he said gently, his anger melting. "I should leave you so you can rest."

"How can I rest knowing I must become a bride with such haste?"

Ashtyn's laughter startled her, and she looked at him questioningly.

"Your first edict as queen is to marry. If only your haste was brought on by the desire to be in my arms."

She glanced quickly at his face, but he was smiling, and she decided he was merely jesting. Still, warmth spread through her. Oh, how she wanted to lie in his arms—but would Ashtyn be thinking of another woman on their wedding night?

"I would ask you to leave me now, so I can spend time with my grandfather before they prepare him for burial."

Ashtyn bowed to her. "As you will."

After he left, Thalia walked back across the corridor to her grandfather's bedchamber. Several people had gathered about his bed, their heads bent, their faces streaked with tears. When they saw Thalia, they bowed and moved away so she could go to her grandfather.

Going down on her knees, Thalia took a hand that was still warm and lowered her head. "Grandfather," she whispered, "I am trying to follow your instructions. I pray the gods take you safely in their arms, and may those same gods stand beside me to guide my footsteps in a way that would make you proud."

She remained there for a long time, trying to untangle her feelings. At last she became aware that the others were waiting at a respectable distance, so she stood. Her gaze met the lord chamberlain's. "Lord Parinez, will you accompany me? I have questions. I want you to send your most trusted courier to Egypt with messages for my family and Queen Cleopatra." Thalia watched his face, fearing he would refuse, but he nodded, following her to the door.

"If you will prepare the documents, Majesty, I will see this done at once. We have a small swift ship, the *War Hawk*, that can be outfitted within hours and ready to sail with the morning tide."

Relief poured though her. Her family would soon know where she was and that she was unharmed. "Then let it be done."

❦Chapter Twenty-Two

In deference to her grandfather's death, Thalia decided on a private marriage ceremony. But it seemed a queen had little privacy when it came to matters that concerned Bal Forea. Lord Parinez had explained to her that the marriage must be witnessed by high-ranking lords and ladies.

Thalia had lain awake most of the night, feeling as if her life had spun out of control. She longed for her mother to direct and guide her though these turbulent times when so much was expected of her.

But in the end, she must stand alone.

Thalia felt her body tremble when she swept across the chamber to stand at the dais where Ashtyn waited for her. He looked magnificent in gold and black armor, his long dark hair falling across his shoulders, his silver-blue eyes fastened on her. He stepped to her side, his features immobile, his eyes hooded.

Words were exchanged, and Thalia mourned on the inside, wishing her marriage was uniting two hearts seeking love, rather than serving political necessity. Her hand trembled in Ashtyn's firm grip. He seemed to be avoiding her eyes.

He was doing his duty, as was she.

* * *

They came to the part of the ceremony where Ashtyn went down on his knees. When he turned his face up to Thalia, he was swamped with so many emotions, he could not sort through them. As he took her hand, he was aware, as the others were not, what she was sacrificing for them. He felt pride in how regally she held her head, never letting those present know she was frightened. Sunlight streamed through the high window, falling on her loosened hair, whose color rivaled the golden crown that was set atop her head. Her shimmering purple gown was adorned with the black hawk of Bal Forea.

"Queen Thalia," Ashtyn recited the age-old words that had united royal Bal Foreans in marriage for hundreds of years. "I, Count Ashtyn of the house of Tyran, do take into my keeping Your Majesty's safety, and pledge to protect the realm of Bal Forea. If blood is to be shed, let it be mine." He touched his lips to the royal seal that now graced her finger. "I am yours until death takes me. This I swear."

He felt her fingers tighten on his, and she spoke unhesitatingly. "I, Queen Thalia the Third of the royal house of Forea, take you, Count Ashtyn, as my husband. In so doing, I appoint you second only to me in the house of Forea and all my realm."

Thalia reached for the crown that Lord Parinez held out to her. Meeting Ashtyn's gaze, she placed the golden circle on his head. "Only my crown places me above you, Ashtyn of the house of Forea, and Prince of Bal Forea."

Ashtyn stood and stepped up to the second step of the dais, while Thalia stood on the top step. With hands clasped, they faced the lords and ladies, who all swept into a low bow.

"Thus unites the House of Tyran to the House of Forea," Lord Parinez proclaimed.

Thalia stood stiffly, wondering why she felt nothing inside. She had just become Ashtyn's wife, and he her husband—surely that should have stirred some emotion inside her. Her gaze swept across the faces in the crowd as she wondered if one of those brightly dressed women could be the one Ashtyn loved. Perhaps her new husband had sacrificed more than she should have asked of him.

Lord Parinez concluded the ceremony. "There will be no festivity, and Her Majesty has asked that instead you give alms to those in need, and let it be done in the name of King Melik. Go now and celebrate this day in your hearts, for the house of Forea still stands, though it is mourning."

When the chamber was cleared of wedding guests, Thalia seated herself on the throne since her legs were too shaky to bear her weight. "It is done," she said, looking at her new husband, who stood so solemn and grave. He had not moved from the second step.

"Aye. It is done," he agreed.

Thalia glanced at the lord chamberlain questioningly. "Have I fulfilled all my grandfather required of me, Lord Parinez?"

The kindly old man dipped his head to her. "You have done much, but not all. There must be a child so the throne will be secure."

Thalia's face reddened, and Ashtyn held his hand out to her. "I believe the queen is weary and in need of rest."

"Aye," Lord Parinez agreed, suddenly looking weary himself.

Thalia realized the honorable old lord had lost a king he loved, and his grief still showed in his eyes. "How goes the loading of the *War Hawk*, Lord Parinez? Will it be ready to sail on the tide?"

"Aye, Majesty. All is as you ordered."

Thalia allowed Ashtyn to help her down the steps, and he accompanied her from the chamber. As they moved down the corridor, five guards fell in behind them.

Thalia arched a brow at Ashtyn. "Will there be guards wherever we go?" she asked in frustration, taking quick steps to stay even with Ashtyn's long stride.

He hesitated only a moment before he answered, "There will be for you. You must know that you will be in danger until we crush the rebels. These are my most trusted men, specially trained by Captain Darius. They will see to your safety at all times."

She sighed. "Life as I once knew it is no more."

He nodded. "For either of us." He paused a moment before he said, "If you will forgive me, I need to send Captain Darius with a message to the front lines. I was expected there today."

"But instead, you were married," she said coolly.

"Thalia—"

She moved away, trying to keep her footsteps slow and even, when in truth she wanted to run and run, and never stop running.

When she finally reached her bedchamber, Thalia noticed that the guards positioned themselves outside the doors.

Uzza and the handmaidens were waiting for her

inside. "Majesty, would you and Prince Ashtyn wish a meal brought to the chamber?"

Thalia shook her head. "Nay, I want nothing. Later you can ask the prince if he is hungry."

Nothing seemed real to Thalia as the handmaidens undressed her and rubbed her skin with exotic oils, then helped her into a thin white robe. Thalia endured the fuss, hardly paying attention as they brushed her hair and added oil of frankincense to her long tresses.

Thalia's thoughts were fixed on what would happen later when her handmaidens left and her husband came to her. Her heart raced when she thought of lying beside Ashtyn.

Uzza finally shooed the others out of the room. "Majesty, forgive me for speaking plain, but you are just a girl. Has your mother prepared you for this night?"

Thalia's eyes widened as she shook her head. "Had I been betrothed to a man of Egypt, my mother would have told me what is expected of me."

Uzza picked up the brush one of the handmaidens had put down and began brushing Thalia's hair. "I have observed that Prince Ashtyn admires you. I have seen how his eyes follow you whenever you are in the same room with him. He is a man of great honor and will teach you what you need to know."

Thalia wanted only to get this night behind her. She was embarrassed, but had to know, so she asked, "Is it assured I shall be with child after this one night?"

"Nay, Majesty. But your husband is a virile man— he will soon plant his seed in you, and a child will come of it."

Thalia motioned Uzza away and stood. "I will not be needing you anymore tonight."

Uzza bowed and backed toward the door, closing it softly behind her.

"Mother," Thalia whispered, glancing upward. "I do so need your wisdom. What am I to do?"

Thalia froze when she heard the door open and the sound of bootsteps behind her. Turning slowly, she watched Ashtyn advance toward her. He'd removed his armor and wore only a short tunic. When he stood before her, he made no attempt to touch her, but his eyes swept her from head to toe, lingering on the golden hair that lay like silk against her creamy shoulders.

"You are an exceptional beauty, Thalia. I believe there has never been a woman born who could rival you."

He was flattering her—it was what she expected. "I would like you to get this thing done as soon as possible."

He smiled slowly. "This thing?"

"Whatever you do to plant your seed in me." She reluctantly met his eyes. "I am not completely unintelligent. I know something of what will happen."

He spoke gently, "You are frightened, and there is no need to be. I will do nothing you don't want me to do. If it is your wish, I will go to my own quarters until you are ready to receive me."

She closed her eyes and let out a long breath. "I would have you do it now."

"Thalia, there is no reason to fear me." He took her trembling hand and raised it to his lips. "Do you trust me?"

"You know I don't!"

He turned her into his arms. "There is no reason you should. I am grieved that you have been forced into so many situations that were not of your choosing. But I promise I will be gentle with you."

Ashtyn's understanding touched her heart, and her head dropped onto his shoulder. "I do not know what is expected of me."

"Yet you have no fear of standing before me in this thin robe." His lips touched her ear, and he felt her shiver. "It does not bother you that I can see all of your beautiful body."

She remembered how he could seduce with words, and she had felt the power of his seduction before. Oh, aye, he was good with words, but she would not be trapped by them—not tonight, not ever.

"My mother once told me that in Egypt we do not put as much emphasis on nakedness as they do in other countries. I suppose it is because our garments are made to keep us comfortable in Egyptian heat." She looked at him. "Are you offended by my apparel?"

Ashtyn's calloused hand drifted down her arm, and she could feel the raw power radiating from him.

"Thalia, I can scarcely think when I am near you. I dare not look too closely, or I will not be able to breathe."

She stepped away from him and gathered the filmy robe about her as if to cover herself. "I know this is as difficult for you as it is for me."

In truth, Ashtyn could hardly catch his breath as he looked at her long, shapely legs clearly defined through the gauzy material. His hungry gaze climbed up her body, and he saw that she wore nothing at all underneath. If she had a flaw, it was not visible. He quaked inwardly at the thought of taking her to bed and introducing her to the joys of the flesh.

"What if I told you I am exactly where I want to be?" he asked gently. "You must understand, my whole life has been moving me toward this moment. I have known since boyhood that you would one day be my wife. I don't think I ever doubted you would eventually be found." He stepped toward her. "I cannot tell you what I felt that night in your mother's garden when I saw you for the first time."

Thalia stared into his eyes, searching for the truth.

"I saw how much you were admired by those men, and I thought to myself: that cannot be—she belongs to me. There was one man in particular I wanted to run through with my sword. He kept touching you. But I soon saw you were annoyed with him, and I watched you leave the room." He touched his lips to her forehead. "And then you came to me in the garden, and I thought one of the goddesses had come to play a trick on me."

"You speak pretty words. Have you said these same words to other women?"

Ashtyn watched her eyes flame like fire, and when her gown fell open, his mouth went dry. "Nay. I have waited a long time for you—but none of the wait was as difficult as the voyage to Bal Forea."

Her eyes were wide with doubt. "Why was that?"

His arms slid around her, and he brought her closer to his body. "To see you every day and not be able to touch you was agony."

"You were untruthful with me," she said accusingly. "You never told me I would be forced to marry you, yet you knew it would come to pass."

"An untruth by omission. There are many things I did not tell you about me, but if there is anything you want to know now, you have but to ask."

"What can you say that I do not already know?" she asked, her voice still edged with anger, though she did not pull away from him.

Ashtyn's mouth rested on her forehead, and he could smell the fragrance of her hair. Closing his eyes, he called on all his strength not to ravish her. "As I grew older, Thalia, you became more real to me." His mouth moved to the tender spot just beneath her ear, and he felt her shiver as he continued his slow seduction. "Each night before I sought my bed, I would say your name aloud. It became a ritual with me, as if you were somewhere speaking my name." He gripped her shoulder and planted a kiss there. "Of course, you did not even know I existed at that time."

"I do not believe you," she whispered, her head falling back against his shoulder.

"Yet, it is true. I have known for a long time we belonged together, while you have had only a short time to learn that your fate was joined with mine." His long fingers tangled in her hair, and he brought her face close to his. "On the voyage to Egypt I felt the space between us narrow, and when I stepped onto Egyptian soil, it was as if I could feel you all around me. That night in the garden, I thought my heart would burst out of my chest." His mouth touched her brow. "In Egypt I could finally put a face to the one I was to marry."

"None of this seems real," she whispered, nestling tighter against him.

"We were destined to walk through life together."

Thalia's blue gaze was filled with uncertainty as she looked at him. "Help me understand."

"I am not sure I can even help myself," he murmured, just before his mouth touched hers. At first Ashtyn felt her body stiffen, but then it become pliable and shaped to his. Her arms twined around his neck, and he lifted her against his body. She was so small, so light to carry, he feared he might hurt her in the heat of his desire.

Ashtyn placed her on the bed and then removed his tunic so he wore only a loincloth. He watched Thalia's eyes widen and her lips tremble, and he knew he'd stirred her passion.

Sitting on the edge of the bed, he lifted her onto his lap, cuddling her against him. "I want more from you than this one night." He brushed her hair out of her face. "We are tied together, Thalia. Do you not feel that?"

Thalia swallowed, aching and throbbing with emotions that were so new to her, she didn't know how to react. What she felt was his hard muscled body against her naked skin. At last she found her voice. "We are tied together out of necessity."

He frowned and stared at her. "I await the moment you feel as I do. I wish for it."

"Then you may have to wait forever, Ashtyn."

Chapter Twenty-Three

Ashtyn pulled Thalia close and tilted her chin, whispering, "Sweeter than honey is this mouth I waited so long to claim."

Thalia's lips parted to receive his kiss. She felt herself floating back onto the bed as his warmth gravitated toward her. Her eyes drifted shut when she felt him lie down beside her and press his body against hers.

She whimpered deep in her throat as he eased her out of the thin gown and tossed it aside. This time when Ashtyn pulled her against him, he had slipped out of his loincloth. Thalia felt the swell of him against her thighs, and heat washed over her in waves.

Ashtyn tilted her head so he could look into her eyes, but Thalia closed them, fearing he would read too much of what she felt. She gasped, and her eyes flew open when she felt his mouth touch her breast.

"Do not fear," he said gently, his head dipping once more to take the nipple into the warmth of his mouth.

Thalia felt like she was melting inside as he suckled her breasts. She had never known a woman could feel this way.

Touching his mouth to hers, Ashtyn's hand moved down, circled her navel and moved across her stomach. Her mouth opened to his as his hand moved even lower.

Her heart was beating so fiercely she could scarcely breathe. When Ashtyn's hand touched her most intimate place, she moaned with need. A cry tore from her lips when he slid his finger inside her, stroking a spot that made her call out his name.

"Sweet wife," he said in a husky voice. "We will discover each other tonight." His mouth was so near hers, she turned to catch it with her lips. "You have only to say the words, and I will stop."

She shook her head, her lips pressing against his while he gently massaged her. "You touch me deeply, my heart," he said, tearing his mouth from hers.

Thinking he wanted her to touch him, she shyly wrapped her fingers around the swell of him, but was startled when he grabbed her hand.

"Nay." His voice was deep. "If you do that, it will be over before it begins."

Thinking she'd done something wrong, Thalia jerked her hand back. Ashtyn caught it and kissed each of her fingers. "My heart, it is just that everything you do brings me closer to pleasure."

She did not understand, but it did not matter because he continued to massage her, and Thalia threw her head back as his finger moved farther inside her. His touch made joy sing through her body and tears spring to her eyes. If she died now, she thought, she would have known what it was to live. Her body trembled, her breath caught, and Ashtyn kissed her tears away.

Wave after wave of pleasure moved through her body, and Thalia could do no more than tremble and quake. She stared into Ashtyn's eyes, feeling the wonder of what he'd done to her.

He moved over her and gripped her hips, lingering a moment as if he feared he might cause her pain. She waited, hardly breathing as their gazes locked.

He entered Thalia, then paused, pressing his lips to hers. She groaned as he slid farther inside her, and her arms wrapped around his waist as if she needed to be anchored. She felt him tremble and knew instantly that he was trying to control his desire.

Ashtyn set a slow rhythm, and her eyes closed in pure ecstasy. He was tender and gentle, moving farther inside her with each thrust. Thalia hardly felt the pain as he broke through her virgin barrier.

"Ashtyn," she said, pressing her lips against his shoulder.

"I know, sweet one—I know what you feel."

She felt him stiffen, and his seed poured into her body.

Thalia was disappointed that it was over. Yet had she not wanted to get the thing done? She looked questioningly into his silver-blue eyes.

He rolled over, holding her close to him, his hand stroking soothingly across her hip. "I know I left you longing for more," he murmured against her ear. "But I feared I would hurt you."

There was a tightening in her stomach as she lay her head against his shoulder. "I did not know how to give you what you needed."

His laughter was warm. "Sweet, sweet wife, if you

had pleased me any more, my heart would not have survived."

They both fell silent for a moment, but his hands continued to move, touching her hip, sliding across her breast, stirring passion anew. When he heard her gasp with pleasure, he gently rolled her over, his mouth taking possession as he entered her once more.

This time he was not so gentle. She could hear his heavy breathing as he pushed all the way inside her, his thrusts hard and deep. Wave after wave of joyous feelings shook her body as she raised her hips to meet his thrusts. They rode the storm of passion, and her body trembled again and again as he brought them both to blissful release.

His weight pressed down on her, and she held him in her arms. "So this is what it feels like to be a wife," she said, smiling.

"How I have yearned for this moment," he whispered, watching her turn her head, which caused her magnificent hair to slide across her face. "I so often imagined what it would feel like to hold you in my arms and make love to you." His lips brushed across hers. "None of my dreams came close to the feelings I experienced tonight."

Thalia tried not to think about the woman who held Ashtyn's heart. She chose not to imagine that he'd ever shared this same intimacy with her. "I am told a man has many partners over his lifetime. Is that not so?" She hated herself for asking such a question, but the answer was important to her. She warned herself to remember he was a master of words and would say what he thought she wanted to hear.

"No woman could stir my heart like the one I now hold in my arms. I hope I pleasured my queen." His smile went straight to her heart, and then nothing mattered but the touch of his hands.

Thalia surrendered to Ashtyn's lips, and his renewed conquest of her body.

CHAPTER TWENTY-FOUR

Thalia stretched as she awoke. For a moment she thought she was back in her bedroom in Egypt, but when her eyes swept across the elegance of her chambers, she knew she was not.

Remembering the night before, she rolled over eagerly, but the smile froze on her lips when she saw that Ashtyn was not beside her.

As if by some second sense, Uzza appeared in the doorway, bowed and smiled. "Shall I prepare your bath, Majesty?"

Thalia slid to the edge of the bed and swung her feet to the floor, wincing at the ache in her lower extremities. "Aye. Where is Prince Ashtyn?"

"Majesty, the prince asked that I inform you he is inspecting the troops. I am also to tell you he will return in time to eat with you before he leaves."

Thalia had known Ashtyn would be leaving, but she had not thought it would be so soon. Pulling on her thin wrapper, she went into the bathing chamber and descended the steps into the bath. Her handmaidens swarmed around the room, some laying out what she was to wear while others poured sweet oils into the bath and still others changed the bedding in the other room. A dour-faced Uzza watched to make sure everything was done to her satisfaction.

The bath was not as large as the one in her mother's villa in Egypt, but Thalia could still swim in it. She dove underwater, remembering all the wondrous ways Ashtyn had thrilled her the night before. And now he was going away. How could she bear to be separated from him? She belonged to him, and he to her.

Was that not what marriage meant?

When she rose to the surface, she was delighted to see Ashtyn sitting on the side of the bath with only a strip of linen about his waist.

"I sent your women away," he said, slipping into the bath and reaching for her. With a blush on her face, she lay her head on his shoulder.

"You are to leave today?" She could not keep the disappointment from creeping into her voice.

"I must. I have been gone too long as it is." He touched her cheek, slid his thumb under her chin and tilted her face up. "But . . . I have time."

Another blush stole up her face as he pulled her against his naked body. She could not breath when he lifted her, locking her legs about his waist and easing into her body.

Thalia's head fell on his shoulder as he backed her against the side of the bath and drove deeply inside her. They both rode the wave of passion while he kissed and caressed her.

"When I awoke this morning and found you beside me, I knew I was the most fortunate of men," he murmured against her lips.

Thalia could not answer because he was plundering

her body. Throwing her head back, she felt his mouth move along the arch of her neck.

His dark hair fell around her, and he whispered, "Tell me I wasn't dreaming last night . . . you are mine."

How could she tell him anything while he controlled her body and mind? Thalia gasped as he brought them both to full satisfaction. For a long moment he held her, still inside her. "What will I do tonight when you are not beside me?" he asked, his mouth sliding across hers.

Thalia had no time to answer because he hardened once more and roughly took her. She cried out his name and held him tightly.

After a while, he reached for a sponge and ran it over her body, even in the most intimate places. Then he lifted her into his arms and carried her out of the bath. She was surprised when he took a piece of soft linen and dried her body, paying particular attention to her breasts, which he kissed and caressed.

"Time is against us, my queen. Although I am loath to leave you, I must."

"I understand your duty," she told him, wishing with all her heart that he didn't have to go.

Thalia allowed herself the luxury of staring at Ashtyn's muscular body. His shoulders were broad, his hips narrow, his legs powerfully shaped. When he paused to pull on his tunic, he gave her the smile that always twisted her insides.

"We can have the morning meal together before I depart."

When they returned to the bedchamber, it was

empty. But dependable Uzza, who seemed to anticipate what was needed before anyone had to ask for it, had prepared a table with roasted fowl, bowls of fruit and slices of thick white cheese.

Thalia could hardly eat for the lump in her throat. "Where will you go?"

"There is heavy fighting in the mountains, where our men need fresh supplies and reinforcements."

"You will be in danger," she said, taking a cluster of grapes and biting into one of them, trying not to show her distress.

He sliced a chunk of cheese and handed it to her. "No more so than the others. They need to see me and know that I once more fight with them."

"If I had been born male instead of female, I would ride beside you."

He took her hand and raised it to his lips. "And that would be such a pity. I would rather have you waiting for me when I return."

Suddenly she saw him frown, and his mind seemed to be somewhere else.

"How long will you be away?" Thalia asked.

Ashtyn had not heard her, so she asked once more. "When will you return?"

"Forgive me," he said, turning his attention back to her. "In truth I was thinking of King Melik, and the sad news I will have to give the soldiers when I reach camp."

"'Tis not an enviable task. But say to them that I intend to do everything as my grandfather would have wanted it done." She frowned. "Will that comfort them?"

"Aye. More than you can imagine." He raised her

hand and examined it. "'Tis but a small hand, yet it wields the might and power of Bal Forea."

"If only I could do more."

"No more is expected of you."

Ashtyn's words cut deep.

"I am not a decoration to be displayed for all to see. Queen Cleopatra rode out with her armies when she was younger. If it comes to that, so shall I."

"There is much you have to learn here, and Lord Parinez is anxious to teach you."

"The woman you wanted to marry when you were younger, would she have been a mere decoration?" Hurt and anger swept her mind, but she hid it behind a lofty gaze. "What was her name?"

Ashtyn blinked his eyes and frowned, "How can I recall what happened in my youth?" Then his eyes lit up. "I remember—her name was Shajada."

Thalia stood. "You can take your thoughts of her with you when you leave." She raised her head regally. "No doubt you wished it was she with you last night."

He rose, the look on his face one of confusion. "Give me a man, and I'll strip him of his secrets with little effort. But I will never understand a woman, especially not you."

"Precisely."

Ashtyn seemed to be groping for words. "I wanted only you—"

Thalia moved toward the door with long, lithe steps and turned back to him, noticing his bewildered expression. "Leave me and go to your Shajada. This is my chamber."

"You are asking me to leave? Why?"

"I am queen; therefore, I don't need a reason. Just go."

He stalked to the door, not knowing whether to be angry or amused. "Will you send me back to war with harsh words on your sweet lips?" Ashtyn was reluctant to leave her this way. He had just spent the most unbelievable night with her in his arms.

She stood before him, silent and unyielding.

With resignation, Ashtyn swept her a bow. "Most Gracious Majesty, I shall send messengers daily so you will know how goes the war."

Thalia was barely able to hold back tears as she said, "May the gods keep you safe and give you victory over our enemies."

That night Thalia lay in her bed, feeling empty inside. She pressed her hand on her stomach in wonderment, hoping Ashtyn had planted his child in her. She closed her eyes, trying to imagine what he was doing at that very moment. Night shadows crept across the room, and still Thalia did not sleep.

Even into the early morning hours she reached for sleep, but it did not find her.

Lord Sevilin rolled over in bed and patted the woman beside him on the arm. "Get out. I hear my mother's approach."

The curly headed beauty pouted. "Allow me to stay."

He nudged her toward the edge of the bed. "You can return tonight."

Smiling, she slid to the floor and scampered out the hidden door just as Lady Vistah entered. "I have been about our business while you rut with a woman of the street."

Sevilin clasped his hands behind his head. "She isn't a woman of the street, Mother. She is the wife of one of my captains."

Lady Vistah waved her hand in dismissal. "I didn't come here to speak of such nonsense."

He yawned. "Really, Mother—what about the young men you take to your bed? Do you think I don't know about them?"

"You may know, but no one else does. I'm discreet, while you flaunt your women for all to see. But I'm here to speak of another woman," she said, sinking onto the edge of his bed. "The new queen of Bal Forea."

Sevilin's eyes narrowed. "Aye. It will be a bit harder to capture her now, but it can be done."

"Fool! Have you not been told of her marriage?"

Sevilin scowled, bringing an ugly twist to an otherwise handsome face. "Count Ashtyn?"

"Who else but he? But now he's Prince Ashtyn. He was handpicked by the king long ago, even though I tried to persuade the king that you would be a better choice."

Sevilin slammed his fist into a pillow. "And what was the good king's answer? That my lineage was not as elevated as Ashtyn's?"

"Something like that," Lady Vistah replied. "I didn't choose well when I married your father. He had no wealth, and but a minor title."

Sevilin had heard about his father's defects many times before. "If you came with the intention of spoiling my day, you have succeeded. But, if you came here with the notion of harming the new queen, you should know that would not fall in with my plans."

Lady Vistah jumped to her feet. "You have no plans! Now that the people have a queen, they will rise up against us, and we will lose all." Her expression contorted with fury, and resentment flared inside her mind. "That young woman has been given everything I ever wanted, and she has done nothing to deserve it. She has youth, and they say no one can rival her in beauty, while I see my beauty slipping away. She now commands the loyalty and devotion of most of the fighting men. They will follow her like geese in a row—watch and see if I'm not right."

"Mother, we still have those who are loyal to us. We are not yet defeated. We must find a way to capture the queen."

"Foolish, foolish man—how do you expect to accomplish that? Think you she does not have loyal guards surrounding her? They will have been handpicked by Ashtyn."

Sevilin's brow furrowed. "Loyalty can be bought."

"Think of it," his mother said, paying little attention to what he'd said. "This Thalia had a kingdom thrust upon her, and it was said she fought against wearing the crown. All was given to her. And now, to make matters worse, my own son is softening toward her. I have seen you daydreaming about her."

He shrugged. "As you said, she is reputed a beauty. I only try to imagine what she looks like. I recall her mother, a very beautiful woman."

"This queen will never be yours, Sevilin. She has everything else, but she will never have my son!"

Sevilin looked quickly into his mother's eyes. She'd

been behaving oddly ever since word reached them that the young princess had landed on the island. He wondered if her mind had been affected by the death of her ambitions. "Surely the young queen has already been bedded by Ashtyn. If he has her with child, we might as well board a ship and find somewhere to hide."

She turned to him. "I know ways to get rid of unborn babies, so do not look at that as a problem."

Sevilin stared into the distance. "We don't even know that is necessary. We have bigger concerns at the moment. I have been informed some of our troops have deserted us."

"You must issue orders that anyone deserting will be slain on the spot." With those as her parting words, Lady Vistah stalked out of her son's bedchamber. There had to be a way to capture the woman who'd stolen the throne from her. Her eyes narrowed as she became swamped with anger. Sevilin was practically worthless to her now.

But then her eyes brightened—did she not have her own spies in the palace?

❦ CHAPTER TWENTY-FIVE

Ashtyn and his men rode single file along a narrow mountain pass. When they reached a wider path, he motioned Captain Darius to his side.

"Tell me," he said, lowering his voice so the others wouldn't hear, "have you ever loved a woman?"

"Aye, Commander. In my younger years, I loved many a woman, but not so many of late. War tends to interfere with a man's love life. And like you, I'm not interested in those women who are camp followers, so there's an end to it."

"I am not talking about the women who have temporarily shared your bed. I am talking about a woman who gets into your mind, so you can think of little else save her. She takes my breath away."

"Commander, is it not called love when you give joy to a woman and take some for yourself?"

"You speak not of love, but of lust. What I feel is loving one woman to the exclusion of all others. I don't see other women, I don't want them." He lowered his head. "Love is hateful, it tears at the heart and renders a man foolish in his own eyes."

Understanding dawned on the captain. "You speak of the queen? Who would not love such a woman?"

"How can a man understand a woman? Suppose you had a woman who was angry with you for something that happened long before you met her. A trifle—nothing more. What would you do?"

Captain Darius nodded. "I always find if you give them a gift they forget about being angry. They like pretty trinkets."

"And what would you suggest I give a queen who can command anything she wishes?"

"That would be a bit of a problem. But the queen is your wife, and there's an end to it."

Ashtyn applied his heel to the horse's flanks, and the animal jumped forward into a dead run, leaving the others to follow. He'd already said too much about his own affairs. But what he'd confessed to Captain Darius would go no farther. He was Ashtyn's closest confidant and would never repeat what they'd spoken of.

Smoke rose in the air, and the sound of clashing swords broke the silence. Ashtyn motioned for his men to dismount. He unsheathed his sword and rushed into the fray.

Thalia realized glumly that she could never be the kind of queen everyone expected her to be. The more Lord Parinez instructed her on her duties, the more unworthy she felt. Being a queen in time of war was a daunting task. Thalia's thoughts turned to Ashtyn. Had he been wounded? Was he alive?

Although they had spent only one night together as man and wife, she sorely missed him. If only her last words to him had not been spoken in anger.

"Majesty?"

Her mind jolted back to the present, and she realized

Lord Parinez had been speaking, and she hadn't heard a word. "I beg pardon," she said. "Could you repeat what you were saying?"

"I was explaining the troubles the women are facing in the city. Majesty, there is hunger. There are mothers who have lost their children, and suckling babies who have no mother." He sighed. "I fear you have inherited a flawed country, war-torn and bankrupt."

Thalia sat silent for a moment, then looked at the lord chamberlain. "I know nothing about finances or war, but my mother did instruct me on the functions of a huge villa. If this sounds foolish, tell me so: Why could we not match suckling babies with women who lost their own children and have breasts full of milk? Further, it seems the only food source is the sea—why not send out a fishing fleet each day and have them share the catch with the population?"

Lord Parinez smiled with jubilation. "Majesty, it takes a woman to discover ways a man would overlook. I believe it would be prudent to find women to take care of the children—but we have no men for the fishing boats."

Thalia stood slowly, her brow creased in a frown. "Then women will have to man the boats."

"But Majesty, the women know nothing about fishing."

"By the gods, Lord Parinez, they can learn! If people are hungry, something must be done at once—something extreme." She hurried toward the door. "I myself will go into the city and see this thing done. Give me time to change my clothing and meet me in the outer courtyard within the hour."

"But it is not safe—"

She paused and glanced back at him. "What is the life of one woman against a multitude of hungry women and children? Our men risk their lives every day—can we not see that their families are fed and relieve them of that worry?"

Lord Parinez watched in stunned silence as the queen stalked out the door. Then a slow smile lit his eyes. "By all I hold dear, she is magnificent! And a credit to her exalted grandfather."

The scribe glanced up from his reed mat. "Pardon, Lord Chamberlain, should I take that down?"

"Nay. I was just musing on how such a tiny slip of a girl, who had been raised to run a household, was also taught common sense. She sees what is to be done with a fresh eye." Lord Parinez clasped his hands behind him and strolled toward the door, his footsteps lighter than they had been in many seasons. "Watch our queen rise to one day rival even the majesty of the great queen of Egypt!"

Still the scribe was confused. "Shall I record those words?"

"Nay, nay. Fold your tablet. You heard merely the words of an old man that would be of no interest to anyone."

When Thalia emerged from the bedchamber, she saw Eleni moving quickly down the corridor, and wondered how she had gained access to this part of the palace since it was so well guarded.

She had intended to have Eleni brought back into her service, but now was not the time; there were other matters that needed her attention.

Eleni halted when Thalia called out to her.

"Majesty," she said, bowing low, "I have information you should know about."

"Then accompany me."

Without hesitating, Eleni followed the queen to a small garden.

"It is good to see you again," Thalia said, smiling. "I regret I cannot give you much time today."

Eleni lowered her gaze as if she could not look into Thalia's eyes. "Majesty, I must not remain long, myself—the guards could discover me at any moment."

"That should not worry you. I will not allow them to send you away, if that is your fear," Thalia assured her. There was something different about Eleni's appearance—her plain blue shift was soiled and wrinkled, and her hair was tangled about her face. "What are your concerns?"

The woman glanced about furtively. "I dare not call attention to myself."

"Then tell me what you have to say."

"Majesty, there are harmful rumors about you and Prince Ashtyn. It is said your union is not a true one, and that he left without consummating the marriage."

Thalia was appalled. "Who has planted such a rumor?"

"I do not know the individual who started it, but Lord Sevilin could profit by it—he would like the people to believe there will be no child from your marriage with Prince Ashtyn." The girl looked directly into Thalia's eyes. "If there is no truth to such rumblings, they should be squelched without delay."

Worriedly, Thalia glanced toward the palace. "There is a war raging, and our minds are better served by attending to that front than in listening to malicious gossip."

Eleni reached out to Thalia, then let her hand drop. "Such viciousness can spread like wildfire. I have a friend in the rebel camp. Let me discover what he knows, and I will find a way to get word to you."

Thalia shook her head. "Nay, do not. We shall allow the rumors to die from lack of reaction from us."

"I beg you, Majesty, do not take it lightly. Wars are won and lost on just such scraps of information."

"I shall not give in to gossips. Nor should you. You are dismissed now, Eleni."

Eleni bowed stiffly, then turned away and hurried across the garden. Puzzled, Thalia watched her disappear around a hedge. Shaking her head, she pondered their conversation. Were the people of Bal Forea putting too much importance on her marriage?

She lifted her head and dismissed the rumor as so much nonsense.

Widow Craymon felt the touch of the cool breeze on her face as she swept her front stoop. When she heard the commotion from the crowd gathered at the public fountain, she dropped her broom and hurried in that direction. The women she passed had dazed expressions on their faces, and the widow saw why when she reached the town square: The young queen was riding in their direction at the head of her entourage.

With a deep-carved frown on her face, Widow Craymon listened to the murmurings as the women spoke of the wonder of the queen coming among them.

She became irritated when several women elbowed their way to the front. But mostly she was angered by the stooped old hag who used her walking stick to push the others out of the way.

Old Didra's once-brilliant eyes were dull from the afflictions she endured daily. The hands that had once been capable of creating the most delicate beadwork were now swollen and malformed. With an awkward gait, she slowly progressed to the fountain.

Didra was reputed to be wise; it was said she had 'the eye' and could see into the future. She knew about herbs and spices, and made love potions and oils to cure a sour stomach. But Widow Craymon did not believe anything that was said about the old woman except that she was cracked. The widow turned her attention back to the young queen. She was not so ready to believe, as most of her neighbors did, that this queen would help them in their plight.

"It could be that her majesty has heard of our suffering and is coming to help us," one of the women said hopefully.

"She is so young—what can she know of suffering?" Widow Craymon stated huffily. "Many of you still weep for your dead children—can she bring them back to life?"

"She has come to bring us hope," another intoned.

Widow Craymon shook her head. "I don't know why she is here, but it will be to her benefit, not ours."

"Aye," said a young wife who had not seen her husband since the last season and was easily swayed by the widow's harsh judgment. "She marries our good Count Ashtyn, but it is whispered she did not take him to her bed before she sent him off to battle. It is a wife's duty to please her husband, be she queen or otherwise."

Old Didra held up her hand for silence. "I have read the constellations and consulted the bones, and seen a vision: I have seen peace and prosperity brought back to our island. I saw Queen Thalia holding our banner high—I have seen a day without war, and I have seen our fighting men arriving home to remain. Our fishermen will launch their boats instead of wielding a sword, our farmers will till the soil, and we will know hunger no more. *And* I saw the hawks return!"

"Nay," came a cry from one of the women. "The hawks have deserted us and will never return. We are cursed!"

Didra was frightening to look upon—her gray hair was frizzed in clusters about her face. She had only one good eye, and it was bright blue and piercing—the other eye was smoky-colored. "Listen well to me, for I speak the truth."

"How can that be?" Widow Craymon scoffed. "Even if the war ended today, there would be no prosperity."

Old Didra pointed a crooked finger at the widow. "It will come—the bones do not lie, and stars always reveal the truth if you are gifted enough to see what they foretell. The young queen's heart bleeds for us; you will see this for yourself."

"Bah," Widow Craymon replied in anger. "I'll believe that when she walks among us and shares our meager repast."

The queen drew near, and in that moment even Widow Craymon's eyes widened in awe. Lord Parinez rode beside the queen, and the palace guards rode behind them.

"Let us see if she even dismounts her horse," the widow stated snappishly.

"Seeing her this close, I see she is younger than I," said a bride with her mouth agape. "But why is she here?"

"All is just as I predicted," old Didra stated smugly, knowing the skeptics would now be forced to admit her bones had predicted true. "The queen will start helping with small matters, but her ripple shall be felt all the way to Egypt, and she will carry us forward with her glory!"

❧ CHAPTER TWENTY-SIX

Thalia dismounted and removed her cloak, tossing it across her saddle. She wore a plain blue linen shift with a matching sash. Her hair hung down her back and was unadorned. She wanted the women of Bal Forea to believe she was one of them—for in her heart she was beginning to feel she was.

As usual, Thalia tried to imagine what Lady Larania would do if faced with the same situation. Of course, her mother would start with the most important matters. And that was what Thalia must do.

Lord Parinez dipped his head to whisper so only the queen would hear: "You must allow the guards to accompany you."

Thalia smiled up at him and shook her head. "Nay, I shall not. Those women look harmless to me. I want only to speak to them, ask them questions, and make suggestions. We cannot help them if we do not know the problems they face every day."

"But, Majesty—"

"Good Lord Parinez, what I must do today you cannot help me with. You have important matters to attend at the palace. Leave me two guards, but have them remain with the horses. I will not intimidate these good citizens."

"But Majesty, it is my duty to see to your safety."

"I see none here who looks threatening." Thalia glanced at each woman and passed over each one who looked at her with awe. She guided her steps to the woman whose light-blue eyes were filled with skepticism—that woman was the one she sought. Her mother had taught her one could learn more from a disgruntled person than from one who wants to please.

The women all went to their knees before Thalia. "Please rise," she told them. "Today I am here as one of you. Let us talk and see what we can do about our troubles."

The women watched in disbelief as the queen took the clay dipper that the whole community used, dipped it in the water, and took a drink.

Thalia hung the dipper back on the peg and spoke softly. "Tell me your names," she said, going down a row of stunned Bal Forean women. She had always been good at remembering names, and she hoped she would be able to put a face to a name later on. At last she came to the skeptical woman and paused. "And what is your name, madame?"

"Majesty, I am called Craymon. My husband has been dead for five years, and my two sons died but a year ago."

Thalia laid her hand on the woman's shoulder, drawing a surprised gasp from the others. "I cannot begin to understand the grief you feel, Craymon. War makes mourners of us all, and I grieve for your loss." She looked at the other women. "I know fear because

I feel it for my husband, who has been gone for an entire full moon. At first I received daily reports from him. For the last week I have heard naught, and I am worried."

The others stepped closer, wanting to say something, but they were still too much in awe.

"Craymon, will you help me?" Thalia asked. "Lord Parinez informed me of our most distressing problem. Let us try to put our heads together and find a solution. This is the way I see it . . . tell me if you agree."

The widow dipped into a quick bow, but could not find her voice.

"You are an intelligent woman, Craymon; you have run your own kitchen, and that is no small matter. But put that aside for the moment and think past your own home to the needs of your neighbors. Let us stockpile what food we have, and, aye, I shall send what food I can from the palace kitchen. Let none cheat or hoard. We will live or die united, thinking of our men who face death to protect us. Let us be strong and do this for them."

Widow Craymon's eyes widened, and she could hardly grasp the fact that the queen wanted her opinion. The sweet little queen was so young, and Craymon lost her heart to her then and there. "Majesty, I will do whatever I can to help you."

"First of all, take me to the place where the motherless children are quartered. Lord Parinez told me they are all housed together."

"Aye, the poor little mites. They have no mother to hold them. We do what we can, but still they cry for their mothers."

"I would like to put you in charge of matching these

children with women who have lost their own. Would that be possible?"

Craymon nodded vigorously. "I can easily do that for you, Gracious Majesty. We have three suckling babes, and two women whose breasts are filled with milk."

"I am grateful to you. Now please point out some of the women whose husbands were fishermen. Surely, they have gained knowledge of the sea from their husbands."

Later in the afternoon, Thalia sat among the women, a thin bowl of broth balanced on her knee. She drank from the clay bowl as if she was one of them. "Galah," she said to the woman seated next to her, "since your husband was a fisherman longer than the others, will you help us? I'll have some of the palace guards look at the boats and make certain they are seaworthy."

Thalia's gaze settled on the old woman who stared at her with her one good eye. "Didra, you said you live a long walk from the village. If we find you a cottage nearby, can you and two women of your choosing oversee the salting and drying of the fish and see that it is fairly distributed so none will go hungry?"

The wise old eye flickered the merest bit. "Aye, Gracious Majesty, none will go hungry while you sit on the throne of Bal Forea."

"Let us hope not." Thalia rose. "We must all help each other through these trying times." She turned to Craymon, who had easily found women who were willing to take children into their homes. "I will provide you with a horse, and you shall come to me weekly and make your report. Cling to each other, show kindness to those who are not of your own family, for we are all citizens of Bal Forea, and we must help ease the worries of our fighting men."

A loud cheer went up from the women, and when Thalia stood to leave, they bowed to her, this time more deeply and more respectfully than when she had arrived. The villagers fell silent as she mounted her horse and rode back toward the palace.

"I dare any country, large or small, to produce such a queen," Widow Craymon stated with force. "There can be none wiser or sweeter than our good Queen Thalia."

Heads nodded as they all agreed.

"She didn't think herself too grand to eat with us," Galah stated.

Didra smiled to herself. Their problems had not all been solved, but by coming among the women today, the young queen had taught them to work together. Didra watched the queen ride away, knowing the day would come when they would all have something to celebrate. The bones had told her something else that she was not ready to share with the others—nay, the others would not believe her anyway—the queen carried a child in her belly. What a joyous time it would be when the people learned there was going to be an heir to the throne of Bal Forea.

Lord Ramtat stood before Queen Cleopatra as she read the scroll. "Was this written by Thalia?"

"I recognize her hand, as does my mother."

Cleopatra handed the scroll to Antony and turned her attention to her general. "It is hard to credit that our little Thalia is a queen in her own right. But on thinking about it, there was always something special about her."

"As you read," Ramtat said, "Bal Forea is in the heat of civil war. I would like permission to take my Badari and help in any way I can."

Antony shook his head. "I have been studying the maps and have come to the conclusion that it will not be an easy task to gain the advantage. Bal Forea is an island of extreme mountainous terrain. I suspect that is the one reason Rome never attempted to conquer it. I will send my Seventh Legion with you if you like. They are accustomed to fighting on uneven terrain."

"A legion will not be needed, but I will take Marcellus and those that serve under him." Ramtat stared at Antony. "Do not think of taking the island for Rome's gain."

Cleopatra nodded. "I agree. But did you take note that Thalia said the people are hungry. Take four ships filled with grain and other stores. We must help our little Thalia in any way we can."

"I am most grateful, my Queen," Ramtat said, bowing. "And I know my sister will be, too."

"Don't be so grateful," Cleopatra told him. "When their war is over, we shall have a new trading partner. I have been told that their mountains are filled with silver, and my treasury is low on that precious metal."

Ramtat smiled and bowed out of the room. He had hoped Cleopatra would help the island, but as always, his queen had done more than was expected of her.

As he rode back toward the villa, he tried to picture his little sister as a queen. He recalled Adhaniá telling him how Thalia had been a pickpocket when she'd first come upon her on the streets of Rome. Deep laughter startled the man who rode beside Ramtat.

Cleopatra was right, there had always been something special about Thalia.

But a queen *and* a wife?

Ramtat frowned. Even if his sister was a queen, someone was going to answer for kidnaping her! And if they had forced her to marry against her will, he would see an end to that marriage.

Marcellus had already landed in Egypt, and if he knew his brother-in-law, he was readying his troops for all-out war. Even if Bal Forea had escaped the world's notice for hundreds of years, its people were about to feel the combined might of Egypt and Rome.

CHAPTER TWENTY-SEVEN

Ashtyn had been away for two phases of the full moon, and in all that time, there had hardly been a moment in the day when Thalia did not think of him.

Thalia was having her customary morning meeting with Lord Parinez when a mud-splattered messenger came rushing in with news that Prince Ashtyn would be arriving at any moment.

Unable to conceal her joy, Thalia leaped to her feet and rushed out of the chamber, leaving a smiling lord chamberlain hobbling after her. Rushing down the front steps of the palace, she paused halfway to the bottom, listening to the approaching riders.

And then he was there! Riding at the head of his men, dusty and weary, but he was safely home. He rode even with her and smiled, making Thalia's heart sing.

Ashtyn dismounted and tossed the reins to one of his men, his eyes on his wife. "My Queen," he said, bowing his head. "Forgive my appearance." He made an attempt to dust the mud from his breastplate, but his eyes never left her face. "It's good to see you in health."

At that moment, Thalia was not a queen, but a young woman in love, and it was difficult to present a queenly stance when she wanted to throw herself into Ashtyn's arms.

As he climbed the steps toward her, Thalia's heart beat ecstatically. Their gazes met, and his silver-blue eyes held a promise of what was to come later.

"My husband, it is good to see you. I had short warning you were arriving."

With a wide grin, he knelt before her and took her hand, lifting it to his lips. "What a welcome sight to find you waiting for me."

Thalia had the feeling she was falling inside those compelling eyes of his. "Have you news for us, my lord?" she asked in a quivering voice, knowing all eyes were on the two of them.

For a long moment Ashtyn just looked at Thalia, his mouth curved into a smile. Then he waved at those gathered to watch the reunion, took Thalia's elbow and led her into the palace, nodding for Lord Parinez to follow.

When they were situated in the small chamber, Lord Parinez motioned for the scribe to take down what was said.

Ashtyn removed his helmet, and his dark hair spilled over his shoulders. "I am the bearer of good tidings. We have retaken Resnene Pass, and the rebels who didn't flee fell to their knees and begged to be allowed to serve the queen."

Thalia dropped down onto a padded chair, her eyes on her husband's face. "How many captured?" she asked.

"Over two hundred prisoners. Half that number fled,

and twice that number were slain. We have the rebels on the run. Lord Sevilin knows by now he cannot win."

Thalia stood, her white gown swirling around her. "How many men did we lose?"

"Fifty-two good men," Ashtyn said sadly.

"Other than our losses, that is good news indeed." Her gaze fell on her husband's face. "What must be done now?"

Ashtyn wearily seated himself on a stool, his gaze going from his wife to the lord chamberlain. "A decision must be made. You must either pardon the prisoners or put them to death, My Queen."

"What do you advise?" she asked.

"I am merely general of your armies. You must decide the fate of these men." Peering gravely at Lord Parinez for conformation, he asked, "Is that not so, Lord Chamberlain?"

Thalia saw the look they exchanged and knew at once she was being tested. She wavered in her decision. "Is there no third option—can they not be sent home and told to war no more?"

"Nay," Lord Parinez stated. "They must either die or be bound to you by their word. There is no third choice."

Thalia wished for Queen Cleopatra's wisdom. "Where are they?"

Ashtyn shoved his hair out of his face. "Housed in the barracks for the moment under heavy guard."

"Take me to them," she stated unequivocally. "I would see these rebels for myself before I decide their fate." Thalia was quaking inside, knowing she had the power of life or death over so many. It was a power she did not want. But it was she who would make the final decision.

* * *

In the outer courtyard, it took all Thalia's willpower to look into the eyes of the kneeling rebels. The stench of them was unbearable. Many had wounds that needed tending, and some were swaying to stay erect. Pity hit her hard when she saw how young some of them were. One with a deep gash in his cheek was little more than a lad.

Despair filled her heart—now was the time to think what Queen Cleopatra would do in her place, and the answer came to her as clear as if the Egyptian queen had spoken to her. Seeing the fear in the prisoners' eyes, Thalia realized they expected to die.

She raised her head, her eyes moving over each man. "If there be any among you willing to swear fealty to me, let them declare it now."

For a long moment there was only stunned silence. Then a man, older than the others, struggled to his feet, his chains rattling on his wrists. "Aye, Gracious Majesty, you have my fealty, and I beg the right to re-turn to my farm and live in peace."

"You are a soldier," she said in a clear voice, "and only my general husband has the right to give you leave to return to your farm, but you shall not die here today." She looked at him, frowning. "Is your word to be trusted?"

"I swear on the gods that I shall not take up arms against you, and that you are my true sovereign. I will fight to protect you." He cleared his throat. "Majesty, I would die rather than betray my word."

The rattle of chains echoed down the line, and to a man, they all bowed before Thalia, pledging their loyalty.

Thalia wanted to look away from the hope she saw etched on the faces of these broken men. "Lord Parinez, see that these loyal citizens' wounds are treated and they are given food and drink." She turned to her husband. "As the commander of my armies, you will decide if these men continue to fight or if they are allowed to go home." She nodded at the young lad. "Except for him—he must be allowed to return to his home where he can grow into a man."

It was a stunned group of men who watched the small queen move away. None of them spoke, fearing they had not heard her correctly, or that she might change her mind.

Ashtyn watched tears gather in the eyes of many of the hardened fighters who had served Sevilin.

And Ashtyn saw more—those men were completely captivated by a queen who showed them mercy.

They had not expected it, but Ashtyn had—he knew his wife well, and today she had made the wisest choice she would ever make as queen.

CHAPTER TWENTY-EIGHT

Thalia sat motionless on the edge of her bed, staring at nothing, trying not to think. Today she had become vividly aware of the hateful side of war—men who were not only scarred in body, but also in their souls. Or were they merely misled by their devotion to Sevilin?

At the time she had pardoned the prisoners, it had seemed the right thing to do, but now she wrestled with that decision.

Queen Cleopatra must struggle with these kinds of decisions daily—but she had been raised to accept such responsibilities.

Thalia glanced toward the open doorway that led to the garden. It was growing late. Why had Ashtyn not come to her? Perhaps he felt he had already fulfilled his obligation as her husband.

Thalia sprang to her feet with the intention of going into the garden when she heard the door open. Ashtyn stood there, gazing at her with growing intensity, and she could not look away.

"I would have been here sooner, but I had matters to attend, and then I bathed before I came to you."

Thalia's voice sounded strained even to her own

ears. "I imagine a great general has many duties to occupy his time."

"There was nothing as important as seeing my queen," he said, moving toward her, then stopping within her reach. "Nothing."

Thalia searched his eyes. "Did I do the right thing today by giving those rebels their freedom?" she asked, uncertainty in her voice.

Ashtyn saw her stricken gaze and paused. "For a queen, there is no right or wrong decision. Your word is law, and few will question it."

Tears of uncertainty clung to her lashes, and she was still unsure if she had been just. "But was it honorable?"

"I will answer you thus, even though it may seem a contradiction. Ask yourself how you can punish those who brought so much grief and sorrow to the people of Bal Forea. And answer yourself thus—all those fighting are Bal Foreans, some misguided perhaps, but citizens of your realm nonetheless. When you took up that crown, even the rebels fell under your protection."

"I could not have sent them to their deaths."

"I never thought you could."

Thalia stared down at the toe of her sandal, then suddenly glanced up at Ashtyn, catching him unaware; the softness reflected in his eyes took her by surprise, but with the flicker of his lashes, she watched his expression change to indifference.

What had he been thinking?

Before Thalia had time to react, she found herself swept into Ashtyn's arms and felt his mouth touch the side of her face.

"Have you missed me as I missed you?" he asked, his grip tightening. "Have you?"

Thalia's heart was racing, and she was hit by so many emotions, she couldn't put them into words. She turned her face up to Ashtyn, allowing him to read the answer in her eyes, and then watched his gaze drop to her mouth.

"My sweet wife," he said, gathering her closer and planting a kiss on her mouth. "You inflame my blood and I ache for you day and night, even after a long battle has left me exhausted."

With the troubled world swirling around her, joy burst through Thalia at the sound of her husband's seductive words. Ashtyn's heart might belong to another, but at this moment, his thoughts were of her.

In dazed astonishment, she cried out when he lifted her in his arms and laid her onto the bed. Hardly giving her time to catch her breath, he came down to her, holding her against his body.

His lips touched each eyelid and then brushed her mouth, lingering as if he could not pull away. "It has been so long since I have been with you. Forgive my roughness." He pulled back and looked into her eyes, his hand moving over her breast. "It's just that I need you."

Eagerly her mouth sought his as her heartbeat quickened. Her mind merged with his as he removed her gown, and she tore at his clothing. Wild abandon drove them both.

Ashtyn's mouth ground against hers, and his body strained to get closer. She closed her eyes as he slid into her, and met his forceful thrusts. Through a mist of passion, she whispered his name.

Ashtyn drove deep inside Thalia, and she rolled her head, moaning in pure pleasure. She laced her hands through his dark hair and met his gaze. Oh, aye, the other woman might have his heart, but his body craved hers—she could not be wrong about that.

Thalia's body shook and trembled, and her arms tightened about his wide shoulders.

He murmured her name as his body quaked, and he gripped her tighter.

Later, when the breeze from the garden stirred and cooled their overheated bodies, Ashtyn made love to Thalia again, this time slowly and lingeringly.

Afterwards, Thalia tried to hide the tears that formed behind her eyes by burying her face against his shoulder. How safe she felt when she was in Ashtyn's arms. And how she dreaded the moment they would be parted.

Ashtyn's hand moved up and down her arm, and she could tell he was deep in thought. "When must you rejoin your troops?" she asked.

"I told Captain Darius to look for my return in two days' time."

She despised the war that had torn this land apart. "When will we see an end to this war?"

"One can never be sure. The fighting has gone on so long, some of the younger men have never known peace."

Although Thalia made the attempt, she could hardly speak above a whisper. " 'Tis a pity."

He placed his hands on both sides of her face and made her look at him. "Does your heart still long for Egypt, and the family you left behind?"

She nodded and tore her gaze from his. "I love Egypt well. And I miss my family."

"I received word that eight Egyptian galleys were

taking on stores and loading troops, making ready to sail from Alexandria. I have no doubt they will set their course for Bal Forea."

"It is my brother!" Thalia exclaimed, happiness building in her heart. She raised up on her elbow, thinking she would soon be rescued. But that thought brought her no joy. "When will they arrive?"

"It depends on the wind. Our small ship carrying the news arrived only this afternoon. The *War Hawk* was built for speed and carries very little bulk, so she will have arrived well ahead of the Egyptian fleet."

"Ramtat will come with Badarian warriors and Egyptian troops."

"Aye," Ashtyn said dully.

"He will also bring food and grain for the people of Bal Forea."

Ashtyn looked into her eyes as if he were trying to read her thoughts. "You cannot return to Egypt with your brother. You are needed here."

She closed her eyes. "Ashtyn, you are far more capable of leading this country than I. I do not belong here—I never have. You are my husband, and it is within my power to set you on the throne."

He rolled to a sitting position. "What nonsense you talk. You forget you must have a child."

She touched him on the shoulder. "I am with child."

Since his face was in shadows, she could not see his expression, but his hand went out to her, and he pulled her across his lap, cuddling her close, raining kisses on her upturned face. "Why did you not tell me sooner? I would have gentled my lovemaking had I known!"

"I wasn't sure how to tell you. I know the people of

this island are awaiting such news, and I wasn't sure when they should be told."

His hand moved gently over her stomach. "Few rebels will raise a weapon against your troops when they learn of the child, for he will be their future."

Thalia sighed. "Then I shall never be allowed to return home, even should I desire it. You must know I would never leave my child behind, and I will not be allowed to take the child with me."

Ashtyn was quiet for several heartbeats. His tone was deep with meaning when he said, "Nay, you cannot take the child away from Bal Forea."

Her words were bitter and spoken with irony. "I have had no free choice since the night I met you in my mother's garden."

"Nor have I." He bent and touched his mouth to her breasts, feeling the fullness of them in his hand. He gently eased her onto the bed, touching his mouth to each breast and then to her stomach, which was still firm and flat.

"I am to be a father," he said in wonder. "Before now, I have not thought of the child as—" he paused as if he could not go on. "—as mine."

"You are the father of the future ruler of Bal Forea," she told him.

His hand moved lower, and he smiled when he heard her gasp.

"Thalia, I need to be inside you," he whispered. "This time I shall take great care."

Thalia closed her eyes as Ashtyn positioned himself to enter her, and she felt him hesitate. "You are very virile, Ashtyn. I have little doubt the deed was accomplished on our wedding night."

He was impatient to have her. He tried to control the rage of his passion, but it was difficult when his body hungered for her so.

Thalia flirtatiously swivelled her hips and arched her back, inviting him, enticing him, to take what he wanted. With a deep growl, his hot gaze moved over her nakedness.

"You fill my heart," he told her. A slight smile touched his lips, and he rubbed his chin against her cheek. "I would have you every moment of the day, were it possible."

"A provocative thought," she told him, needing him in the depth of her heart. Her hands slid down his back, and she arched her lower body upward, issuing another invitation.

Ashtyn was beyond thinking as he slipped completely under her spell. He gripped her hips and slid slowly into her moist heat.

Thalia touched her lips to his and took his groan into her mouth. She closed her eyes, feeling as if she had always loved this man.

The passion that held them in its grip erupted, and they clung to each other, trembling from the intensity until it passed.

Thalia pushed her fingers through his dark hair and touched her lips to his strong jaw.

When he rolled her over, holding her away from him, he watched her face. "Are you happy about the child?" he asked.

"What woman would not be happy to have your child? But much is expected of this poor infant who has not yet drawn breath. I wish it were otherwise."

His voice sounded distant. "I wonder if you have

considered that you will have power on your side when your brother arrives with his army. Bal Forea cannot stand against Egypt's might. Will you ask him to take you away?"

"I don't deny I thought about it when I sent Ramtat word of where to find me. I have to weigh my own feelings against what is best for the people. I am learning a queen cannot always choose as she wishes."

Ashtyn remained silent for a long moment. At last he drew a breath and said in a deep tone, "Be angry with me if you must, hate me if you will, but never deny me your body."

She felt the pain of his words deep inside. "This is not how I imagined marriage."

"How *did* you imagine it, My Queen?"

"My brother, Ramtat, and his wife, Danaë, have great love for each other—it is a joy just to be near them. Marcellus, Adhania's husband, loves her so much he cannot take his eyes off her when she is in the same room with him. I always supposed that was what marriage was like."

He rolled off the bed and stood. "Duty calls. May I come to you tonight?"

She was hurt by his coldness and struck out at him. "Of course. Is not servicing her husband a wife's duty, be she queen or slave?"

"If that is how you feel, I shall not trouble you again." Ashtyn reached for his tunic and pulled it over his head while she watched. She could tell he was angry by the force he used to lace his boots.

He stood, gazing at her. "I will send you reports of the war when I can."

Thalia knew one word from her would bring him

back to her bed, but pride would not allow her to do that. "You are leaving?"

Ashtyn's voice was devoid of feeling when he said, "I feel I must. Look for me when the sails of Egyptian ships are spotted."

With closed eyes, Thalia listened to his footsteps recede and fade. She wanted to run after him and beg his forgiveness for her cruel words. Instead, she rolled over, placing her hand on her stomach, loving the baby because it was a part of Ashtyn.

CHAPTER TWENTY-NINE

The hour had taken a turn toward morning as a cloaked figure carrying a bundle of clothing moved noiselessly down the palace corridor. Dodging past lighted torches, the person attempted to stay within the shadows and finally slipped out a door into a garden. After avoiding the guards and climbing over several garden walls, the figure came to the queen's private garden. When two guards passed nearby, the person flattened against the wall, waiting for them to leave.

Pausing at the archway that led into the queen's chamber, the intruder quietly stepped inside. The person's gaze flew about the room, making sure the queen was alone. Cautiously, the individual moved forward, and slowly pulled back the curtains to stare down at the queen.

Thalia had not slept the night before. Overcome with doubts, once again she'd spoken her mind and made Ashtyn angry. Lord Parinez informed her Ashtyn had left that morning and he was not sure when he'd return.

If only Ashtyn had come to her before he left.

A slight sound caught her attention, and she lay still, her eyes only half-open, trying to see who it was. Her heart pounding with fear, she was about to call out to the guards posted at her door when a hand landed on her shoulder, and she heard a woman whisper.

"Majesty, it is I, Eleni."

Thalia threw back the cover and slowly rose, trying to shake the fear she'd felt only moments ago. "Eleni? What are you doing here?"

The young woman dropped to her knees. "My Queen, I have come to you with a message, and this was the only way I could reach you."

Thalia pulled on her green wrap, her fear subsiding, but she was still puzzled by Eleni's strange reasoning. "What is so important you come unannounced in the dead of night?" Sharp moonlight spilled across marble floors, and Thalia could see Eleni's careworn face. "I would have seen you if you had asked it of me."

"I did ask for an audience with you, and it was denied."

Thalia frowned. "By whom?"

"The guards at the palace steps. This place is like a fortress."

"And yet you managed to reach my quarters." Thalia was beginning to become agitated with the woman. "Who sent you with a message?"

Eleni glanced at her through lowered lashes. "'Tis Lord Sevilin who begs to speak with you."

Thalia spun around and stared at Eleni. "You dare come here to speak for that man? I thought you were to be trusted—I thought you were my friend."

Distressed words spilled from Eleni's lips. "You can always trust me, Majesty. Lord Sevilin came to me because he knew I cared about your welfare."

The first inkling of suspicion tingled inside Thalia. "What can that man possibly have to say that I would want to hear?"

"Lord Sevilin said the war is lost, and his mother fears for her life. He wants to surrender, but only to you. He has asked if you will allow him and his mother to sail away without harm." She looked dejected. "That is all I was told—I know nothing more."

Thalia placed no trust in the leader of the rebels. "How did Lord Sevilin approach you?"

"Through a man called Turk. I am to remind you that Turk kept his word to you, and you came to no harm from him. He asks that you trust him."

Thalia paced across the chamber and back. "That man is no friend to me, nor do I trust him." She paused thoughtfully. "You may return to Turk with this message: Lord Sevilin and his mother will be given safe passage here to the palace. I will hear their terms of surrender and make my decision at that time."

Eleni rushed to Thalia, then went down on her knees. "I was told to show you this if you should refuse to meet with Lord Sevilin." She reached into her sash and withdrew something small and gold and handed it to Thalia.

Thalia's face froze, and she stared at the signet ring with a gold arrow through a red shield. "That is my husband's!"

Tears rolled down Eleni's face as she clutched at Thalia's gown. "I was not supposed to tell you Lord

Ashtyn was their prisoner unless you refused to see Lord Sevilin alone."

Thalia clutched at the girl's arm and made her rise, searching her eyes. "How can I know what you say is true?"

"Turk said he'd captured Lord Ashtyn a day ago while he was on his way to rejoin his men."

"I don't believe him. My husband would never allow himself to be captured by rebels."

"Then how did they get his ring, Majesty?"

Thalia clutched the ring so tightly in her fist, it cut into her flesh. Staring at the golden gong just over Eleni's shoulder, Thalia wrestled with the thought of calling the guards to her. "Then I shall send a man to wake the soldiers in the barracks so they can accompany me to rescue my husband."

Eleni's face whitened. "I was told if you did not come alone, Count Ashtyn would be slain before you could reach the rendevous point." Eleni looked frightened. "I am sorry, Majesty. I believe they will do just that. What have they to lose?"

Thalia was still not convinced. "How did Turk locate you?"

"I had returned to my village in the mountains to live in the house my aunt left me. Turk sought me there."

Thalia was torn.

"Where am I to meet Lord Sevilin?"

"Turk said he would be waiting near the mountain road to take you to the rebel camp. I have horses waiting in the outer courtyard. I was told you should dress as a servant, and I have brought you clothing so no one will recognize you when we ride out the gate."

Everything was too well thought out, and it sounded like a trap. But if Lord Sevilin was holding Ashtyn prisoner, Thalia had no choice. "I will accompany you, but if this is a trap, you will be branded as a traitor."

Eleni bowed her head, waiting for the queen to dress herself in the plain homespun woolen gown and cloak.

Thalia picked up her jewel-handled dagger and shoved it into her sash, fearing for Ashtyn. "Let us go. But if they have spilled one drop of my husband's blood, they will pay with their lives!"

The yawning guard paid scant attention to the two servant women who rode out the front gate. After all, he was supposed to search those entering, not those who left. He covered another yawn and blinked his eyes to stay awake. If the captain caught him napping, it would be the worst for him.

But a wiser eye than the young guard observed the two women. The old woman, Didra, hobbled onto the roadway to watch two horses disappear around a corner. She hurried as fast as her aching knees would allow her, and watched them take the road leading toward the mountain path.

Her all-seeing eye blinked. Why would the queen sneak out of the palace in the dead of night? The old woman was certain nothing good could come of it.

"Nay," she said aloud. "There is trickery here." She hobbled toward the palace, her pace slow and painful.

The moon was high above the treetops as Eleni led the queen away from the main road to a path that sloped steeply downward. All Thalia could think of was Ashtyn. He would have fought his enemies if they tried to capture him; therefore, he must be injured. Fear crept into her heart. What if he was dead?

Thalia could not allow herself to ponder such thoughts.

At one point the incline was so steep they had to dismount and lead the horses the rest of the way to the bottom.

"Turk said he'd meet us here," Eleni said, glancing around her. "He should have been waiting for us. I wonder why he isn't?"

"Aye. I am here," spoke the man Thalia had hoped never again to encounter. She slowly turned to face him, anger burning inside her. "Where is my husband?"

Turk looked not at her but just above her head, as if he was hesitant to meet her gaze. "Such a stern greeting for an old friend. I was sure you'd be happy to see me."

"We have never been friends. Take me to my husband at once!" Thalia demanded.

At last he looked at her. "I do believe you are blooming. Bal Forea seems to agree with you. Or perhaps 'tis Prince Ashtyn who is responsible for the bloom on your cheeks?"

"I did not come here to trade pleasantries with you. Take me to my husband."

"Aii," he said with a pretended shiver, "you now sound like a queen. How quickly our little mouse turned into a roaring lion."

"You tricked me! You do not have my husband! How did you come by Ashtyn's ring?"

Turk laughed. "It was not difficult to have a gold-smith duplicate it."

A prickle of unease touched the back of Thalia's neck and slid down her spine. She turned to Eleni, who was cowering near her horse. "How could you be-tray me?"

"Don't blame the poor woman. She likes a particu-lar color—gold." Turk tossed a pouch to Eleni. "Enjoy your reward. And remember this," he said, reaching out to grip Thalia's wrists, "no one likes a betrayer, so do not seek sanctuary in any rebel camp."

Eleni refused to meet Thalia's angry gaze, but her mouth narrowed spitefully. She ducked her head and led her horse away. Then she stopped and glanced back. "I did not want to betray you, Majesty. But you betrayed me first."

Thalia was appalled at the woman's accusation. "It is said that the weak thrust the blame for their mis-deeds on others because they cannot look into their own hearts and see the evil there. To have betrayed someone who trusted you is something you will have to live with for the rest of your life."

Turk glanced down at Thalia. "You would never be-tray a friend, little Queen. Your heart is truer than the gold given that woman."

"You let Lord Parinez dismiss me," Eleni stated spitefully. "You never asked for me."

Thalia shook her head in disgust. "It would seem my good lord chamberlain is a better judge of charac-ter than I."

With a grim smile, Turk said, "See how tall trees grow from small seeds. In Eleni's mind, you were sup-posed to raise her up when you became queen—to her way of reasoning, you turned your back on her. It is always the same with those who take the crown." He clicked his tongue and looked at Eleni. "You should have expected it."

"I befriended this woman." Thalia glanced at Eleni. "Had you come to me, I would have found you a position at the palace. You know this to be true."

"I would never have begged," the woman spat. "My family all died for Bal Forea, and where are their rewards?"

"Hear this, Eleni. I am queen, and one day you shall stand before me and be judged for your treachery."

Although Thalia could not see the woman's face, she felt her shrink from her. A short time later, she heard Eleni ride away.

Thalia turned her attention back to Turk. "You did not capture my husband, did you?"

"If we could have captured Prince Ashtyn, he would have been in our prison long ago. But you came, Majesty, just as I knew you would. That's inexperience for you."

"Take me to your puppet master so we may get this thing done. I assume you are taking me to the traitor and coward, Lord Sevilin."

"Mount up," Turk said, reaching out to grab her horse's reins and yanking them forward. He no longer made an attempt to hide his anger as he said, "You will soon discover who is a traitor, and who has honor."

"Turk," Thalia said, knowing she was his prisoner, "I am learning quickly who to trust. I should have remembered how doggedly you hunted me throughout the years. I feared you, I disliked you, but I never considered you would not be a man of your word. You had Eleni bring me here under false pretenses."

The big man blinked his eye as if she'd struck him. He helped her onto her horse and led her toward the distant woods.

❦Chapter Thirty

Old Didra stared at the palace guard through her one good eye. "Let me pass—I must see Lord Parinez at once. If you do not let me through, you'll be the cause of the queen being harmed."

"Get you gone, old crone. What can you have to say that the lord chamberlain would want to hear?"

"Heed my words carefully, fool. Did you perchance see two women ride out of this gate a short time ago?"

"Aye. Servants they were." The guard shifted his weight from one foot to the other, uneasy under her scrutiny. "But what use is that information to Lord Parinez?"

"For this reason: One of them was a betrayer, and the other was the queen. If you don't take me to the lord chamberlain, it will be too late to save the queen. Then you will have to answer to Prince Ashtyn."

The young guard looked uncertain, wondering if the old woman could be telling the truth. "Go there to the guard at the inner courtyard and tell him your tale. If he'll let you in, you can see Lord Parinez."

When it was discovered the queen was not in her bedchamber, Lord Parinez acted without delay.

Just before dawn, a patrol of soldiers rode at breakneck speed out of the courtyard and toward the mountain pass, while Didra was seated at a sturdy table, enjoying a fine slice of lamb and a cup of sweet wine in the palace kitchen.

Didra reached for the carafe and poured more wine in her cup. Closing her eyes, she savored every drop. And if the lord chamberlain was a man of his word—and she had no reason to think otherwise—she would be taken home in a cart.

The overhead trees shut out the moon, making it almost impossible to see the narrow path that led through the woods. But Turk knew the way and led Thalia through so many twists and turns she was dizzy. She was also bone-weary and almost thankful when they rode out of the woods, where a stone fortress was obscured by bushes and trees.

Turk lifted Thalia from her horse. "Have no fear. You will come to no harm," he assured her.

Thalia said nothing as he led her into the fortress, past a room that appeared to be the kitchen, then through an armory. She pulled back when she realized he was leading her down a long stairway. He gently urged her forward to a place Thalia could only assume was the dungeon.

He nodded at a man who unlocked a small cell. "Just so you don't take it into your head to flee," Turk assured her.

Heartsick and frightened, Thalia walked inside, staring up at the small window, where she saw only gray darkness. She stepped lightly over the straw that was strewn on the floor and turned back to stare at Turk.

What was going to happen to her?

No one would know where she was being held, so there was faint chance of being rescued. When Turk turned to leave and the guard followed him, she glanced around at the empty cells, where torchlight reflected eerily on the stone walls, and she wanted to call them back.

Thalia didn't have to wait long before the sound of footsteps echoed through the dungeon, and she braced herself for what was to come. Staring at the woman who came toward her in a swirl of red silk, Thalia thought she might have once been pretty, even beautiful, but a belligerent nature had carved deep wrinkles on her face.

"Do you know who I am, girl?" The woman's screeching voice shattered the silence.

Thalia dropped the hood of her cloak as the woman unlocked the cell and stepped inside. "I can guess who you are."

Lady Vistah stared at Thalia with pure hatred, her mouth compressed in a thin line. "You have cursed my life, caused me years of grief. If it was left to me, I would see you dead, but my son has other ideas." Thalia watched the woman's eyes darken. "My son is sometimes misguided."

"More than a little misguided, Lady Vistah. Your son is responsible for the deaths of thousands of innocents."

The older woman's mouth twisted with bitterness. "Just because you wear the crown of Bal Forea does not make you a queen," she spat. "It takes much more than that to hold the throne."

"One with a malignant mind like your son will never win the people," Thalia said angrily.

Thalia had not expected it, and when the woman delivered the hard blow with her fist, Thalia's head snapped back from the force of it. Then the woman struck her again, causing her to fall to her knees, and it was with great effort that Thalia shook off the darkness that threatened to consume her.

With pride driving her, Thalia rose to her feet, ignoring the pain each movement caused. With an angry glare, she met the woman's cold, cunning eyes. Wiping blood from her mouth onto the back of her hand, Thalia said scornfully, "And it takes more than bars to hold a queen. Do you think I don't know you have no army left? You have lost. It is time for you to admit this and take the justice the people will demand for you."

"Upstart! Impostor! You are like your mother—she also dreamed of the impossible, and you know what happened to her. She died in a fire trying to save you. Little good it did her to run away with her lover."

With sudden sadness came knowledge. A scrap of memory of a horrible fire, and a woman trying to save her—it had been her mother. The once-fragmented childhood memory now flooded her mind—her mother shoving her into the arms of her maid, and the maid running and hiding with Thalia in her arms. She knew that she was now staring into the eyes of the woman who had ordered her mother's death.

Thalia's lip was throbbing, and she could tell it was swollen. She blinked back tears of pain and grief. She would not allow this woman to see her cry. Thalia faced her enemy. "It was you who sent Turk to hunt for me in Rome."

"Aye, it was me. As soon as I heard of your birth, I

decided I must have you under my control. When my son was old enough to understand the significance of controlling you, he sent others to find you. Long have you escaped me, but I have you now!"

Thalia tore her gaze from Lady Vistah when she heard footsteps on the stairs. With growing fear, she watched as a tall man with piercing blue eyes walked toward her, flanked by Turk. He stood at the bars, looking at her for a long moment before he entered the cell.

"Mother, why is this woman bleeding?" Sevilin asked in a hard voice.

"I gave her some of what she deserved," Lady Vistah said spitefully, moving to slap Thalia once again—but her son caught her wrist and held it firmly.

"Do not touch her," he ordered through clenched teeth. "I want no mark on her." His hard gaze went to Thalia. "Remove your cloak so I can better see what we have here," he demanded.

She was trying to push the memory of that horrible night when her mother had died out of her mind, but her anger helped her defy this man. "Nay," she said with iron-willed stubbornness, "I will not."

The man seemed undaunted by her refusal. "I am Lord Sevilin, and this is my mother, Lady Vistah. I am sure you have heard of us."

"I have heard both of you mentioned, though nothing good was said of either of you. But let me amend that," she said, staring at Turk. "Your sycophant here speaks of you with praise and believes anything you tell him. More's the pity."

Turk frowned, and Lord Sevilin smiled. "I like a woman with spirit. Tell me, what did Turk say about me, Majesty?"

"He said you were handsome." She looked over his blue eyes, long flowing golden hair and broad shoulders. "You are handsome. 'Tis a pity you are a man without honor, because that makes you repugnant in my eyes."

Sevilin's brows came together in a frown. "For years I have wondered what you look like, and now I will see for myself," he said, reaching for Thalia, but she quickly drew back until she came up against the wall.

Sevilin shook his head, then advanced toward her. With an easy smile, he unhooked her woolen cape, and it fell to the floor.

For a long moment he stared at Thalia, and even laughed when she lifted her head to a royal tilt.

"I have long dreamed of you," Lord Sevilin said. "But no dream can do you justice." His hand moved down her neck to cup her breast. "Sweet and young. I will have all of you before too many days have passed."

Thalia thrust his hand away. "I would rather die than have you touch me, snake."

His smile was as frightening as his mother's anger.

"But you will not die, Majesty, and I shall touch you. You will be my wife—how would you like that?"

"I have a husband," she said, glaring at him. "You do not seem a foolish man to me—if you value your life, you will set me free before Ashtyn arrives."

"Beautiful and brave. What a pair the two of us will make."

"Never!"

"Strike her for speaking so insultingly," his mother cried. "Show her the power of your fists!" Lady Vistah gripped the bars. "Strike her down!"

"Nay, Mother. Hold back your anger. Would you

have me bruise such a jewel when I have her where I have always wanted her?"

"What do you intend to do with her?" Lady Vistah demanded, eyeing Thalia with a jaded gaze. "She's already wed to the enemy. So he will have to die."

"Perhaps." Sevilin caught Thalia's face between his hands, bringing her into the light. "If she were to become a widow, our plans can still work."

"The Destroyer will not be easily killed, or the deed would already have been accomplished," Turk reminded him. "Have we not tried in the past, only to fail?"

Thalia studied Sevilin. He had a weak chin and a predatory light in his blue eyes. She saw evil lurking there and shivered. "You cannot win," she told him.

He laughed as he took his mother's hand, leading her out of the cell toward the stairs. "I have already won. What man would not come looking for such a prize?"

Turk laced his twisted fingers so tightly the knuckles whitened. There was surprising kindness in his gaze when he looked at Thalia. "It will be better for you if you do not resist. I would not like to see you come to harm."

"Leave me alone," Thalia said. "You are nothing but a puppet of that evil man and his twisted mother."

Turk studied her face for a moment. "Prince Ashtyn will come for you, and that will be the end of him because he will be falling into a trap."

Fear gripped her heart. "You are evil."

Turk looked taken aback by her assessment of his character. "Nay, Majesty. I merely follow orders."

"I wonder how many men cover their own vice by claiming they are only following orders." She reached her hand out to him, thinking there might be a shred of decency left in him. "Turk, you protected me when you served my mother. There is something I must tell you, and I hope you will keep my secret. I am with child. Do not let them harm my baby."

He walked a few paces toward the stairs and then came back to her. "Put on your cape; it's damp and cold in the dungeon." He looked toward the stairs and lowered his voice. "And say nothing more about the child you carry."

Thalia watched Turk disappear up the stairs, wondering if he would help her or betray her. Stooping, she retrieved her cape and pulled it about her shoulders.

In the torchlight she examined her surroundings. As far as Thalia could see in the dimness, there were three more cells—one was beside hers, and the other two were directly across. The dungeon seemed to have been carved out of the ground, with stone steps leading upward.

She examined the walls and saw many names scratched into the stone. Her fear had kept her from being affected by the stench, but she smelled it now and pressed her hand over her nose. Dirty water pooled on the uneven floor outside the cell, and she shuddered when she saw a rat creep out of the darkness.

Thalia closed her eyes, hoping Ashtyn would *not* come for her. Lord Sevilin's plan was clear—he meant to murder Ashtyn and force her to marry him.

She gripped the bars and leaned her head against them. She must not give up hope.

Having intercepted the lord chamberlain's messenger, who was on his way to Prince Ashtyn's camp, Captain Darius discovered the queen was missing.

Charging the messenger to proceed to the camp with all haste, Captain Darius rode through the inner courtyard of the palace with his bedraggled, battle-weary soldiers, who had been on patrol for three days.

As his men were saddling fresh mounts, Captain Darius studied a map, while Lord Parinez anxiously watched him.

"One among the captives we took today told us the general direction of Lord Sevilin's stronghold. Let us trust to the gods that they have not harmed the queen, or I'll tear it down stone by stone."

"I cannot bear to think of the sweet queen being in that evil man's hands. Make haste, Captain, before it's too late!"

❦ CHAPTER THIRTY-
ONE

In the cold morning mist, Ashtyn stared at the messenger who was babbling and waving his arms. "Curb your exuberance and speak slowly. What about the queen?"

The young recruit took a big gulp of air and met the commander's gaze. "They have taken the queen!"

Ashtyn's eyes narrowed. "Who took her?"

"I don't . . . they did not tell me. Captain Darius wanted you to know he would attempt to track her majesty to the enemy stronghold."

Ashtyn's voice cut like a knife. "Get me a fresh mount at once," he said, racing toward his tent to gather his sword and dagger.

Moments later he reappeared, issuing orders, and then leaped onto his horse. A group of startled soldiers watched their commander leave the encampment, his horse at an all-out run.

The day had come and gone, and no one came to see Thalia. She had sat near the door all night, refusing to lay on the filthy straw mat that served as a bed. Thirst made her tongue stick to the roof of her mouth, but when she glanced at the grimy clay jug that held water, she shook her head. There was no way of knowing how long the water had been there, or what was in it.

Pacing up and down the cell, trying to ignore her hunger, Thalia guessed Lord Sevilin and his mother were trying to wear her down. But she would not give in to them. Her one fear was that Ashtyn would come to rescue her and fall into their trap.

By mid-afternoon thirst drove her to the water jug, and she took only a small sip. It tasted fresh, so she drank deeply. Then she wearily began to pace once more, although her stomach churned and she feared she was going to be sick.

Gripping the bars, she bowed her head. As wave after wave of nausea washed over her, she resisted the need to lie down. Thalia eyed the straw mat with revulsion—it was most probably lice-infected. Instead, she wrapped her cloak around her and sat with her back against the wall. She dared not fall asleep because she did not want anyone to come upon her while she was unaware.

But sleep finally claimed Thalia, and her head fell back against the wall. She had no way of knowing how long she'd slept when she was jerked awake by the sound of scuffling on the stairs. Scrambling to her feet, she heard the sound of clashing swords.

Stumbling to the bars, she gripped them so tightly her knuckles whitened. She hoped it would not be Ashtyn! If Sevilin had both her and Ashtyn as his prisoners, the war would turn in his favor. Or he might try to strike some kind of a bargain with the lord chamberlain.

Suddenly Thalia's heart clenched: she heard a muffled cry of pain and then silence. She held her breath, waiting.

When she saw flashes of light from a lantern streak across the wall, she tensed as several men dragged two prisoners down the stairs.

Ashtyn and Captain Darius!

Captain Darius appeared to be unconscious, and it took two burly men to bear his weight. Blood streaked down Ashtyn's face, and her heart stopped when she saw him stagger. Three men escorted him: two dragging him forward, while the other held a sword to Ashtyn's back.

When he neared her cell, their eyes met. "Are you hurt?" he asked, looking her over.

Before she could answer, one of the men struck him in the head with the hilt of his sword, and Ashtyn went to his knees. Shaking his head, he glared at the man who struck him. "I'll remember your face," Ashtyn warned him.

"There will be no talking," the man said, unlocking one of the cells across from Thalia and shoving Ashtyn inside. Captain Darius was placed in the other cell, still unconscious.

"Please don't hurt them!" Thalia cried out.

One of the men, broad-shouldered with long black hair, spun toward her, advancing with quick steps. "I'll wring your pretty neck if you say anything more. You're the cause of all our trouble," he said angrily.

"Hold," Turk said, suddenly appearing at the foot of the stairs. "You will not speak to the queen with such disrespect. You were told to deliver the prisoners to their cells, and nothing more."

"That one," he said, indicating Ashtyn, "said things I didn't like."

Turk's mouth stiffened into a cruel smile. "Your life

has no worth. But that man," he nodded sharply at Ashtyn, "is married to the queen."

"Little I care," the man mumbled. "She'll soon be a widow."

Turk grabbed the man by the neck and held him above his head while the man struggled and kicked, making a strangling sound. As Thalia looked on in horror, Turk dropped the man, who coughed and clutched his throat, trying to catch his breath.

"Never disobey one of my orders," Turk intoned harshly. "For the next time, you will die." He glanced at the other men, who had been watching the commotion. "Get up those stairs. You, Mored," Turk said, tossing the keys to a slender youth with shoulder-length black hair, "you I place in charge of the prisoners' needs. Have a care for the queen."

Thalia waited until the men left before she spoke to Ashtyn. "You are hurt. How bad is it?"

Her husband shook his head and rose to his feet, wiping blood out of his eyes so he could see. "I am more concerned about the dried blood I see on your face." He gripped the bars and shook them, needing to get to her "What did they do to you?"

"Think not of that." She met Ashtyn's gaze, agonizing over the fact that she'd been the cause of his capture. "I fear by my foolishness we are lost." She quickly told him everything that had happened with Eleni, and watched the growing dread gather in his eyes. "I trusted her, and she betrayed me."

"Betrayal is a bitter dreg to swallow," he told her. "But the guilt is not yours. It was the king who placed that woman near you, thinking he could trust her."

Thalia gathered her cloak tighter about her because

the dampness of the dungeon had chilled her to the bone. "Why did you come after me? Did you not sense you were riding into a trap?"

Ashtyn lowered his voice. "Knowing Sevilin as I do, I had no doubt he was trying to lure me to him. But I didn't come without a plan to get you free." He glanced toward the stairs with a frown creasing his brow, then looked back at Thalia. "First, we will have to get out of these cells."

Thalia felt somewhat relieved because Ashtyn was so confident. "I fear for Captain Darius," she said, looking over at him.

At that moment, the big man moaned and struggled slowly to a sitting position. Using the bars for leverage, he stood, blinking. "Where are we?"

"Never mind that," Ashtyn told him. "The question is how we are going to get out of here."

Thalia smiled. "Leave that to me. I know just what to do."

As the two men looked on with concern, she bent over, clutching her stomach. "Help me!" she cried, loud enough for her voice to carry out of the dungeon and up the stairs. "Someone help me!"

The guard, Mored, came running down the stairs. "Here now, what's this commotion?"

"Help me," Thalia said, dropping to her knees. "I'm in pain." She lowered her head so he would not see her eyes. "Terrible pain."

Mored, who was in awe of the queen even if she was the enemy, quickly unlocked the cell and shoved the keys in his belt while he bent to help her stand. "Can I get you something? Water? Would you like wine?"

Ashtyn gripped the bars and shook them. "Let me out! Let me help the queen!"

Thalia was moaning, and she threw her arms about the big man's waist. "I feel sick," she cried. "The water here is foul. Perhaps if you brought me a fresh jug?"

With growing concern, Mored gently seated Thalia on the floor and hurried out, locking the cell behind him.

"Are you ill?" Ashtyn said, shaking the bars, frustrated because he could not get to Thalia.

"Shh! I am not ill."

The guard reappeared with a fresh jug of water. Bending, he held a dipper for Thalia to drink from. "How fare you now, Majesty?" he asked, knowing he would be held responsible if anything happened to her.

Thalia pushed tangled hair out of her face, giving the poor guard a smile that made him smile in return. "You have been most kind. Help me up, and let me lean on you for a moment until the dizziness passes."

He was most compliant, and held her while she reached around his waist. "I shall not forget your kindness. Should the time ever come when I can stay someone's hand from causing your death, I shall do so."

Puzzled, the young guard looked at her. "I do not think that time will come, Majesty."

All Ashtyn could do was watch helplessly. "Bring the queen to my cell so I can have her with me," he called.

"Nay," Mored replied, as Thalia moved away from him. "My orders are to keep you separated." He watched the queen for a moment. "Are you still dizzy?"

She reached out to Mored, and he took the hand she

offered. "Just stay with me for a moment more," she said, looking pale and shaken.

It was easy for Ashtyn to see that Mored's attitude was softening toward Thalia, or perhaps it was the man's fear of retribution from Turk that made him attentive. Whatever the reason, Ashtyn was infuriated by the guard touching his wife.

Mored's hand was gentle as he patted the queen on the shoulder. "Rest a bit. That's what you should do." He smiled as he stepped out of the cell and turned the key in the lock before fastening it to his belt. "Is there anything else you need?"

Thalia reached through the bars and caught his hand. "Just stay with me a moment. I am frightened."

The concerned guard slid his hand up her arm, and when Thalia glanced over at Ashtyn, she could tell from his expression that he wanted to kill the man. She gave her head a slight shake so her husband would know she was only acting, but she wasn't sure he understood what she was doing because he glared at her.

"I am feeling much revived," Thalia said, smiling at Mored. "Perhaps I shall lie down."

Mored looked her over carefully. "If you need me, call out—I'm just up those stairs in the armory, so I will have no trouble hearing you."

All three prisoners watched the guard leave, then both men looked startled when Thalia laughed. "What was the meaning of that little display?" Ashtyn demanded.

Dangling the keys, Thalia said, smiling, "Husband, you know I was a very fine pickpocket on the streets of Rome. It seems that becoming a queen has not caused me to lose my skills."

Ashtyn watched in amazement as Thalia unlocked her cell, then hurried to unlock the other two. He grabbed her and held her in his arms as if he would never let her go.

Captain Darius was busy looking about for something to use as a weapon.

"At first I feared you were in pain. Then you—" Ashtyn's grip tightened. "Don't ever do that again."

"I had to make it look convincing for the guard to believe me." She smiled up at him proudly. "Are you not impressed by my skills?"

He held her to him for a moment longer, then released her. "We have to find a way out of here, and I don't have a weapon."

She dangled her own jewel-handled dagger from her fingers. "They did not search me before they locked me in the cell." Thalia arched her brow at Ashtyn. "Despite my skills as a thief, I must have an honest face."

He touched her cheek. "Thalia. My Thalia."

"Commander," Captain Darius said, gripping a long wooden pole that had been propped against the wall, "if you don't mind my saying so, we would be better served if we got out of here."

Ashtyn's face took on a guarded look, and Thalia saw his jaw harden and his eyes narrow as the warrior in him emerged. He shoved her behind him and gripped the dagger. "Let us make our way to the armory."

Silently they crept up the stairs, with Captain Darius in the lead and Ashtyn keeping Thalia just behind him.

When they reached the armory, Thalia saw that Mored had nodded off, a jug of wine on a table next to him.

With a quick thrust, Captain Darius's staff came

down on his head, and the poor man crumpled to the floor, never knowing what had hit him. When Captain Darius would have struck him again, Thalia reached out and grabbed the staff. "I made him a promise. He will live."

Footsteps sounded outside the door, and Ashtyn grabbed one of the swords from the wall hook, turning to face the three men who rushed at him. Before the guards knew what was happening, Ashtyn and Captain Darius were before them. In a short time the rebels were disarmed, two bleeding, the other probably dead. They moved hurriedly toward the door when a shadow fell across the wall, and Turk stepped into their path.

"Yield or die," Turk said to Ashtyn.

"It will not be me who dies here today," Ashtyn said, striking the first blow, which Turk easily sidestepped.

Thalia could do no more than watch. Turk had been a gladiator, a trained fighter, and he was at least a head taller than Ashtyn, and much larger. Turk swung his sword and caught Ashtyn across the arm, barely scratching the skin.

"I shall make the queen a widow this day," Turk threatened, swinging wide with his sword.

Ashtyn caught the thrust with his own blade. "You boast, but I see sweat on your brow. Age has dulled your sight, and you are losing your skills," he taunted, knowing that if he could anger Turk, the big man might become careless.

Turk swung swiftly, his blade clanging against Ashtyn's. The two men fought, neither gaining the advantage, while Thalia could only watch, fearing for her husband.

Suddenly Ashtyn stumbled and went to his knees.

Pain twisted his features as Turk's sword struck again, but Ashtyn managed to roll away quickly so the sword struck his breastplate. Still, the blow was delivered with great force, and Ashtyn reeled backwards.

Turk raised his sword, ready to deliver the final blow. Thalia cried out to him. "Turk, no—please don't!"

For the merest moment, Turk turned his gaze to the queen, and that gave Ashtyn the advantage he needed. Slamming his sword upward, he buried it deeply into Turk's chest.

For a moment the big man looked amazed. He crumpled to his knees and reached out to Thalia. ". . . My Queen," he uttered, falling forward. He twitched, and then died.

Tears sprung to Thalia's eyes. Some part of her pitied the man, but at last she was free of him.

Ashtyn gripped her arm, hurrying her out of the armory. Silently, they slipped out the side door and made their way away from the stronghold, into the woods.

Once they were under cover, Ashtyn went down on his knees and took Thalia in his arms. "I thought I had lost you," he murmured.

She touched his face. "I am not so easy to lose. But you are injured. Let us find a place where we can treat your wounds."

Suddenly they were surrounded by Ashtyn's own loyal troops, who had been waiting for the signal to strike the fortress. "We weren't sure when you'd come out," one of his men stated. "We considered going in after you."

"We will never have a better time to hit the enemy than now, when he is at his weakest," Ashtyn told his men. "I am taking the queen away from here. From what I gathered, there are but a few men holding the stronghold. If Lord Sevilin is in there, spare him if you can. He has much to answer for. I shall return as soon as I see the queen to safety."

Moments later, Thalia found herself on a horse in front of her husband.

Captain Darius moved back toward the sound of fighting and called over his shoulder, "We'll make short work of these rebels, Commander."

As Ashtyn's horse climbed the hill, there was already the sound of swords clashing all around the compound. Ashtyn held Thalia against him and felt her tremble. "Do not fear defeat—your soldiers will win the day."

"There were moments in that dungeon I feared I'd never see you again," she said, resting her head on his shoulder.

"There was no danger of that. The rebels had something that belonged to me, and only the gods could have kept me from getting to you."

Thalia felt his arms go around her, one of his hands resting on her stomach, where his baby was nestled.

"Thalia," he whispered, his voice breaking. "My sweet, unpredictable Thalia."

CHAPTER THIRTY-TWO

When they reached the road that led to the palace, Thalia saw a sight to behold. Her citizens, young and old, women and children alike, were hurrying toward them in large numbers. They all clutched whatever weapons were available to them—brooms, rusted spears, limbs from trees.

She glanced up at her husband. "What can this mean?"

A roar of joy shattered the countryside as the crowd saw their queen.

"I believe," Ashtyn said with humor, "your loyal citizens were coming to rescue you."

Nestled in her husband's arms, Thalia smiled at her subjects as they gathered around Ashtyn's horse. "Thank you," she said with tear-bright eyes. "Thank you with all my heart."

When Thalia entered the palace, she was immediately surrounded by servants. Uzza had food and drink brought in for the two weary travelers, while Lord Parinez dismissed everyone and led them to a small chamber.

Ashtyn quickly explained to the lord chamberlain

how they'd escaped, and Lord Parinez beamed. "Your Majesty," he said with a teasing tone that few had ever heard in his voice, "You are to be commended for sneaking the keys away from the guard." He leaned forward and laughed. "As word spreads of your deed, you will gain even greater glory."

Thalia was seated on a low stool and began to tremble. "You must also know, my Lord Chamberlain, I was frightened. Lord Sevilin is a truly evil man, and his mother even worse."

"Yet you are safe now, Majesty, and all your subjects will celebrate your return."

Ashtyn stood, tightening the buckles on his breastplate. "The queen needs food and rest, and I must rejoin my troops."

Thalia came to her feet, noticing how weary he looked. "Surely you can rest first! That wound on your head needs tending."

Ashtyn took Thalia's hand and led her to the door so they could speak alone. "Remain in the palace, and do not go about without your guard. If Sevilin escapes my men, he will be dangerous."

"I will take no more chances with our baby."

His eyes softened, and he touched her face. "Rest." Without another word, he walked away, leaving her staring after him.

Lord Parinez came up beside her. "He's right, Majesty. You should rest now."

"I fear for my husband," she admitted.

"Majesty, there is not a mightier warrior in this land than Prince Ashtyn." His face suddenly creased into a frown. "We captured the servant, Eleni. She awaits your judgment."

Anger tore through Thalia. "Bring her to me at once!"

"Should you not rest?" he asked kindly.

"Nay. Not until I see the traitor."

Evening shadows had crept across the chamber floor as Eleni stood before Thalia, her hands clasped in front of her, her head bowed. Thalia silently walked around her and then spoke, "I wanted to see what a traitor looked like, so I will recognize friend from foe the next time I meet with one of your kind."

"Majesty," Eleni pleaded, "have mercy! I have heard that you gave pardon to the rebels who fought for Lord Sevilin. Have you none for me?"

"There is a difference between you and the rebels: I knew them for the enemies they were, whereas you masqueraded as a loyal citizen. Surely you can discern the difference."

Eleni raised tear-bright eyes to Thalia. "It was the gold, Majesty. Gold corrupts when you haven't any."

"And therein lies the malignancy. A person who can cast aside loyalty for gold is tainted."

"What is to be my punishment?"

Thalia turned to Lord Parinez, who was watching along with two fierce-looking guards stationed at the door. "Where is the gold she was given by Turk?"

"It was placed in the treasury."

"Give it back to her."

The lord chamberlain frowned. "Pardon me, Majesty?"

"This person sold her honor for that gold, and she shall keep it. But this is my judgment on you, Eleni. You are to be banished from Bal Forea for the rest of your life. The time will come when the gold is used up, and you will understand what your greed has cost you."

Eleni was sobbing and reaching out to Thalia. "Please, Gracious Majesty—my life is here. I know nothing else. Do not send me away!"

"Take her from my sight—keep her confined until the next ship sails for Rome. Perhaps the Romans will welcome her."

Without a backward glance, Thalia left the room, closing her eyes as she walked down the corridor, listening to the traitor's cries fade into silence.

A messenger arrived the next morning. The rebels had been flushed out of the stronghold, and many captured. Some had died. Among the dead was Lady Vistah, who had been thrown and trampled by her own horse while trying to escape.

There was no personal message from Ashtyn, but the rider assured his queen that the prince was in health and in pursuit of the last of the rebels.

As Thalia lay in her bed, she sent all her thoughts to the gods, beseeching them to put an end to this war. The people had suffered enough, and she wanted them to know what peace felt like.

Hot tears scalded her eyes. She was no longer the free-spirited girl who had driven her chariot into Alexandria that day not so long ago. Before too many months passed, she would be a mother. Her stomach was softly rounded, although she had not yet felt the baby quicken within her.

Thalia had little doubt that the conflict was all but over, and Ashtyn would be returning home. They had a country to rebuild—a bankrupt country where the people had barely enough food to survive.

She sighed and turned over in her bed, wondering if Ashtyn was thinking about her. Though they had been through so much together, Thalia had no knowledge of what his feelings were for her.

He respected her, she knew that.

He honored her as his queen, she knew that.

He was loyal to her as a husband, she knew that.

But was his heart still bound to the other woman he had spoken of? She did not know the answer to that.

Heavy-hearted, Ashtyn sheathed his bloody sword. So many of his countrymen had been slain in this useless conflict. And now the war was over, and he'd have to deal with peace. Weariness swamped him, for he hadn't slept in four days. The last battle had been the bloodiest, as the defeated rebels fought for their lives.

There was one last requirement that needed his attention before Ashtyn could go home and lay down his sword. He dismounted and motioned to Captain Darius. "Bring me the prisoner."

Moments later Sevilin was led before Ashtyn, his shackles rattling as he stumbled forward. Sevilin's hair was matted and so dirty it was hard to see what color it was. His armor was bloodied and battered, but he stood erect, with a snarl on his lips.

"It is over, Sevilin."

"If you expect me to beg, you will be disappointed. But I would ask that you meet me in battle so I can die with honor."

Ashtyn met the cold blue stare. "I do not expect

you to beg—I expect you to die like the traitor you are. I will not cross swords with you; that death is offered only to the worthy."

Sevilin's mouth thinned. "You think you have it all—Bal Forea, the beautiful young queen. But there are many who will always be loyal to me—they will never forget that we fought for a great cause."

Ashtyn shook his head. "There is no one left who is loyal to you, and, if you are remembered at all, it will be as a defeated man. When Bal Foreans hear your name mentioned, they will despise you for tearing their country apart."

There was a long silence before Sevilin spoke. His hands were trembling, and he went to his knees. "It's her doing—it was her plan."

"I suppose you speak of your mother?"

Sevilin dropped his gaze. "I am not sorry she died."

Ashtyn turned to Captain Darius. "When this traitor is dead, bury him in the woods so no one will ever find his remains."

Hearing the chains rattle as he walked away, Ashtyn felt his heart lighten. The people would soon be reunited under one banner. He thought of Thalia and the part she had played in the victory, although he doubted she understood how important that part had been. She had seen to it that the women and children had survived hunger, and she had given the men hope, and someone to rally around.

He frowned. Word was that eight Egyptian ships had been sighted on the horizon. He doubted there would be a fight. Thalia would not allow that. Her brother Ramtat was coming to take her back to Egypt.

To live without her would be like death, but he would

not stop her if she wanted to leave. His only hope was that she would stay for the sake of the people . . . and for their child.

His mind was filled with thoughts of golden hair brushing against soft shoulders. Eyes so blue they rivaled the blue of the sky. He thought of making love to her and groaned. No woman had ever stirred his passion as deeply. He missed the sound of her laughter, and even the way her eyes sparkled when she was angry. He reached out his hand as if to touch her.

If she left him, he would never know another happy day until his death.

Whatever happened, he would be there early in the morning so he could ride beside Thalia to meet the arriving ships.

❧ CHAPTER THIRTY-THREE

Bal Forea had never seen a sight such as the fleet of Egyptian ships sailing into the harbor. Frightened women scooped up their children and ran into their huts, barring their doors. Battle-weary men gathered what weapons were available to them, even knowing they would be useless against the might of Egypt. Although the rebels had been dispatched, a far more deadly foe was sailing into their port.

But for Queen Thalia, watching from the palace balcony, it was the most beautiful sight she'd ever seen. Eight Egyptian warships were entering the harbor, their white sails rippling in the wind.

She turned to Lord Parinez. "Send someone with a message to our own ships to take no overt actions against the Egyptian fleet. They have come in friendship, laden with food to feed the hungry."

Lord Parinez's forehead creased in a frown. "Perhaps they have come to take you back to Egypt."

"My brother Ramtat will be on one of those ships, and he will have many questions." She looked into the blue eyes of the elder statesman she had come to love. "I have a decision to make."

"Do not consider leaving us. You are sorely needed

by your people," he said with feeling. "We love you, Majesty."

"The war is over; can you say with assurance that I'm still needed?"

He reached out to her, but stopped short of touching her hand. "Gracious Majesty, you have done Bal Forea much good. But your subjects are still in need, and they trust you to see them through the rebuilding of the kingdom. This is where you belong."

She lowered her head. "I had a life and people I loved before I came here. My mother was ill when I was taken from her. I fear her health might have worsened. I need to see her, and she needs me."

Lord Parinez bowed low. "May the gods help you decide wisely."

Thalia placed her hand on his blue-veined one. "Lord Parinez, you have stood at my side and taught me what it means to be a queen. You are very dear to me, as are the people of this island. Whatever I decide will be difficult."

"I will see that your guards are made ready. I know you will want to meet the ships."

"I must wear the royal crown to meet my brother— perhaps it will help him understand why I am here," she said, rushing to her chamber.

There was a great uproar when the Egyptians came ashore, leading their spirited war horses down the ramp, their armor gleaming in the sunlight. The people crept to their windows, staring at the two resplendent generals who rode at the head of their troops.

General Ramtat wore his blue and gold Egyptian

uniform, while Rome's General Marcellus wore red and gold. Red silken banners of Rome intermingled with blue Egyptian standards, rippling in the afternoon breeze.

Thalia had just ridden out of the gates of the palace with her honor guard, when Ashtyn suddenly appeared beside her.

She halted her horse and looked him over carefully. Although he was dressed as befitted a general who was about to meet another general, he was weary, she could see it in his eyes. There was a gash on his cheek and one on his hand, evidence of the fierce battle he had fought.

"I did not expect you."

He studied her face with grave scrutiny. "Did you think I would let you face your brother alone?"

Joy spread through Thalia, and she reached out to touch his hand. "Ashtyn, how glad I am the war is ended!" Unashamed tears dampened her eyes. "The people can live in peace at last."

He raised her hand to his lips. "Aye. But after so many years of nothing but war, they must be taught the ways of peace."

In that moment, Thalia recognized her brother riding at the head of his troops, and renewed joy burst from her heart. She dug her heels into her horse's flanks and galloped toward Ramtat in quite an unqueenly manner.

When she neared him, she didn't remember dismounting, but she was suddenly in Ramtat's arms. "My brother!" she cried as he crushed her to him. "How glad I am to see your face."

He pulled back and looked her over carefully, from

the golden crown on her head to the royal purple she wore. "It's true then—you are a queen."

She was unaware that her own people were venturing out of their houses, though they were still wary of the fearsome-looking army.

"It would seem so." She laced her fingers through his. "Tell me about the family—are they all well?"

"Why don't you ask how I am faring, little sister?" Marcellus said, dismounting and pulling her out of Ramtat's arms. "I had not thought to see you so splendidly gowned. And with your shoes on, too."

She lay her head on Marcellus's shoulder. "Tell me about Adhaniá. Is she well?"

"You can ask her yourself. Do you think she would have remained behind?"

Thalia was not sure she could take more happiness. "She is with you!"

"Aye. And Danaë."

Thalia felt sobs building in her throat. "This is a blessed day." She turned back to Ramtat, almost afraid to ask, "Our mother—is she in health?"

"That, too, you can see for yourself. Nothing would keep her from coming on the voyage with us."

Suddenly Ashtyn appeared at Thalia's side. Ramtat reached for his sister and pulled her to him, while Marcellus drew his sword and placed the point at Ashtyn's throat.

Ashtyn had known he would have to answer to Thalia's family, so he did not reach for his own sword, as instinct drove him to do.

"No!" Thalia cried, pulling Marcellus's sword arm away from Ashtyn. "Marcellus, Ramtat, this is Prince Ashtyn, my husband."

"I don't think so," Ramtat said, pulling her back against him. "I will hear all that has happened before I sanction such a marriage."

"I have much to tell you, but first, let me calm my people's fears." Thalia looked at her brother pleadingly. "I beg of you."

Reluctantly, Ramtat nodded, and Marcellus sheathed his sword.

"Have you brought food, as I requested?" Thalia asked, noticing the villagers were venturing closer.

Ramtat nodded toward the ships. "Queen Cleopatra sent enough food to feed this island for years."

Thalia reached for Ashtyn's hand as she spoke to her brother. "Please excuse us while we explain to the people why you are here."

Ramtat glanced at Marcellus as his sister moved away with Prince Ashtyn. "She fears I will harm that man."

Marcellus nodded. "She is wise to keep him with her. Did I not feel the heat of your wrath when I married your other sister?"

Ramtat was watching Thalia closely. "She is different."

"Aye. Our Thalia is a queen in every sense of the word," Marcellus said with pride.

"People of Bal Forea, please gather around, for I have much to say to you." Thalia raised her voice so all could hear. "First of all, you need not fear the Egyptians or Romans. Both generals are my brothers, and they will not harm you."

A murmur rippled through the crowd.

"Also, the ships are loaded with foodstuff from Queen Cleopatra of Egypt. Lord Parinez will appoint an overseer to distribute the food fairly." She turned to her husband. "Prince Ashtyn will now speak to you of glorious tidings."

Ashtyn met her gaze, and then looked back at the gathering crowd. "We have much to celebrate this day. Not only have your queen's kinsmen come to our island, but the war that has lasted so long and taken so many of those we love is over. Lady Vistah and Lord Sevilin are both dead. Take heart, all is well!"

After the roar of happiness had finally subsided, old Didra hobbled to the front of the line, pointing up at the sky, which was filled with hawks circling and riding the wind currents.

"The hawks have returned!" she said, glancing at Widow Craymon. "Just like I said it would happen." There was glee in her heart, and a renewed strength in her aching bones. "You wouldn't believe me when I said this queen would save us—but you can now see it for the truth."

Widow Craymon's eyes bulged as others pointed at the sky. "Aye, there has never been such a day," was all the widow could manage to say past the thickening lump in her throat.

A stunned silence fell over the crowd as they watched the Egyptian and Roman soldiers begin unloading food from the ships.

❧CHAPTER THIRTY-FOUR

It was a happy group that gathered on couches in a small chamber where they exchanged information on what had happened since the day Thalia had been abducted.

Ashtyn stood apart, near the arched doorway, his gaze on his wife's face. He watched her laugh, he watched her smile, and when he saw how much she loved and was loved by her family, his heart ached.

Servants with downcast eyes served food and wine, while Ramtat asked the questions they all wanted to have answered.

Thalia explained to him how she had first been kidnaped by Turk. She caught her husband's eyes as she said. "Ashtyn rescued me from that man."

A short time later, Thalia was seated next to her mother, clasping her hand while they had a private talk. "You look wonderful, Mother."

"My dearest daughter, I knew not what we would find when we arrived, but I find you happy. I am not wrong about that, am I?"

Thalia tried to put her feelings into words to this woman who had always understood her so well. "I have come to know joy in the simplest matters: seeing an orphan cuddled by a woman who lost her own child, seeing my people free of war, and knowing none shall hunger." Thalia looked into her mother's eyes. "I suppose those are not really simple matters. They mean the difference between life and death on this island." She shook her head, not wanting to think of sad events on this wondrous day. "I suppose my four white Badarians and my chariot were stolen?"

"Nay, daughter. Jamal found them and brought them safely home. They will be shipped to you as soon as it can be arranged."

Thalia felt relief, for she had worried about her whites. "I would ask if you would also send Jamal and his family to me. I feel sure he is in disgrace because he could not prevent Turk from taking me."

"He was sent to the Badari encampment in dishonor, but he has been made to suffer enough. He shall be sent to you."

"Jamal could not have saved me, Mother—I would not have him blamed."

Lady Larania nodded toward Ashtyn. "And what about him? He watches you guardedly while pretending to listen to Marcellus, who is trying in his own way to befriend him. No doubt Marcellus remembers when he was forced to face Ramtat's stinging rebuke, so he knows well how your husband feels."

Thalia glanced at her husband and saw uncertainly in his gaze. He was overwhelmed by the family reunion he was no part of. "I love him. He is the finest man I have ever known, honorable and loving, and right now he fears I will leave with you and take his unborn child."

Lady Larania looked uncertain. "And yet, he is the man who abducted you."

"I . . . now know Ashtyn had little choice in the matter," Thalia said hesitantly, hoping she could make her mother understand the circumstances that had brought her to this island. "Ashtyn and my grandfather feared I would fall into the rebel leader's camp. The war might very well have gone differently if Turk had taken me to Sevilin."

Her mother's eyes clouded. "I was so fearful we had lost you."

"I must admit, Mother, there were many dark days for me. But those times have passed." Thalia smiled brightly. "Now that I have been reunited with my family, I can wish for nothing more."

The two women were joined by Adhaniá. "Look at my little sister—a queen!" She leaned close to Thalia and whispered with humor, "Can this be the little guttersnipe I rescued from the streets of Rome?"

"Part of me is still that child," Thalia said in all seriousness. "But I am finding out how difficult it is to be responsible for the well-being of so many people." Thalia turned to her mother. "Much of what you taught me about running a household helped me make many difficult decisions here on the island."

Danaë gave voice to the question they all wanted answered: "Do we take you home with us, little sister?"

Thalia knew in that moment she could never leave Bal Forea. She loved the people, they needed her and she needed them. And Ashtyn, she could never leave him. "While I will grieve for each of you when you leave, my place is here, beside my husband." Thalia searched the room for Ashtyn, but he was not there.

Danaë saw Thalia's distress, and knew the reason

for it. "Your husband asked to be excused. He said something about a matter that needed his attention."

Lady Larania patted Thalia's hand. "I believe that young man could not face the possibility of losing you, my daughter. Go to him, put his mind at ease." She gently shoved Thalia. "Go to him with haste! We shall have plenty of time to talk later. I have decided I shall remain with you until my grandchild is born."

Thalia stood, walking out of the chamber with her family watching her disappear through the curved archway. When she reached the corridor, she started running.

Bursting into her bedchamber, she did not see Ashtyn until he came in from the garden and stared at her.

"I can see why you missed your family. They are quite extraordinary."

"The women in my family are strong-willed, and when they want something, they pursue it."

"And you want to return home," he said dully, his gaze sweeping her face.

"I *am* home."

"Why would you say that?"

Thalia saw hope flicker in his eyes and smiled. "I should have thought that would be obvious."

He searched her face. "Where you are concerned, nothing is obvious to me."

She saw the misery in his silver-blue eyes and knew, in that moment, that he wanted her to stay, not for Bal Forea, but for him. With that knowledge came another revelation. What she saw in his gaze was not worship for a queen, it was love for his wife. Thalia moved toward him. "Name me a reason I should stay, then I shall tell you mine."

"There are the matters of state, and the country needs its queen." He reached for her, then allowed his hand to drop to his side. "But my true reason is more personal. Stay for me." Grief poured from him, visible on the sharp planes of his face.

"Ashtyn, do you not know when a woman loves you above all others? Wherever you are *is* my home. I hope we are never parted, beginning with this night."

He looked doubtful for a moment, then he smiled, drawing her tighter into his arms. "I was so certain you would leave me. I have been agonizing over what to say to keep you here." He held her face between his hands and kissed her. "My dearest love, I have been in the depths of torment."

"Because . . . ?"

"You want me to say it?"

She spoke in earnest, "I do."

"Beloved, I cannot take a breath without thinking of you. Years before I met you, you were a shadow in my mind, and I wanted and desired you. The first time I saw you, I knew my life would never be the same, and it hasn't been. Love has done that to me."

Thalia slid her arms about his waist. "What about the woman that you once wanted to wed?"

Ashtyn looked confused. "I don't know who . . ." Then he smiled. "You mean Shajada."

"I was jealous of your feelings for her," Thalia admitted.

He gave her a slow smile that melted her insides like hot honey. "Were you indeed?" He laughed. "Shajada is nothing to me. She is now the wife of one of my officers and has given him six children. The poor man has to listen to her lecture him from day to night. My Thalia, when you first asked me about her, I could hardly recall her name."

Thalia placed her head on his chest, listening to the beating of his heart. "Did you ever think we would find happiness together?"

He tilted her chin and gazed into her eyes. "I hoped we would." He lifted her in his arms and carried her toward the bed. "Tonight there will be no shadows between us." He laid her down and joined her. "Beloved . . . how many times I wanted to call you by that endearment," he whispered, pressing his mouth against hers. "Has ever a man loved a woman more than I love you at this moment?"

Thalia felt tears on his face, and it brought tears to her eyes. The Destroyer had one weakness, and it was her.

"We shall build a new Bal Forea together so that our sons and daughters will know only peace and prosperity. I will ask Marcellus, who is a master architect, to remain for a while and help us rebuild. And I will ask Queen Cleopatra to open trade with us and help our people prosper." She frowned in thoughtfulness. "And Ramtat will send a herd of Badarian horses, and I will ask him to send Heikki, his master of horse, to train our men in raising the rare breed."

He could not speak as he listened to her plans that would bring peace and prosperity such as Bal Forea had never known. She had the power and family connections to do just what she said.

Ashtyn took her face between his hands and looked

deeply into her eyes, and Thalia could see he was still troubled.

"I have something to ask of you." He hesitated, swallowed and traced her lips with his finger. "Forgive me for taking you out of Egypt in such a harsh manner. I should have gone to Queen Cleopatra and laid the facts before her."

"Ashtyn, do not suffer over what you were forced do. I have come to understand you had no choice. Your one aim was to save Bal Forea, and you did that."

"Then you forgive me?"

She touched his face, loving him so much it hurt. "Without hesitation."

He gathered her close, his body trembling. He buried his face in her silken hair, wondering why the gods had favored him with such a wife.

"You once considered yourself a daughter of Egypt, but you, Gracious Majesty, are the queen of my heart."

❦ EPILOGUE

Egypt

Cleopatra stood on her balcony as she had so many times, staring out at the turbulent sea that splashed waves against the high garden walls. There was a restless stirring within her, an inkling of trouble to come. Octavian was making noises in the Senate of Rome, stirring up the people with the intent to set them against Antony.

Had her ambitions taken her too far—was she the cause of Antony's troubles? True, she was ambitious, and she had convinced Antony to share her ambitions.

But Antony was no Caesar.

How her heart burned with love for Antony. Perhaps it would have been better if she had been happy to remain Queen of Egypt with him at her side. But it was too late to turn aside now—the die had been cast. Trouble was coming their way, and she would have to be prepared.

Cleopatra frowned. Tomorrow she would have the builders begin construction on more war ships. If Octavian came, she would be ready for him.

She heard Antony stirring in the bed, just waking.

With hurried footsteps, she went to him, and he pulled her into his arms.

As his lips touched hers, she felt a coldness in her heart. She would lose him, just as she had lost Caesar, but his loss would take all the joy from her life. She snuggled closer to him, trying to fight against her growing dread.

"Antony," she whispered, "you are the true love of my heart."

His dark gaze settled on her face. "Even more than Caesar?"

How often did she have to convince Antony that her love for Caesar was nothing compared to the love she felt for him? "I love you more than my own life," she admitted.

Even as his mouth found hers, troubles still haunted her mind. She had felt this same emptiness just before Caesar had been assassinated.

Her arms tightened around Antony, as if by holding him to her she could stave off any trouble that came to Egypt.

Love stung like a dagger in the heart. She closed her eyes. Truth to tell, her greatest love was Egypt, and she could feel it slipping out of her grasp. . . .

☐ YES!

Sign me up for the Historical Romance Book Club and send my FREE BOOKS! If I choose to stay in the club, I will pay only $8.50* each month, a savings of $6.48!

NAME: _____

ADDRESS: _____

TELEPHONE: _____

EMAIL: _____

☐ I want to pay by credit card.

☐ VISA   ☐ MasterCard   ☐ DISCOVER

ACCOUNT #: _____

EXPIRATION DATE: _____

SIGNATURE: _____

Mail this page along with $2.00 shipping and handling to:
Historical Romance Book Club
PO Box 6640
Wayne, PA 19087
Or fax (must include credit card information) to:
610-995-9274

You can also sign up online at **www.dorchesterpub.com**.
*Plus $2.00 for shipping. Offer open to residents of the U.S. and Canada only. Canadian residents please call 1-800-481-9191 for pricing information.
If under 18, a parent or guardian must sign. Terms, prices and conditions subject to change. Subscription subject to acceptance. Dorchester Publishing reserves the right to reject any order or cancel any subscription.